Stone of Fear

by

Margaret Izard

Stones of Iona

The Wild Rose Press, Inc.
PO Box 708
Adams Basin, NY 14410-0708
Visit us at www.thewildrosepress.com

Publishing History
First Edition, 2024
Trade Paperback ISBN 978-1-5092-5537-5
Digital ISBN 978-1-5092-5538-2

Stones of Iona
Published in the United States of America

Dedication

To my favorite Uncle John in heaven, thanks for the corny jokes. (He's my only Uncle) To my husband for encouraging me to chase my dreams. Thank you for your love and support.

Chapter 1

Marie stood alone next to the Chapel in the Woods, studying the castle grounds at Dunstaffnage Castle, Scotland. Bree, her friend and colleague, told her, "Not everyone single is lonely, and not everyone taken is in love. You should embrace you for you." She sighed. Alone remained alone, no matter what anyone said. *Embrace myself. Well, that's history.*

She took a deep breath, closed her eyes, and imagined what this area might have been like in the seventeenth century, a small village of squat huts lined in rows, some lived in, and some made an aisle for a market. Folks scurried about as they attended to everyday chores. Others slowly lumbered along on their regular duties. Closer to Loch Etive's shoreline sat a series of buildings that stored and repaired boats. All around, serfs, guards, maids, and craftsmen all lived and worked to support the enormous castle behind her. This would've been a small village today, a large community in the past. She opened her eyes to the land before her. Being a specialist in historical buildings was what she loved, and she anticipated the next portion of the project from the Historic Environment of Scotland.

Hands closed over her eyes and startled her. At first, she grew concerned, but the familiar scent of clean male musk with an undercurrent of light aftershave wafted to her, and she recognized who held her.

A breath blew gently against her ear as he whispered, "How do ye get a geologist girlfriend?"

Marie giggled and shrugged as she leaned back against John's muscular chest. Her head fit perfectly under his chin. John removed his hands, but she kept her eyes closed as he turned her in his arms, then kissed her lips. She returned his kiss and rose on her toes as she wrapped her arms around his neck.

He lifted his head. "Well, how do ye get a geologist girlfriend?"

Another of John's corny rock jokes, she opened her eyes to his expectant stare. "I don't know. How?"

He smiled and replied. "Ye best *esker* out!" He paused. "Get it? Esker is a long, winding ridge of stratified sand and gravel…"

She giggled and kissed him quickly as she stopped his speech. "Are ye asking me to be yer girlfriend or asking me out?"

John hugged her and replied, "Both, be my girlfriend and have lunch later today. But first, I need to exercise."

John took her hand as they strolled toward the Chapel in the Woods. "*Woman of the rocks*, were ye examining the excavation site ye and Bree believed to be a small village during the eighteenth century? Yer project starts today, right?"

She smiled at his endearment. He called her "Woman of the rocks" in their emails and phone conversations when they first spoke about Bree's chapel renovation project, over a year ago.

She glanced around. "Aye, the lads are due any minute, and we'll begin on it." Bree confirmed the small village site *had existed*. She accidentally tripped back into the eighteenth century the previous year. She saved her and her now-husband Colin MacDougall from the evil Fae when they recovered a magic Iona stone, the Stone of Love.

God, if she had visited the castle and village in the past. That would be awesome. But not the way Bree did with her life threatened and the mission to search for a magic Iona stone. No, Marie would've loved to stroll through the grounds in the past.

She recited the project description in her memory. "A charter of 1572 refers to a place on the property called 'sen dun,' apparently an attempt at the Gaelic word Sean Dùn, old fort. The Historic Society identified the location as Chapel Hill, a rocky ridge about one hundred and sixty meters southwest of the castle." She stared at the Chapel in the Woods. This past year, she and Brielle MacDougall, then DeVolt, managed the renovation of the chapel ruin for the MacDougall family. Brielle—Bree—headed up the project, and Marie oversaw the mosaic floor restoration. The Historic Environment of Scotland selected them for the special project, and their friendship quickly developed.

During that time, she fell in love with John MacArthur, captain of the castle at Dunstaffnage. She squeezed his hand as they continued their stroll. They flirted via email and phone while they coordinated the project.

John stopped them and turned to her. "I wanted to say last night was exceptional for us both." The morning breeze blew a blonde strand of hair across her face. His hand brushed the piece behind her ear, and his palm caressed her cheek as he gazed into her eyes. Last night *was* remarkable for them. It was the first time they declared their love.

Marie smiled and returned his gaze with all the love of her heart. "Aye, it was."

He bent, brushed his lips over hers, and whispered, "If I don't get jogging soon, I'll never leave and end up spending my day telling ye how much I love ye." He pecked her cheek and took off on his run as he headed toward the castle for his daily roundabout route, which ended at the chapel beside her.

As he jogged away, she recalled his appearance when she first met him. He stood at the top of the castle steps, appearing younger than she first imagined. Tall with light brown hair and a strong nose. She noted his very muscular body as her gaze traveled over his form. His arms shifted, and her eyes snapped back to his face. He smiled as she drew closer. A warm sensation spread over her when she returned his smile.

He seemed more than she first assumed. From phone calls and emails, he seemed an older, educated man with a dry sense of humor, not the young, intelligent, witty man she got to know now, yet his soul was old and held knowledge beyond his years. His appreciation for life and all around him sparked her interest, which grew a few months later when she first examined the chapel floor, then swelled in the following weeks. When she arrived and stayed for months to work on the chapel renovation, they dated, and the romance led up to last night.

She smiled as she remembered. Marie giggled aloud as she recalled what John had said. He opened his mouth, then stopped like he had trouble saying what stayed on his mind. John opened his mouth again and told a rock joke.

At first, Marie was a little put off since his jokes were always so corny, but when she registered what he said, "Marie, what did the infatuated boy volcano say to the beautiful girl volcano?"

He brushed her lips and whispered, "I lava ye."

"Excuse me, my dear." The deep voice startled Marie.

She glanced up and found a priest in full black robes with a white collar stood close to her. So close she smelled his aftershave, leather, and musk with an undercurrent of rosemary. Marie had never met a clergyman who wore so much aftershave. She turned her head and breathed fresh air as she searched for the lads from the wharf. Ronnie, Ian, and Conner were the workers hired for the projects at the castle, but they weren't around.

She turned back to the priest. "May I help ye, Father?"

The man beamed, and the hawkish gleam in his eyes made her skin crawl. "I heard about the chapel renovation, the Chapel in the Woods. You are the woman they say renovated it. Am I right?"

He put her immediately on guard. People rarely appeared unexpectedly on the castle grounds. A tour boat docked daily at the castle near Loch Etive during the spring and summer, but the season had passed. She remembered they expected no tourists in the area today. She glanced around again and found no one. The father stepped closer. She stepped back.

In full black robes, the priest reminded her of a recurring dream which haunted her for weeks. She dreamed it again last night, and no matter how much she focused on the Chapel on the Woods project, the memory flashed there now.

She stood before the historic display of Ardchattan Priory. "They say she had an affair with a monk. She hid beneath the floor of his room to visit her lover at night, but the Prior found her and buried her alive."

The dream flashed, changed, and she stood in a hole. She couldn't reach the opening. The hole seemed barely large enough to turn around in. Her fingers grazed the dirt as more dropped upon her face. She clawed the walls repeatedly as the soil packed under her nails, but she didn't care. Grime landed on her head, stuck in her hair. She leaned back and tried to find fresh air, but more dirt fell. *No, this could not be happening.* As she tilted her head back for air, the monk's red, sweaty face appeared at the top of the pit.

She stretched toward the opening again, like a lost soul who reached for heaven, but a shout answered. "Women are the temptation placed on the earth to foul men. You shall pay the price of the priest's sin. Die, whore!"

Debris fell continuously now and covered her legs. She cried for help, but none came. The monk shuffled around at the top. The dirt fell in large clumps and piled up as clumps gathered around her body. *Please, God, don't let my life end, not this way, not without John. Please let me see him one last time.*

The soil covered her chest, pressed in, and she struggled for air. She couldn't stop the dirt's fall, and the mound trapped her arms. She couldn't reach her face. Earth piled around and covered her. She drew in a breath but failed. Left suspended, her lungs desperately burned as she tried to breathe.

Marie was startled awake and gasped. She drew in another precious breath. Her chest hurt from her nightmare's struggles, but she breathed. Her hand pressed her chest. Her tee, bathed in sweat, stuck to her. The dream's image faded as her breathing turned to normal. She glanced around. She lay in her bed at the castle, not a dirt pit. She took a deep breath and calmed her nerves.

Her heart finally slowed, and her mind cleared. The vision came every morning for weeks, and the dream was always the same: a nun buried alive. John told her the ghost story during their visit to Ardchattan Priory. Marie closed her eyes tight and banished the images. She took a deep breath and released it, as she tried to focus on other, more pleasant thoughts.

After a while, she opened her eyes, and at the end of her bed stood The Green Lady, Dunstaffnage's resident ghost. The ghost's appearance foretold the fates of the people in Dunstaffnage Castle. If she smiled, she preceded good tidings. If she cried it meant bad. A visit from the ghost rarely occurred, the person chosen, important to the MacDougall clan. Marie felt honored until she noticed the spirit silently cried.

"You are Marie Murray?" She blinked, and the priest stood before her. He smiled as he spoke. "The Historic Society of Scotland mentioned you were the one who managed the mosaic flooring renovation. I spoke with Odell McEntyre. She said you were still on the property for the next project."

Marie nodded and recognized the name of the director of projects for the Historic Society.

"I'm Father Matthew Clarke." He held his hand out for a shake.

Marie stood and glared at it.

"I am addressing Marie Murray, right?"

Marie shook herself. *Don't be rude to a colleague.* She placed her hand in his and encountered a sweaty palm. He gripped her hand for a moment.

She pulled her hand back and turned as she wiped her palm off her pants. "Aye, I am Marie. Why did Odell send ye?"

Father Clarke nodded. "Oh, I would love to see the mosaic tile floor. She said you restored the building to the original eleventh century pattern." He smiled at her, but it didn't extend to his scrutinizing eyes. "I would very much like to see it."

Marie glanced around again, still not spotting anyone else on the property. *Where were the men? They were supposed to be here by now.*

She glimpsed back at the priest. Father Clarke followed her gaze. His head slowly turned as he surveyed the property. When he came back around, his eyes met hers, and stared at her. He took a deep breath and smiled.

Her stomach fluttered. Maybe breakfast hadn't settled well.

As he spoke, the priest waved to his side, his eyes still focused on her. "If it's too much trouble, I can return another time." Father Clarke folded his hands behind his back. "But I'd love to see your work."

He grinned again, but his face looked off. Marie couldn't quite place it.

"I was told the quality matched some of the restoration done on the Iona Abbey."

His statement caught Marie's ear as praise rarely came from the Historical Society director. "Odell said that?"

She glanced at the chapel, then back at the priest. He said he came from the Historical Society.

Marie stepped around him, then strode toward the chapel. Father Clarke quickly stepped beside her, so close his arm brushed her shoulder. He looked the same height as John, close to six feet tall. Now that the priest strolled close, she noted how large his body was. Marie glanced at him again, and his stomach filled his robes and pulled on the fabric.

His arm brushed hers again as he leaned in to speak to her. "Yes, my dear. Odell has extolled your work, said this was some of the best she had seen in a long time."

Marie blushed under the praise. Odell came out last month and said Marie did a good job but never mentioned this merit level.

The trip to the chapel seemed short, and Marie opened the heavy wooden doors for the priest, who gestured for Marie to proceed with him into the Nave. As she strode inside, she sensed he followed close behind.

"My, what a magnificent achievement in the mosaic work you have completed in the glory of God." Father Clarke spoke as he strolled in behind Marie, who turned when she reached the center of the chapel.

Marie blushed again under his praise. "The floor is stone pieces placed here in the eleventh century. The floor depicted Christ on the cross with the sun halo around his head, spanning twelve feet. We've duplicated near exact based upon drawings recently discovered."

Father Clarke stepped closer as he studied the tile.

"You have replicated the pattern well and in such detail. You positioned the center of the cross in the center of the chapel, pointing east/west as the building should." His eyes traveled the chapel slowly, his gaze resting on the open door, then snapped to Marie.

His smile shifted swiftly. "Most impressive."

The priest glanced toward the circular stained glass above the altar. Marie followed his gaze; the cross in the stained glass reflected the light against the opposite wall in perfect duplication.

"Ms. McEntyre mentioned you believed the chapel held magical properties but found no evidence or stories in your research. Said you hoped more research guided you to what you believed that was." He stepped back as he spoke, his gaze still on the stained-glass window.

Marie crossed and stood under the window.

She loved those windows. "Emily MacDougall, the last Lady of Dunstaffnage, believed light from the west window at dusk hit the center of the chapel and the stained glass matches the floor or, at minimum, the cross."

The father shifted behind her, and she assumed he approached to look at the window with her. She always enjoyed staring at the stained-glass windows. They were magical, and Bree said they were. She claimed they transported Colin back from purgatory after he battled the evil Fae as he sought a magic Fae Iona Stone.

The father whispered behind her, "Yes, my dear. The stone dipped under the cross shall show us the power of the Stones of Iona."

Marie gasped. His phrase sounded like he referred to the magical Fae Stones, the Stones of Iona. She turned to ask the priest about his wording, but before she fully twisted, a searing pain exploded in her skull.

****

As he jogged down the hill from the castle, John's attention focused on Marie. She never strayed far from his mind. And these days, he was delighted at what their future promised. He stopped close to the Chapel in the Woods to catch his breath.

When he strolled toward the chapel, he smiled. She would stay there much longer now the Historic Society of Scotland approved the next project, the excavation of what Marie and Bree believed to be the village from the eighteenth century. Last night remained magical and marked the beginning of their new life together.

Magical. The word sparked John's memory of the first time he observed Marie from the wall walk the day she arrived for Bree's renovation project. Laird Ronald and Lady Emily MacDougall remained alive, back when things were simpler. The laird and lady were away, which left John to show Marie around. He never forgot the first time he viewed her.

From his perch on the wall walk, John waited for the scholar. She stepped out of the car, grabbed her bags from the back seat, and glanced at the chapel. She possessed bright golden hair she pulled back in a ponytail which flapped in the wind. John's eyes followed her gaze to the chapel as the building sat in the morning light. Like a beacon, it glowed brightly in the sunlight. The dew cast shimmering flecks of light which reflected off the water like jewels in the woods.

He sensed her step as she rounded the car. John viewed her more clearly. Marie's petite body strode with a lively bounce to her step. She came here for the chapel renovation—her specialty, rocks. Well, old churches, but Marie came here for the mosaic flooring. They communicated over the phone and email for some time before she made the trip to see the floor. Over time, professional banter quickly turned into romantic flirtation which made John search for any excuse to speak with her again.

John turned to go down to greet her when he sensed a tweak at his heart.

She stopped and glanced up. Time slowed. They stared into one another's eyes. A spark of awareness washed over John. His soul said *mine*. It felt like they floated and drifted together.

Someone startled Marie, and she turned, the spell broken by Mrs. Abernathy, the main housekeeper who called Marie inside the castle.

John pulled up short of his run. So lost in thought, he stood at the doorway to the chapel. The door stood wide open. John glanced around the yard and didn't see Marie. Now that he looked, he didn't see Ronnie, Conner, or Ian, the wharf workers hired to help with the excavation project.

John strode into the chapel and called Marie's name but only encountered an empty aisle. He called her name again, and his voice echoed lightly as dust particles danced in the sunlight that shone through the stained-glass windows. A chill spread up his spine as a bead of sweat dripped down his back. Something wasn't right.

He marched out of the chapel and scanned the area. Certainly, she couldn't have gone too far. Movement in the distance by the dock caught his attention. A man in all black carried a sack over his shoulder and lumbered toward a boat docked there. This seemed strange. There were no tourist boats due on the property today.

John strode to the man and, when he turned, John saw what he carried wasn't a sack, but legs dangled in front of the man. His heart skipped as he ran near the man and never took his eyes off him.

The man flung the body into the boat, and that's when realization hit him. A blonde ponytail flapped from the head. John almost lost his breath but ran faster and harder now; he would recognize that hair anywhere.

"Ye, stop. Stop!" John yelled as he ran hard to the man.

The man glanced over his shoulder, spied John, and clambered into the boat.

John pushed harder. *I must get there before he gets away. God, I have to help her. He's hurt her, and Marie needs me.*

John could kick himself. The safety of everyone at the castle was his duty. Today he failed. He pressed harder, but his body was slow to respond, weary from his morning exercise.

A shout came from his right. Conner ran toward him, blood dripping down his face.

John slowed as Conner yelled, "Get the priest. The bastard attacked us!"

The boat motor started, and he turned just as the boat steered away from the dock.

John took off again. He must get to her. "No, Marie. That bastard took Marie!"

When he finally reached the dock, the boat cleared the Firth of Lorn and headed into the open ocean. He jerked his head around and searched for a boat, but there wasn't another one nearby. He left his cell back at the castle. His heart dropped.

Conner made it to him.

John grabbed him by the shoulders and yelled in his face. "What the hell happened? Why did he take Marie?"

Conner shook his head, tried to speak, and fell forward in a faint at John's feet.

John tried to catch him, but his body remained exhausted.

Giving into his body's needs, John fell to his knees as he tried to catch his breath. He glanced up and stared at the ocean.

That man kidnapped the love of John's life. His Marie had vanished.

Chapter 2

John paced the length of the study again. He glanced at Colin, who arrived at Dunstaffnage Castle this morning after John's urgent summons. John turned and stared out the window. The Chapel in the Woods stood in the distance. God, he just wanted her back, back in his arms again.

Colin approached from behind. "Well, we still have not talked over the *Fae Fable Book*. The damned thing makes little sense, and it is a story I've never heard my ma mention before."

John barked a sharp laugh. "Since when do those damned Fae sisters make any sense, and that book?" He waved at the *Fae Fable Book*, half expecting the book to thump or flip a page to vex him. "Has never made sense."

Colin raised an eyebrow as he lounged against the desk and crossed his arms and legs. How could Colin be so relaxed and composed? John hadn't slept, hadn't bothered to shower, and stood before Colin in what he wore yesterday, his exercise clothes. John felt like crap and smelled like it, too, but he didn't care. All he cared about was Marie.

Colin smirked. "Well, no, it doesn't. At least not till ye need it most, like when I needed it. Then the book makes total sense."

The Fae sisters. John rolled his eyes. The sisters'

father, Dagda, was king of the good Fae and charged Morrigan, his family Fae, and Brigid, Colin's family Fae, to assist John and Colin protect the Stones of Iona from evil for all mankind. Many centuries ago, the Fae gifted the *Fae Fable Book* to the MacDougall family, and inside were stories which outlined the stones' fates. But they weren't always cut and dry and most times didn't help at all.

Last year, the Tuatha Dé Danann Fae, the good Fae, discovered the evil Fae, the Fomoire, created three evil stones, the Stones of Fear, Lust, and Doubt, which track the three good gems, the Stones of Love, Faith, and Hope. When an evil Fae almost discovered the good stones' hiding place, Dagda cast the good stones through space and time which prevented them from falling into the hands of evil. That Fae killed Colin's parents, traveled back in time, and used the Stone of Fear to find the Stone of Love.

Once Dagda recognized the Stone of Fear locked in on the Stone of Love, he sent Colin through the chapel door, a Fae portal dedicated to time travel, to the eighteenth century to locate the Stone of Love. In a mishap, Bree followed Colin. They both found the Stone of Love, defeated the evil Fae tracking it, and took the Stone of Fear. Colin became stuck in purgatory. When Bree used the Stone of Love with her love for Colin and returned her true love, Colin lost the Stone of Fear.

Once reunited in the present, Colin and Bree placed The Stone of Love in the Chapel in the Woods, now protected by Fae magic.

John stood as he remembered yesterday. "The book changed pages after Marie disappeared. But when I began reading it, the pages turned on their own so I could read the entire story." John glanced at the book, secure in its glass case next to the window. He clenched his fist, exhaled, and stared out the window. "Marie is out there with a strange cleric, and I'm stuck here." He drove his fist into his hand. "God, Colin, I have to do something."

He ran the fable, *The Stone of Fear*, back through his mind. There must be a clue which explained why a priest took Marie.

One day, a man sat by a stream, depressed beyond belief.

A Fae approached the man. "Lonely are ye?"

The man sighed. "So much so."

"What can I grant ye to cure yer loneliness?"

The man sat up. "Ye can grant me a wish?"

The Fae giggled in her tinkling voice. "A spell, I can cast a spell. What would ye like most in the world right now?"

The man didn't hesitate. "I want my wife by my side, forever."

The Fae giggled again, but this time it didn't have the tinkling sound but a mirthless, deep laugh.

"Done." She flew over his head as waved her arm and chanted.

And on all hills that shall be dug for the place of God,

No fear shall be cast upon anyone on his hallowed ground.

For there, you shall bury all fear to hide it from the doom of man.

This is our cross to bear.

John turned to Colin. "What does a man who

bargains with the Fae to return his dead wife have to do with Marie and me?"

Colin shrugged. "Hell, at least this time ye got to read the whole story before ye must chase after Marie. I only got one or two lines before. The damn book only changes pages when an evil Fae seeks a Stone of Iona. The tale leads us on a trail searching for a rock. Now it's open to the Stone of Fear fable. This time they want us searching for the Stone of Fear."

Damn the Fae and their games. He needed a clue which explained why the priest took Marie, and the damn *Fae Fable Book* didn't have an answer.

A plan. They needed a plan, and John remained in no state of mind to make one.

Colin cleared his throat, and John glanced up as Colin raised an eyebrow.

He ran his hand through his hair and tried to focus. "Damn the Fae! I need to find Marie."

Colin stood and sat at his desk. "Calm down, John. The beginning. Start at the beginning."

John took a breath, released it slowly and allowed the motion to relax him. "Colin, I cannot understand how it happened. I was out jogging like I usually do. I stopped by the chapel to see Marie, and she wasn't there." He held his hand out in front of him. "That's when I saw him, the priest. He had her, Colin. God, he hurt her." John clenched his fists. "Before I knew it, I ran. Then Conner showed up, injured." He exhaled as he unclenched his fists. "The bastard flung her unconscious into the boat, then whisked her away before we reached her."

Colin glanced up at John. "I know it's hard to witness the one ye love hurt." He sighed. "But let's look at what facts we have. Then we can form a plan."

John strode to the fireplace, thankful his boss and childhood friend came when he called. Colin remained the mastermind and he would formulate a plan that helped him find Marie. It's what Colin did best.

John leaned on the fireplace's mantel and mumbled. "Marie was at the chapel…"

Marie, the chapel. God, was it over a year since he first met her? When she first arrived to work on the renovation project. He stared into the flames as he recalled the day, clear in his mind as if it were today.

****

Marie stepped out of the back entrance of the castle. "Ye don't have to come with me in the rain."

"Nonsense"—John flipped open the umbrella—"I insist on coming along. The trail can be treacherous in the rainfall." He couldn't allow her to walk along the pathway alone. She might slip and fall, and he didn't want her to get hurt.

The shower stayed a slightly cool rain that stayed at a steady pace as it dropped hard drops and hit the umbrella John carried. He shifted the umbrella into his other hand, and they inched closer as they shifted beneath the covering.

He glanced at her profile; she was more than John expected. Their friendship quickly grew as they communicated via text and email for weeks. Marie was short; her head stopped at his middle chest which made him want to protect her more. Her dark-blonde hair flopped in its ponytail bounced on her back as Marie bounded along the route. She reminded him of a sprite, what a bright, happy Fae.

She slipped on a stone. John's arm wrapped around

her and prevented her from falling. He drew her closer to him, and the side of her face pressed against his chest until his chin rested upon her head.

He stopped on the trail. John turned toward her and leaned closer to her face. "Ye okay?" John caught a close glimpse of Marie's eyes, frost blue, like ice with silver flecks. They gazed at him in honesty and struck him immobile.

Marie blinked and nodded her head. "I'm sorry. I wasn't watching where I was going. I was so eager to get to the chapel."

John smiled as they continued. "Oh, that's okay. I'll make sure ye're safe."

They proceeded on the trail slowly, close under the umbrella. John kept his arm around her waist as he held her close in case she slipped again. Their hips bumped, and Marie leaned into him.

When they arrived at the chapel, Marie shifted away, stepped across the doorway, gasped, and stood still as she studied the stone flooring. The chapel possessed no roof as the wood had long rotted out. The trees provided a little protection from the rainfall, but droplets still dripped from the branches into the chapel. It wasn't raining as hard now, so John closed the umbrella and leaned against what the passage of time left of the doorway frame.

Marie crossed to the altar and examined the tile from front to back of the nave. Her springy energy enchanted him, and her bright smile lit up the room. Marie pulled a measuring tape, pad, and pencil from her backpack.

John, not missing a chance for a rock joke, asked, "Ye know what the ruler said to the rock?" He winked at her. "Ye rock, I rule."

Marie rolled her eyes as she dropped her backpack but grinned back at John before she bent to take measurements of the flooring.

She crisscrossed as she measured the space until she reached the rear. Portions of the mosaic design were gone, long washed away from weather and time which left the stones smooth, with the edges rounded in wear over a lengthy period, some light and some dark. The head of Christ, part of the original design, was long gone, but his hair, ear, and neck remained, the face blank as it rested near the center of the Chapel. He viewed the flooring multiple times, but today he imagined how Marie might view it. While he imagined empty spaces and broken rocks, she probably saw the floor, new and complete.

Marie stepped in front of his vision as she marked in her notepad. She chewed her nail then mumbled to herself.

John chuckled.

She glanced up and blushed. "I am certain others look at this and see a ruin. A pile of worthless rocks."

"Oh, no." John waved his hand. "I've worked with Emily putting this project together. I understand the passion she has for the chapel." He glanced around, his eyes landed on her. "As a boy living with my da, I always sensed the chapel seemed sad as it sat here rotting. He called the building a lonely lost soul."

Marie's eyes twinkled as she crossed to the center of the chapel and turned, her eyes wandered over the building as she spoke. "The history of this building has inspired me in my graduate studies at University. Since researching it for Emily, I've become caught up in the chapel's lore. The death of Lady Mary, the wife of the eighteenth century Laird MacDougall, is such a sad story, to be stabbed to death at yer son's christening. The spiritual implication is moving."

The way her eyes sparkled when she spoke about the history, he believed, caught him in a spell.

"In some lore, it's rumored the tile design is magical. The floor comprised of stone pieces placed here in the eleventh century and depicted Christ on the cross with a halo around his head spanning twelve feet. When the MacDougalls built the chapel, they positioned the center of the cross in the center of the nave." Marie pointed to the empty circular window above the altar. "Emily MacDougall believes the original design of the circular stained glass above the altar held magical properties, but we found no drawings or depictions. She hopes more research will guide us to what that design was." Marie sighed as she stared out the window.

"Emily believes when the sunlight at dusk from the west window hits the center of the space and the stained-glass matches the flooring or, at minimum, the cross." As raindrops hit her head, Marie folded her arms and hunched. "She believed the chapel holds mystical power but can't figure out what or how."

John grabbed the umbrella, crossed to the center of the nave, and opened it so the canopy covered them both. "Ye are getting wet standing out here in the middle of the chapel."

He stepped closer and lifted his hand to her face. He wiped the water from her nose, then her cheek. John sensed time slow. As his fingers cleared her face, he leaned in and brushed his lips against hers. He dropped the umbrella and cupped her face as he kissed her deeper.

He drew his arms around her as she moaned into his kisses. She felt so good in his arms. Her lips followed his caress's energy and returned his kiss with enthusiasm. John shifted and kissed her neck as raindrops followed his path. He spotted a small mole on her neck and kissed it. Marie shivered, and he tightened his embrace. Heat spread over John as he yearned to take her close. He trailed his lips up the other side of her neck and brushed his lips against hers. As he ended the kiss, John's chest swelled with his breath. His hand caressed her face. The sun broke through the clouds and shone on them creating a perfect halo. They stood together and gazed into each other's eyes, stunned by their reaction.

A raindrop dripped on Marie's cheek, and John wiped the drop away with his thumb. "Ye should get inside, get something warm to drink. Ye wouldn't want to be catching a cold." John glanced around the chapel, settled his gaze on Marie, and his thumb caressed her cheek. "The rain will stop tomorrow, and ye can spend all yer time here. Let's go inside for a cup of tea."

John waved to the doorway. Marie stepped through it, and he snapped open the umbrella and stepped beside her. Huddled close, John led her out and down the trail.

John grinned as they strolled down the slope. "Where do rocks sleep?"

Marie shrugged.

He gave her an impish grin. "In bedrocks."

They continued to her bright laughter.

****

"Ye haven't heard a damn word I've said, have ye,

John?" Colin's voice snapped John back to the present. He blinked at his friend, his mind still in a haze.

Colin stood, stepped to the table of spirits, and poured a generous portion of whisky into two glasses.

He strode to John, handed him one, and then placed his hand on John's shoulder. "We'll find her. Don't worry. We've been through worse." Colin referred to his adventure when he courted Brielle, which included a trip back in time to restore The Stone of Love for the Fae. An evil Fae threatened her life. Colin risked his life to save her.

John sipped his whisky and stared into the glass at the brown liquid as the liquor glittered in the sunlight reminding John of Marie's golden hair and bright smile.

Next to him, Colin paced in front of the fireplace, sipped his whisky as he counted off the facts. "So, we know she's on a boat with a priest." John ran his hand through his mussed hair as Colin stopped. "Hamish's friend at the Iona Abbey says they were there, confirming they landed in Iona."

John nodded, crossed the study, and stood in front of the window. "I know; ye said as much."

Colin spoke from the fireplace. "Aye, Hamish's friend reported she's conscious and not hurt, but the man isn't nice to her. His friend tried to intercept them, but they disappeared from the property. But ye didn't hear me say they are on their way back here. A fishing boat spotted them and radioed Hamish. They tried to double back, but the shipping lines traveled through. Once they passed, it was too late to catch them."

John turned fast. "They are coming back. My Marie is coming back?"

Colin smiled as he spoke. "Aye, we've laid a trap.

Ronnie, Ian, and Conner lie in wait, in shifts. They'll notify me when they spot them around the point coming into the loch."

Colin had a plan. He always had a plan, a backup plan, and a backup to the backup plan.

John took a deep, soothing breath. "Then what do we do?"

Colin grinned. "We get them at the dock and get yer, Marie, back."

Colin's cell phone rang.

John stared at him and his insides shifted. Was she back already?

Colin glanced at the caller I.D., then at John and shook his head.

Damn, it wasn't the guys from the wharf who warned they spotted Marie.

Colin answered his cell and whoever spoke on the other side came clear.

"Bree? Aye, I'm here and in one piece." There came a brief pause, and Colin glanced at John. "Aye, John's a mess. No, we haven't found her yet." Another pause.

"No, Bree, ye will not come to Dunstaffnage. No, I don't care who all ye can get to watch after the twins. Ye are not coming near the stones *ever again*." The last Colin bellowed loud enough his voice shook the stone walls.

There came a long pause, and Bree's very American voice, high-pitched and angry, yelled from the speaker. Colin and Bree had twins almost a year ago, a boy and a girl who created havoc for their parents. John grinned as he recalled when they dumped maple syrup in Colin's "stinky" boots.

"Damnit, Bree, I said no. Ye will not come here, and ye will not bring the kids. That's final." Colin pushed the button on the phone, ending the call.

He practically panted as he ran his hand through his hair. "Ye sure ye want to find yer woman? They are hell on earth at times."

John stared at his friend and replied, "Aye, I'm already hooked."

Chapter 3

Marie jostled and woke. Stars danced behind her eyelids, and her head bobbed with heaviness. She opened her eyes to black fabric which moved as the man who carried her strode. She flopped upside down, carried over a man's shoulder.

She kicked and connected with something soft. The clergy's jolt and groan told Marie she landed a good kick. He dropped her to the ground, and she landed on her side with a grunt.

Marie glanced up and the priest kneeled, doubled over as he moaned in pain. This was it! Her chance to get away. She scanned the area. Marie caught the cleric off guard just outside of a small church. She quickly scrambled and rose, but the father tackled her before she got to her knees. He slapped her temple, and stars danced before her eyes as he tied a fabric strip around her wrists.

"Come on. We must get to my cottage. I have to hide you away before nightfall." His gaze traveled the yard. "No one can know you are here." He pulled her to stand and dragged her beside him.

She pulled back on the ties. "Wait, where are we going?"

Father Clarke stopped and spun her around. "My home, you Scottish trash." He sighed audibly. "If that is what you want to call it. I must plan how to go about this without alerting others. I'll need to hide away for the evening."

Marie pulled on his arm again, but he remained so much larger than her, her short height unable to gain any leverage.

He dragged her to a small house behind the old church and mumbled, "This is my church, the one I serve." He held her tied hands and shoved her through the door. "If that's what you want to call it. Slaving is what I am doing here."

He slammed the door and locked it as she turned to a modest, quaint cottage. Father Clarke pulled her toward a small room near the kitchen. When she passed the door, she glimpsed a sturdy padlock outside. Anyone on the other side of the door became a prisoner. He planned for her captivity and would lock her away. Her breath hitched. Alone. He would bolt her in and leave her alone.

He dragged her inside and dropped her on the bed. She sat there as she tried to stop the spinning of her head and the roll of her stomach. Once righted, she lay on a short bed, next to a wooden box for a nightstand, with a small lamp on top. He had painted the window black, and nails stuck out from where he hastily nailed it shut.

He cut her bindings, turned to leave, and spoke as he passed through the door. "I'll be back for you in the morning. We'll begin the search. The rock's here, and you will find it. You harnessed the power of the chapel flooring. You can harness the power of the Stones of Iona for the glory of God."

As he shut the door, Marie jumped up and grabbed at the edge. "Ye can't leave me here alone."

The priest pulled on the door.

Marie gripped the edge harder and pulled back. "Not alone all night. What is going to happen to me?"

He glanced at her fingers as they gripped the door, then at her through the tiny crack. His eyes shifted, and they reminded her of a wild animal caught in a trap. But she remained the one trapped.

Her stomach growled in a reminder; she hadn't eaten all day. "What about food, water?"

The cleric stopped. "I'll be back later with your daily meal."

He jerked the door, and her fingers slipped off before it slammed shut. The padlock clicked and her heart dropped to her stomach.

She turned and checked the walls for any doors or hidden windows. Nothing. She remained boxed in, four plain walls with a blackened window the priest nailed shut. She ran to the window and tried to pry the nails to open the window, but it wouldn't budge. He had replaced the glass with boards. She backed away and stood in the middle of the room.

The father unlocked the door and came in with a tray of bread, cheese, cold meat, and jug of water. He glared at her for a moment, his gaze hard, then disappeared behind the door. The lock clicked, and his footsteps retreated as he left her alone.

Alone. Marie's breath grew shorter. Her panic rose as her heart raced. The last of her oxygen squeezed out of her lungs. The walls closed in as her ears rang. Marie covered her head as she crouched to her knees. She curled into a ball on the floor, lay on her side, and squeezed her eyes shut as tight as possible. She willed the ringing to go away. *Go away, go away, go away.*

The ringing continued until it echoed in her head, bounced around in an endless circle. She curled farther into herself and drew her hands to her chest. Her fingers brushed against her stone necklace, the one her grandmother gave her, which held a magical crystal from the isle of Iona. Marie's fingers wrapped around the stone like an anchor in the vast whirlwind, and the spinning slowed.

She lay there for a moment. She remembered John, sweet, kind John. Her breathing slowed, and her body relaxed. She glimpsed his face as he smiled at her, his tender expression when he gazed at her and spoke words of love. She sensed his hands caress her face, felt his lips kiss hers. A tear slid down her cheek. Would she ever see him again?

Marie took a deep breath, then another, and opened her eyes. The area looked the same but less restricted than before. The chill she suffered left, and her stomach growled. She glanced around the room and spied the tray of food.

She dragged the tray toward her. Marie sipped the cool water, then chugged the whole glass. She set the cup down and nibbled some meat and cheese. At least the priest didn't throw her in some cold, dark crypt like Brielle when she searched for a Stone of Iona.

Once fed and her fear subsided, Marie ran the events back through her mind. Father Clarke arrived filled with compliments on her work to inspect the chapel flooring. She should have been leery of someone who showed up without an appointment. It didn't take her long to figure out what he wanted, even if she must suss it out from his ramblings about the cross over a stone. But she realized once he said the Stones of Iona, he hunted a magic Fae rock. Marie didn't let on that she understood about the mystic rocks, but she did.

What she believed helped became a trap. She felt like a fool. All she wanted was to return to Dunstaffnage, John, and home. This was the first time she considered the castle as home. Realization hit her; the castle wasn't home. Home was John. She rolled over, curled herself into a ball, and tried to sleep.

****

Father Clarke stood before St. Martin's Cross at Iona Abbey just after sunrise the following morning and yelled the phrase at the cross again.

And on all hills that shall be dug for the place of God.

No fear shall be cast upon anyone on his hallowed ground.

For there, you shall bury all fear, hiding it from the doom of man.

This is our cross to bear.

Marie sat on the grass next to the cross, her hands tied with fabric in front of her. She would recognize this landscape anywhere since she studied this location for college work. They were near Iona Abbey. Her history class spent an entire month reviewing the plot plan since the Historical Society recently retrofitted and modernized the main building with bedrooms and community areas. The project also boosted a completely renovated refectory, new kitchen, a scullery with a dumb waiter, comprehensive rewiring, insulation, and a new plumbing system. She glanced at the abbey in the morning light. The building looked as magnificent now as it remained in the past. This stayed her favorite part, the abbey's renovations—her dream to oversee renovating a historical religious building.

She gazed at the property as she took in the view, this being the first time she saw the abbey in person. The gray buildings stood amidst perfectly manicured grassland and gardens which stretched to the loch's coast. As the sun peeked over the horizon and cast the sky in crimson and marigold hues which shifted to bright lavender as the light reached the mountains, the scenery rivaled any photo she had seen. Her eyes turned toward Ben Chruachan mountain range in the distance and John at Dunstaffnage Castle.

Her stomach turned and reminded her this morning's meal was no quaint bed and breakfast greeting but a quick cup of tea and stale toast. Father Clarke refused her bathroom privileges until she threatened to pee on the kitchen floor. She smirked; she would've done it to anger the priest.

He seized her arm again and was beside her as he glared at her. His face held a forced look like he concentrated too hard. Bree mentioned what a human looked like when a Fae possessed them, extreme anger and a hard expression which seemed insane. Black eyes, she said, the eyes went totally black. Father Clarke's eyes looked normal, but if someone told her his behavior was what the spell seemed like when a Fae possessed a human, she believed them.

He opened his mouth to say something, then dropped her arm and bent to read an old book.

A plan. Marie needed a plan, a plan to outsmart him, but how? The abbey opened soon and people would arrive to view the gardens and graveyard. She realized he needed to leave quickly. If she kept him occupied, maybe she could alert someone or escape.

She glanced back, and he held the book away like he needed glasses. He yelled the quote again.

She leaned forward for a peek. As he flipped the pages, Marie recognized some illustrations which looked like the Book of Kells, but there was no way this was the actual religious tome. The real book sat in a museum at Trinity College in Dublin, Ireland—she had visited it.

Father Clarke slammed the book closed and yelled at her again. "You, you need to call forth the stone. God has called and I fear his wrath."

She rose and stood before the cross again but did nothing. Father Clarke kicked her leg, and she yelped as she fell hard. Her knees hit the ground as her tied hands scraped on the rough surface.

Father Clarke yelled as spittle flew from his mouth. "Kneel. Now call forth the stone."

She glanced at him. "I don't know what ye are talking about."

He tapped the book against his hand and uttered a groan. As he stood next to her, he opened the pages again. He held the book away at just the right angle so Marie could read some of each page. If she were careful about how she studied them, maybe she would gain some insight into what he intended.

He examined an illustration page with various crosses drawn on it. She recognized St. Martin's Cross. There were biblical scenes on the shaft, and the cross's center represented the Virgin and Child. He mumbled, and she tried to read along with him.

She made out the MacDougall Cross and recognized the relic well since she and John visited Ardchattan Priory near Dunstaffnage, where the cross sat. She remembered the MacDougall cross was wider, and the drawing depicted both sides, a crucifixion scene on one side and an image of the Virgin and Child on the other.

Father Clarke flipped the page, and she spotted text. Latin, a language she became familiar with as a religious buildings expert. All the ancient text was in Latin or Hebrew. As she read parts, she realized this page spoke about the Fae portals between the world of Fae and man. He flipped a page and she swore she stared at a drawing of the door to the Chapel in the Woods at Dunstaffnage Castle. She recognized that door anywhere since she renovated the mosaic flooring over the last few months.

Father Clarke glanced sharply at Marie, then slammed the book closed. She didn't get to read it all, but enough to know. A chill spread up Marie's spine as she glanced away. *Oh, please don't let him figure out the Fae's portals.*

"That's it. We aren't at the wrong cross. We are at the wrong time."

Her heart sank—time travel. From what Bree told her, the portals opened and closed at the command of the Fae, not humans. He couldn't figure this out. She glanced at his face, but he squinted at the sunrise. Her heart dropped to her feet, and his expression shifted to a wide grin. Dear God, had he figured it out? How had he learned the chapel door was a portal between times? From what she read, the book didn't mention time travel. The book only said a portal between the realms existed. He viewed something in the book she hadn't.

Father Clarke grabbed her tied hands and marched back to his cottage. "That's it. We'll need supplies, and more money." He mumbled along the way, "The power of God resides within the Stone of Iona."

She wanted a better glimpse of the book, but he hid it in his bag.

He mumbled again as they marched to his church's small chapel on the hill. "God is the giver of power, and I shall have all the power willed to me in the power of the stone."

He stopped at the church door and slammed it open. "I'll need something to use in the past for money." He dragged her along and grabbed an ornate cross necklace from the pulpit. He stole a holy relic. One she understood the church kept for prayer and inspiration. Marie dedicated her life to the pursuit and preservation of history.

She yanked on her bindings. "Ye can't take that from the church. It's not yers to take. It belongs to the people of Iona."

Father Clarke grabbed her arm as he waved the cross in her face and shook her with each word. "Anything which can bring me the power of the stone will be for the glory of God."

As he waved the cross in her face, Marie got a good look at the cross. The relic was made of solid gold and likely from the thirteenth century. It was large and likely heavy; how could he wave it so easily? Each end held a round, bright ruby gem and the arms showed beautiful scroll carvings. In the center sat a large oval purple gem, so deep a color Marie had never seen.

A memory flashed in her mind fast with clarity. Brielle's voice described her entrapment in the crypt when she traveled to the eighteenth century, and Colin's cousin, possessed by an evil Fae, handed Brielle the Stone of Fear.

"Marie, it was an oval gem, a deep purple, almost black. When activated, it glowed dark and sinister. When I held the gem, my deepest fears rose without control, and the stone–froze in my hand. Pure evil flowed through me as I held it." Marie peered at the cross again and the deep purple gem set in the center. Could it be?

Father Clarke grabbed the ties on her hands. A large gold cross with a center gem and four stones on each arm reminded her of the picture of a crusader's cross she viewed in class once. In her mind, the cross belonged in a museum. In the priest's mind, the relic became his ticket to a Stone of Iona.

People spoke in the distance, and she glanced at the priest who stood over her with the cross in his hand. He swung the cross at her, and a burst of pain exploded in her head.

Marie woke to rocking and the sound of a boat motor. The salty scent of the ocean filled her nose. She shook her head and shifted a bit as she woke her blurred mind. *Wake up!* She needed to be conscious.

She peeked over the side as Father Clarke steered them out to the open ocean. He turned and headed to the mainland, which meant he departed for the chapel, the portal, and back toward Loch Etive, to Dunstaffnage Castle. Maybe if she got to someone and alerted John, but her head hurt too much to think.

As the boat rocked again, she almost heaved. She pulled at her bindings he had tied to one of the boat cleats the docking ropes tied around. She sat farther down in the seat as she tried to get out of the wind; her lightweight jacket did little to keep her warm. To ward off the cold, she closed her eyes and allowed the motor engine to drown out everything. It began to rain, and as she covered her head, the rain hit her jacket. The pings of the drops brought her back—rain, a storm, John.

****

Rain pelted the castle in a steady beat. Marie held her candle and tried not to burn down the place. The flame danced and her other hand covered the fire. Thunder boomed so loud it shook the castle and startled Marie. Her hand shifted too close to the fire and she burned her palm. She yelped, then waved her hand to ease the sting.

When the storm blew in, the electricity cut off. With the thunder so close to the castle, it became hard to fall asleep, so Marie figured a cup of tea might be nice. As Marie floundered down the hall, she recalled Bree stayed afraid of dark places and storms. She hoped she remained okay tonight.

Marie made her way down the stairs and through the great hall toward the kitchen. She stepped inside and set the candle on the counter. The first cabinet she opened found no cups. Marie shifted to the next cabinet. The cups must be here somewhere.

A creak sounded behind her, and Marie whipped around. No one was there. She stood still for a moment in the dimly lit room. She could've sworn she saw a movement in the shadows. She breathed in an uneven pattern as the light from her candle cast ominous shapes on the wall and doorway. She turned back to the cabinet and opened another, grabbed a cup, and her candle went out leaving her in pitch dark. She gasped and gripped the cup to her chest.

She turned around as she tried to detect the candle

in the dark to light it. Lightning lit up the room, and she spied the candle for a moment. Marie placed her hand on the counter and patted down, only to find the sink. Thunder boomed again, and she yelped as she gripped the cup. She extended her hand out again, but this time encountered something warm.

Marie screamed as she held the cup for dear life. Large arms wrapped around her in a warm embrace. Her face rested against a man's naked chest which wiggled as he chuckled. She took a deep breath, smelled John's scent of light musk, and relaxed in his embrace.

"Sorry, *a nighean*," *my girl*. "I only meant to play with ye. I didn't think I'd scare ye."

Marie huffed and pushed against him. "Well, ye scared me all right. Thought I found the ghostie, the Green Lady of Dunstaffnage, in the flesh." She lifted her head, peeked at him, then rested her hand on his naked chest.

John stepped back as he took her cup. It clinked as he set it on the counter. She felt him move away as his form shifted toward the stove. The clank of the kettle told her he'd picked it up.

His body moved to her and he reached around her to turn on the water. The kettle filled with a gurgle. He amazed her at how he easily navigated the kitchen in the darkness.

In a flash of lightning, his white teeth glowed as his voice calmed her. "Didn't ye want some tea?"

Marie blinked as her eyes adjusted to the darkness and his face outlined in the dark, close to hers.

She took a deep breath. "Aye, tea would be nice."

John chuckled as he moved away. "This happens

every storm." At the stove, with his eyes on hers, he opened the drawer, took out a long lighter, and held it up. He smiled, flicked it on, then lit the stove manually casting him in shadow. He stretched over her and lit the candle. A warm light illuminated the room and cast a golden glow around them.

As he pulled back, he stopped when their faces were a mere breath apart and stared into her eyes. He stepped closer and smiled as he reached to the cabinet behind Marie and retrieved another cup.

Marie shifted out of his way, but he placed the cup on the counter stopping her motion. He put the lighter on the other side. John leaned on the counter trapping her between his arms.

He gazed into her eyes as he opened the drawer next to her hip. His hand shifted around, then pulled out the tea and tea strainers and set them on the counter. His gaze held hers.

Marie raised an eyebrow. "I see ye've made tea in the dark before."

John smiled. "Aye."

Lightning lit up the room, and thunder reverberated off the walls. Marie jumped, and her hands gripped his shoulders. John took her hands into his, kissed one, then placed them around his neck as he wrapped her in his embrace. She rested her head on his chest, her ear aligned with his heart. Beneath his warm skin, its steady beat calmed her. Marie took a deep breath, and they stood there in the night as they held each other. The rain made shadows on the moonlit window and ran down the glass in wavy patterns. Thunder rumbled, but farther away now.

She wasn't sure who moved first, but she gazed

into his eyes. He shifted closer, and his lips brushed hers lightly. She didn't stop to think, only feel.

Their lips twirled and his heart beat against hers, then her heartbeat rushed. His hand caressed her face while the other anchored her to his body. She relished the play of their mouths as warmth spread from her neck to her toes, making her knees weak. Her hands traveled over his chest as she ran her fingers through the soft hair.

He deepened the kiss, and she molded her palms over the muscles of his shoulders, then trailed them back to his chest again. John's kisses sent tingles from her fingertips to her toes. She tilted her head and moaned as John trailed kisses down her neck.

The tea kettle whistled loudly. Marie jerked away, but John held on to her.

He whispered, "Stay here. Don't move an inch." John crossed to the stove, shut off the gas, and shifted the kettle to another burner. He stopped and lowered his head as he rubbed his neck. They stood there momentarily. She glanced down, took a deep breath, and turned away.

Before she proceeded farther, he came beside her and took her into his arms, her face in his hand. "Where are ye going?"

Marie wouldn't look at him. "Back to bed."

John's thumb shifted under her chin as he tilted her head till their eyes met. He gazed at her a moment, glanced over her face, eyes, and mouth.

His hand caressed her hair. "Sit up with me, please?" His eyes shifted to her face again. "I can't sleep in storms. Spend the time with me over a cup of tea. We can sit by the fireplace in the hall."

Marie blushed. "Aye, I can't sleep either. I'll sit up with ye."

John kissed her nose, then stepped away. His easy manner soothed the storm jitters away. John moved close to her, handed her a cup, and placed his hand on her back as they made their way out of the kitchen.

Marie stopped. "John, the candle. Ye need to blow out the candle."

He leaned down and blew out the candle. "That's the second time I've blown that candle out tonight."

Marie gasped.

He laughed as they made their way out of the room.

The fireplace flickered low in the Great Hall which kept a warm shimmering circle around the sitting area. John set his cup down and gathered the plaid from the back of the sofa. He wrapped himself in it, sat on the couch, and held the plaid open in invitation.

She smiled, sat, and curled up in his embrace. He wrapped the plaid around them and his warmth enveloped Marie.

He grabbed his teacup, and they cuddled together as they watched the flames as they danced. Lightning lit the room, and a moment passed. Thunder echoed in the distance. In John's embrace, Marie became so warm and relaxed.

She jerked a bit, and John's arms squeezed her. She must have fallen asleep. John chuckled, set his cup on the table, and took her cup as well. He gathered her against him and kissed her lips lightly. He stopped and stared into her eyes as the shadows of the flames flickered on his face and reflected in his eyes. Such a handsome man who sent chills through her. She could sit like this all day and not have a care in the world.

He caressed her face and shifted her close to his heart. She nestled her cheek on his chest, took a deep breath, and then let it out slowly. They lay for a while, and she drifted off to sleep to his steady heartbeat.

****

The bump of the boat rocked Marie and pulled her from her daydream. Cold and stiff from sitting in the same position, she sat up and glanced around. Now late afternoon, and this dock she didn't recognize. She believed they headed back to the pier at Dunstaffnage Castle, but she had never seen this one. She glanced around, and the castle wasn't near either. Her stomach dropped, and her heart skipped into her chest. She didn't know where they were.

Chapter 4

John stood on the castle wall walk that overlooked the castle property. The chapel sat solemnly in the woods. Beyond, the dock where he last saw Marie sat empty. After the damned priest took her, John berated himself repeatedly since he couldn't get to her in time. The sunlight shone off the loch, the waters calm as they reflected the most beautiful scenery in Scotland. Images of Marie in the priest's hands flipped through his mind instead of the beauty of the land before him.

Two days! Missing for two days felt like an eternity. Everything went too fast, yet not fast enough.

His earlier conversation with Colin rang in his mind. "John, a fisherman witnessed the fool priest take Marie from a church to the dock in Iona. Claimed the priest yelled they headed back to Dunstaffnage. The fisherman tried to stop them, but he was too far away to intercept them before the priest's boat hit the open ocean. I ordered the lads from the wharf to position around Dunstaffnage docks for the best chance to intercept them. We'll know the minute the bastard gets back."

John wracked his brain as he tried to figure out what the priest came after. Horrible images ran through his mind day and night. Try as he might, he couldn't stop them. Was she harmed? Had he done more than drag her all over Iona island? John rubbed his face; he must stop thinking that way. *She is okay. They said she is okay.*

Men's voices reached him. At the car park below, the officers from Scotland Yard got into their car and drove away. What a sorry lot. They claimed Marie wasn't gone long enough to declare missing and even suggested she might willingly be with the damn preacher. John nearly slugged the officer before Colin took the official out of the study. John stepped outside to the castle wall to calm himself and breathe fresh air. He closed his eyes. *I must focus and not allow my imagination to get the best of me. She is okay*. He took a breath. S*he is okay*.

A faint sound stretched from a distance, and his eyes snapped open. *Was that a scream?* He scanned the wooded area and observed nothing. He held his breath and listened…a distant cry echoed. He searched the site again, and in the far-left distance opposite the main dock, he made out a man in black with a woman in mild-colored clothing. The people were too far to tell, but his heart screamed, it's Marie.

When a blonde ponytail flipped on her head, he yelled, "Marie!"

He tore down the wall walk through the bailey, and out into the woods. John ran toward the far side of the chapel as he kept them in sight. The priest used the binding tied to her hands and dragged her as he crossed toward the chapel. Boiling rage gave John strength as he pushed faster. He had to make it this time. He must catch her.

Their gazes connected, and Marie screamed, "John!"

Her voice, the panic, tore John's heart into pieces.

They lumbered on the path as they approached the back of the chapel.

He sprinted harder. John's gaze shot between the chapel and the priest. They were closer to the chapel than him, and he wouldn't beat them there.

Conner yelled from the right as he ran toward John from the main castle dock. "I saw them come up the trail. I'm coming, John!"

Once they all arrived at the chapel, he and Conner trapped the priest between them. The cleric had nowhere to run. They would capture him, and he would get Marie back.

The priest stopped at the chapel door, and Marie pulled on her bindings.

John ran harder toward them.

The father pulled a book out and yelled, but John couldn't understand him.

Marie yanked at the priest's grasp.

Her eyes widened as she glanced over her shoulder, and she screamed, "John, hurry!"

His heart dropped to his toes. Marie's eyes locked with his, and time slowed.

The priest chanted something.

Marie yelled over the father, and the one word she said shot fear into his soul. "Portal!"

The chapel door disappeared, and the frame lit up in bright white light. The priest's maniacal laugh echoed through the woods.

John pushed harder to get to Marie, who pulled against the clergy as she tried to escape. John ran faster—almost there. Only three strides from Marie, and he would save her.

Marie's eyes connected with his as she screamed,

"I love ye," as they both disappeared into the light.

John's body slammed hard against the door, knocking his head against the hardwood. He roared and opened the door to the chapel's interior. John missed Marie by a mere second. He turned a full circle and searched for them. John turned the loop again and hoped he would find them. His eyes teared up. He missed her by a mere second.

John fell to his knees, threw his head back, and roared until he had no breath left.

****

Dunstaffnage Castle 1498, the Chapel in the Woods

Father Clark fell on top of Marie, and she kicked him hard. "Get off me, ye son of a bitch, get off!" She landed a good hard kick in his groin, and he rolled over and groaned. Marie jumped up and scrambled for the door.

Father Clarke pulled her feet out from under her.

She screamed as her body hit the floor.

He put a rough hand over her mouth. "No, now we can't have any yelling from you." He panted as he caught his breath. "People will come, and we can't have that." He pulled a strip of fabric from his bag and tied it through her mouth and around her head.

She shook her head hard as she tried to avoid him tying her.

Father Clarke was stronger and manhandled her till he tied the knot at the back of her head. "This will hold you till we get away." He stood and pulled her next to him. The light shone through the stained glass in a warm haze as dust flurries flew around them. It seemed near dusk.

Marie panted around the cloth. Saliva dripped down her chin, and she wiped it with her sleeve. She glanced around the chapel. The building was similar but different. The mosaic flooring was the first thing she detected. By lying on the rougher stone, she recognized this was another rock. The altar changed. Wait, Marie corrected herself. We're in the past; her altar remained different in the future. Thinking gave her a headache, and she rubbed her forehead.

Father Clarke opened the chapel door, peeked out, and glanced from side to side. He picked up his bag and pulled her outside the door.

Father Clarke dragged her down the trail which led to the castle. The woods were heavier than the future, where a groundsman kept them clear. The dense forest made it easier for him to hide them both.

They neared the stables, and Father Clarke hid them behind hay bales. Something about the stables nagged in her memory. The stones seemed familiar. It hit her. The entrance to the stables was the stone archway ruin, where John and Colin practiced their swords.

A stable boy crossed her line of vision as he led two horses, fully saddled and loaded with gear.

Marie jolted and stood to signal the boy as she grunted to gain his attention. Father Clarke grabbed her around the middle, and his hand covered her mouth as he held her tight.

The lad tied the horses to a post. "Aye, sir. The horses be ready for the laird and lady's trip. Loaded with their bags and foodstuffs as Laird Alexander wanted for the trip to Lady Anabelle's family. I'll tie them here." The boy left the horses.

The priest snickered.

After the lad disappeared, Father Clarke dragged her along, grabbed the two horses, and strode into the night.

****

He shoved a shift in front of her. "Put this on. You will need to look the part."

She shoved it back. "I'm not helping ye with shite."

Father grabbed her head and pulled her till her face came nose to nose with his.

His eyes glared at her. "You will do as I say, or I will repeatedly hurt you." He twisted her hair hard enough to elicit a cry. Father Clarke let her go and stepped away while he rummaged through the saddlebags.

He tossed the other clothing about as he fumbled through the bag. They rode a short way from the castle, set up camp for the night, and Father Clarke surprised her when he produced matches and built a fire. He would've impressed her if he had rubbed rocks together.

In the distance, the lights of the marina flickered, fewer and smaller than in the future. Nothing but woods surrounded them. She must rethink her strategy. Going along hurt and tied up wasn't the best way to plan her escape. She needed to gain the father's trust, then get away when he became unaware. At least he took off the mouth gag, and she breathed easier. He even took mercy on her and gave her water to wet her dry throat. One step at a time. A plan.

The priest tried to assemble the clothing, but the pieces were mismatched. The man's shirt with the woman's skirt, and he left the woman's bodice on the ground. Earlier, he didn't know how to mount a horse or ride one. He traveled away from the marina instead of closer. He needed a boat to get back to Iona island if he wanted to examine the Iona cross in this century. She understood a lot about history. This became her leverage, her knowledge. His lack of intelligence turned into her power. If she convinced him she helped, he would let his guard down. Then she could escape—one step at a time.

She took a deep breath. *Courage, Marie*. "I tell ye what, Father. I'll help ye, even cooperate with ye on two conditions."

He huffed a reply.

Marie squared her shoulders. "First, ye will leave me untied at all times and not hurt me, and I will go where ye want and stay where ye want, willingly."

He lifted his head and glowered at her. Good, she'd got his attention.

"Second, I'll even help ye with yer book and find this stone ye want. I'm a history expert and likely can interpret the book better than ye, but there will be a price."

The father folded his arms over his chest and glowered at her. "I'm listening."

She must say it now and make sure he understood. "Ye have the vow to be chaste, and ye'll honor it. Ye'll not violate me."

The father slowly walked toward her, one step at a time. His smile grew as he approached. When the clergyman arrived before her, he bent his head down till he came eye to eye with her. Would he honor his vow, or had she pushed him too far?

"That's three conditions, and it doesn't matter. I don't like Scottish whores, and I would never sully myself with the likes of you."

Marie released her breath. "So, we have a deal?"

Father Clarke strode back to the bags and rubbed his chin. "I'll only bind you when we sleep and lock you up when I am not near." He glanced at her over his shoulder. "If you go back on your word, there will be punishment, and I can guarantee it will hurt."

Marie raised her tied hands and lifted an eyebrow.

He stood and glared at her. "I mean it. You try anything, and I will hurt you badly."

Marie didn't take her gaze from his and slowly nodded.

He strode to her, untied her hands, and stood close to her. She picked up the clothing, flipped the pieces around as Father Clarke returned to the saddlebags and selected up another, rummaging through it again.

Marie huffed. "Ye don't know much about period clothing. Parts are missing. To get dressed, I'll need all the pieces."

"Make yourself useful then." Father Clarke tossed the saddle bag, and it hit her chest. "Figure out our clothing and impress me."

Marie gathered her apparel and shifted behind a tree.

Father Clarke jumped up and grabbed her arm. "Just where do you think you are going?"

Marie glared at him. "Behind the tree to change." Marie blushed and added, "Plus, I have to pee."

Father Clarke laughed. "No, you won't. You can change here and pee on this side of the tree." He released her, and she shivered. Would he stick to his vow? She wasn't ready to test his limits.

He crossed to his side of the fire, sat as he took off his collar, and tossed it into the fire. "Which are my clothes?"

Marie gathered his clothing and strode to him. She needed to show him how to wear a tartan. She doubted the English man understood how to fold one in the old style.

She held each piece as she explained each in the most straightforward way. "This is yer shirt. Ye tuck it into the plaid, which ye fold like this." She knelt, laid out the large cloth, and started pleating the fabric.

The priest stripped his shirt, and Marie averted her gaze from his white pudgy chest vastly different than John's tanned, muscular one.

He drew on the puffy medieval shirt which swallowed his flabby body. "I'll not wear a damned skirt as some light foot wore."

Marie stood and folded her arms. "Ye'll stand out in this age wearing pants. We are in Scotland, and based upon the laird and lady's name, I'd say around the fifteenth century."

He stood and glared at her. "No skirts!"

Marie picked up the plaid and crossed back to the pile of clothes. She collected her clothing and glanced back at Father Clarke.

Father Clarke sat by the fire, lounged on his elbow as he stared at her.

Marie backed up a step.

"Not too far, dear," the father growled.

Marie stopped and gaped at Father Clarke. "Ye said ye weren't interested."

He smiled, "I won't touch you, but I plan to enjoy

the show."

Marie shivered. She glanced at the clothes and contemplated how to change hers while revealing nothing. The larger shift glowed in the firelight. Lady MacDougall was more sizable than her. She smiled as her solution popped into her mind. Marie pulled the shift over her head only, and it dropped past her knees. The shift puffed out large and billowy on her tiny, petite body. She kept her body under the large tent and removed her button-down shirt and bra under the dress. She quickly stripped her khaki pants while averting her gaze from Father Clarke.

Father Clarke mumbled, "Probably not worth looking at, anyway."

After she adjusted the shift correctly, she put her bodice on and found it possessed extended ties to tie herself in without his help. The skirt easily slid on over the undergarment. Sitting, she pulled on the woolen hose leg by leg and tied them at her thighs. She even found sturdy shoes which laced up. Not bad. She dusted her hands and folded her modern clothing into the saddlebag. She stepped behind the tree to do her business, and Father Clarke didn't comment. When she emerged, he rested beside the plaid. Marie sat across from him.

He moved around the fire and handed her dried beef and an oatcake. "Found this in the bags. Bon appetite." Marie nibbled on the oatcake, then set it aside.

After some time, Father Clarke stood and towered over her as he waved the fabric strips. "Stand up, Scottish hag."

Marie rolled her eyes and stood with her hands out.

The priest tied her hands together, pulled her closer to him, and then tied her to his left hand with a longer cloth strap. She moved as far away from him as the ties allowed and sat hard on the ground. She gathered the woman's wrap, the arisaid around her. The plaid warmed her as she tucked herself into the wool, picked up her food, and nibbled some more.

Father Clarke glanced at her. "Remember our deal, no running."

Marie shivered and curled up in her plaid. At least the dress was sturdy wool, and the thick stockings kept her warm. When she closed her eyes, her first images were of John. She let her mind drift for a minute and smiled in the darkness.

When she nipped more food, her head cleared. She had eaten better dinners than this. Dinner—the first dinner she and John shared happened the first night she came to the castle for the start of the renovation project.

****

Marie headed to the dining room at Dunstaffnage. She arrived that day to commence work on the chapel renovation project and planned to have dinner with Brielle, Colin, and John.

She turned the corner and strode toward the far end of the Great Hall. When she neared, John stood outside the dining room, alone. Did this mean he would cancel? Marie slowed her steps as she approached him.

Their gazes locked as she walked closer. "Good evening, John."

John's smile went wide. "Good evening, Marie. Colin and Brielle have other dinner plans, so we won't be dining with them."

No dinner plans left her alone. Her gaze lowered.

"Would ye like to come to the marina pub for dinner with me? They've booked a band. I've heard they're good, so maybe we can stay a bit?"

Marie's gaze snapped to John's. "Aye, I'd like that."

John offered his arm as he walked her to his black SUV.

The drive to the marina wasn't long, and the view from the castle cliff at dusk took Marie's breath away. Nothing was more beautiful than the Scottish mountainside. She glanced at John as he drove. His profile looked relaxed.

He glanced at her, smiled, and then looked back at the road. Tonight, with John, she hoped would be a chance to get to know him better and tell him she looked forward to the project and her time at Dunstaffnage.

John pulled into the crowded parking lot, parked, and cut the engine.

He hopped out of the car and ran to her side to open the door. "This way to the best beer and fish 'n chips this side of Loch Etive." She stepped down, and he took her hand as he escorted her to the pub.

John grunted as he opened the heavy pub door and held it for her. He picked a table farther to the rear where the floor-to-ceiling window overlooked the marina. The boats bobbed a bit but seemed at rest in the deepening dusk, like shadows of fishermen who sought rest.

A tall, thin man approached, and his booming voice, an unmistakable welcome. "John, what have we here? A beauty she is, and she's yers, eh?"

John blushed. "Hamish, this is Marie Murray from

Glasgow. She's part of the chapel renovation project."

Hamish took her hand and shook it hard. "Aye, such a great project." He released her hand and clapped John on the back. "Wait till yer granny hears about this. Ye on a hot date!"

John cleared his throat loudly as red flushed his neck. "Just the usual, Hamish, fish 'n chips, and beers."

Hamish walked away and waved. "Aye, and keep 'em coming till ye signal. Right!"

Marie turned to John and raised an eyebrow. "Hot date?"

John smiled as he shrugged. "My granny's tried to set me up for years. I keep turning them down. They are girls I grew up with, more like sisters."

Hamish returned with a wink and two stout beers, Marie's favorite.

John held his aloft. "To the chapel."

Marie clinked her mug and took a sip. The bite of the hops hit her tongue, but the smoothness of the brew went down easily.

John set his glass down and took her hand.

He rubbed his fingers over the back. "Marie, I am glad ye are finally here in person. I wanted to spend more time with ye."

His caress set tingles through her, and she gazed at him as she smiled. "I am glad to see ye in person as well."

He rotated their hands till he held them palm to palm. "Ye know, when I started working on the renovation, I assumed the project was another duty, another part of my job." He linked their fingers together. "But as I got to know ye, I found the chapel wasn't a chore." His eyes shifted to hers. "It was a pleasure. I found myself looking forward to our conversations, then regretting when they ended." He pulled her hand close to his face and brushed his lips over it. His breath tickled her skin when he spoke, sending chills. "I hope we'll spend much time together, Marie."

So caught up in what he did, the sensations his caresses sent through her, Marie's only response was, "Me too."

Hamish stood beside the table and held two plates piled high with fried fish and chips. "Aww, now that's romantic."

They broke apart, and Hamish set their dinner on the table. As he walked away, he called over his shoulder, "Don't let me interrupt ye. Kissing over fish 'n chips and beer is how I found my love."

John placed his napkin in his lap. "I hope ye brought yer appetite. These are the best."

Marie glanced over hers, comfortable enough to pig out. Over dinner, they shared another round of beers and a conversation about the stone delivery from the quarry for the renovation. Then the rock band started, and the room's chat rose with the sounds of the music.

Marie yelled over the band's music, pointing to the porch. "Can we go on the porch for a bit?"

John's gaze followed her finger, and he nodded. He grabbed both beers in one hand, pulled out Marie's chair, and waved them toward the back door.

Outside, the dock overlooked the loch, and the boats bobbed lightly in the water. They reflected perfectly off the loch, a mirror image in line with the water. The moon lit the loch in a mix of deep indigo and wine haze. Silver flashes danced along the water like fairies floating in the sky.

Marie sighed as she leaned on the railing as she took in the breathtaking view.

The music from the pub faded.

Marie sensed John's approach, and he set the beers on the railing. A breeze blew her neck and chilled her.

John stepped closer, rested his hands on the railing, and enclosed her in his arms.

Marie sighed and leaned back as she rested her head against John's chest.

He wrapped her in a soft embrace. "I've thought so much about ye, Marie." He squeezed her lightly.

She rubbed her hands on his arms. "John, I've thought about ye too."

John turned her in his arms and caressed her face. He dipped his head and kissed her lips lightly.

John lifted his head a little and spoke softly as their breaths mingled. "Standing here in the moonlight, it's lit ye in bluish purple, like fine a gem." He caressed her cheek. "Ye look like a little sea nymph who has jumped from the waters and graced me with her presence." John bent and brushed his lips against hers. "It's mystical."

Marie's lips tingled as his lips brushed hers. She trailed her fingers up his arms, curved her hands around his neck, pulled him down, and deepened the kiss. Mysterious, this night seems like a Fae cast a love spell, and she, a willing recipient.

John tilted farther. Their tongues danced as he molded his body to hers, and his hands stroked her back. He lowered his hands to her rear and gently squeezed.

Marie moaned as she dropped her head back, and John trailed kisses down her neck up to her ear and sucked the lobe. Desire burned through her. A flash of heat near weakened her knees.

John kissed her mouth lightly. They both panted, and he left her a little dizzy.

John took a deep breath. "God, woman, I could kiss ye forever and never grow tired of it."

She giggled. "I never grow tired of yer kisses."

John rocked back on his heels till his gaze met Marie's. "Why were the paleontologists kissing?"

She shrugged.

John smiled. "They were carbon dating."

****

Time slowed, and Marie blinked out of her daze as a tear fell from her eye. A man's voice echoed. It wasn't John or the priest but in her head.

"…hiding from the fear of man. This is our cross to bear."

After waiting a while, she hoped the priest would fall asleep. She tried to untie her hands, but the knots stayed tight. She shifted and crawled toward the priest, hoping to find the tie to his left hand. The fabric jerked. She fell forward and hit her chin on the ground.

She cried out as the priest laughed.

He spoke in a low deep voice. "I knew you'd try to escape. Go to sleep, and don't try it again. I'm a light sleeper and will catch you every time."

She crawled back to her plaid and curled up in it as she tried to sleep. Escape was not for tonight, but another time.

Chapter 5

Dunstaffnage Castle Present Day

John glanced at Colin as he shrugged. "I assumed our Fae would show up."

John looked around the chapel and spied Colin doing the same.

Colin peered around them and smirked.

John huffed a laugh. The irony of the situation did not escape them. Colin did this very thing over a year ago when he traveled back in time to find the Stone of Love and return his ancestor to the right place.

John frowned. "Those two damn sisters won't show. Ye know when ye didn't come back, I came down here one night. I yelled for my Fae Morrigan. When she didn't show, I yelled for yers, Brigid, till I lost my voice. They didn't show then, and they won't show now."

John strapped his broadsword to his back and double-checked his supplies. Dressed in period clothing from the reenactment event Dunstaffnage Castle hosted each year, he stood ready. Well, as prepared as he could be for someone about to time travel. As John stood in the graying dusk, the rain beat against the chapel roof. He smirked, thankful the building possessed a top now since Bree and Marie had spent the last year renovating it.

Colin huffed. "Those sisters are supposed to serve

as guides on our duty to the stones, but they tend to do whatever they damn well please, regardless of a need or not." Colin stared at him. "Do ye have a plan on how ye will locate her?"

John peered around the chapel as he searched for Morrigan, his Fae. She had to show he must go back in time to save Marie. Damn, he needed her.

He glanced at Colin. "I'll concentrate on her. I'm bound to be steered toward her if I focus enough."

Colin nodded. "Simple enough. So, how do we open the portal? Yer Fae story said nothing 'bout that."

John grinned and held up a small red book. "I got Bree's poem book. She opened the portal with a poem, so I'll use it and hope for the best."

A burst of tinkling laughter echoed, and both men started.

"So confident ye are, John." Brigid's form coalesced, and she sat on the altar, small like his Fae Morrigan. The only difference between Brigid and Morrigan was Morrigan's long jet-black hair.

Colin growled lowly. Brigid's appearance always preceded trouble.

Morrigan appeared beside her in a burst of brightness.

The room grew lighter in a warm, dusk-like glow. The sisters sat next to each other, identical in form, two small women, maybe three feet tall, and were almost pure light. Brigid with her white-blonde long hair glowed in an ethereal light and Morrigan's jet-black hair flashed purple in the rays of dying light. Each possessed a beautiful soft face with pale, almost translucent skin. Their bodies flashed in and out of form, the way flames of fire shift in a breath of air.

John's gaze scanned his Fae Morrigan. Today was the second time she visited. She flashed in a dream last year. Now that he had time to study her, her eyes shone light blue, glowing like a hypnotic orb. Her gaze returned to him and held him immobile. He felt sinful as he gazed upon her, and thinking of her reminded him of angels. Colin said no mortal man denied the attraction of the female Fae. The little woman smiled knowingly, and her glow dimmed, and she released him from her imprisonment.

Morrigan nodded as her translucent wings fluttered fast.

When she shifted her gaze to her sister, her hair fell aside, and the point of her ear showed. "Stop teasing the man, sister. He's got a lot on his mind."

The two Fae sisters' arrival meant he would go back in time to rescue Marie. "So, what can ye tell me? Where or when is Marie?"

Brigid flickered. "So demanding, as if we would tell ye."

John drew his sword and pointed it at Brigid, who vanished.

Her voice sounded through the chapel. "As if yer wee toothpick could do me any damage."

Morrigan sighed. "Brigid, stop. No more games." Morrigan leveled her gaze on him. "She is in the fifteenth century. We'll drop ye back the day after because that's today's equivalent. It's the only way we are permitted to travel humans through the portals."

John's head snapped up with his mouth open ready to ask about Marie.

Morrigan held up her hands. "She's safe and fending for herself. She's part of Fae's plan to retrieve the Stone of Fear Colin lost. Ye can seek aid from the MacDougall laird, Alexander MacDougall."

Brigid laughed. "Brawny boy dropped it when I cast him into purgatory, and the Evil Fae hid it. It turns out Marie is my da's choice for finding it."

Colin growled. "I didn't drop it, ye stinking sprite. It disappeared."

John sheathed his sword. "Let's get on with it. I will not find Marie and bring us back to this time if I am standing here arguing."

Morrigan nodded as she gazed off into space. "Yes, ye will go back, find Marie, and she will find the Stone of Fear."

A chill spread down John's spine, unsure whether Morrigan viewed or planned the future. And what did Brigid mean by Marie was her da's plan for the stone? The damn priest took her. What did Dagda, the King of the good Fae, have to do with any of this?

Colin approached John, and they grasped in a hug. "John, ye can do this. I have faith in ye."

Colin stepped back and nodded. "See ye when it's done. We'll be here for ye."

John strode toward the chapel doorway, took a deep breath, and drew his dagger to draw blood for the portal spell.

Morrigan flew in front of him. "No blood. We must use a different spell. Blood was already spilled for ye." John tilted his head as he sheathed his dagger. Someone spilled blood for him?

Morrigan floated above the entrance and bowed her head. The doorway disappeared, and the frame glowed white.

Colin barked at the Fae, "Why didn't ye just do

that for me instead of making a hole in my hand?"

Brigid's voice rang through the chapel. "What's the fun in it if ye don't spill blood for a spell? Sis, ye are boring."

Colin growled. "Ye cut me for fun?"

Morrigan clapped her palms together in prayer and chanted,

We have all been through the weather,
Now, I bring us back together.
All is healed. All is well.
We are reunited, as my words tell.
No harm shall it cause one,
So reunite them and be done.

Morrigan opened her eyes and locked gazes with John. "Ye must remember the Fae Fable Story of The Stone of Fear; without it, ye are as doomed as yer father."

His da? What did his missing father have to do with this? Determination overcame him. It didn't matter. *Marie; focus on Marie.* He closed his eyes, and she appeared in his mind. Her face, her smile, and he sensed her, *Marie.* He passed through the portal, and the light vanished as soon as he cleared the frame.

****

In a flash of light, Colin stood alone in the chapel. He stared at the doorway for a moment, unsure if he made sure John made it back in time or if John might pop back to the present. God, he hoped John found Marie, and they returned safe. He couldn't stand another thing to go wrong with the stones.

He shook himself and glanced around. The sisters left the chapel darker in the dusk as the rain beat steadily on the wooden roof.

Colin approached the altar and kneeled, praying out loud. "God, please look after John and Marie. Please get them safely back. They've become family to me, and it'll mean a great deal to me to have them back, safe. Amen." He stayed there for a minute with his head bowed and eyes closed.

A burst of light flashed before him, and his head snapped up. Brigid sat on the altar as she faced him with a smirk.

Colin growled, "Now what, ye foul fairy?"

She smiled widely. "I have a surprise for ye, Colin."

He stood with his hands fisted at his sides. "I'm done with yer surprises, ye damn troll."

She cackled. "Aw, Colin, but ye will like this one. It's a riddle."

She chanted in her supple singsong voice.

Rain falls and water flows,
Through yer door a storm wind blow.
Sweet and ripe, she comes to ye,
and brings the twin fruit ye both bear to see ye through.

Colin frowned. "What the hell does that have to do with John and Marie?"

Brigid's tinkling laughter echoed. "It doesn't, Colin. Me poem has to do with ye."

Colin repeated the riddle in his mind. *She comes to ye and brings the twin fruit ye both bear to see ye through.*

His gaze snapped to Brigid's. "The hell she did not." Colin ran out of the chapel.

Brigid's laugh echoed as he ran the entire route to the castle in the rain.

Colin burst through the main castle doors, and water dripped from him as he ran to the middle of the Great Hall and bellowed, "Damnit, Bree, I told ye to stay away."

Bree and Mrs. A. emerged from the kitchen hallway, each holding a toddler. Mrs. A. was what Marie called Mrs. Abernathy, and it stuck with everyone.

Ewan and Evie held their hands toward Colin and squealed together, "eeeee!" Colin ran his palms through his wet hair and shook the water from his hands as he strode to his family. He took Ewan from Mrs. A.

"Okay, I'll let ye go to yer daddy, but both are all mine tomorrow," Mrs. A. huffed as she marched away. "Ye're getting the wee one all wet, M'Laird!"

Colin's fingers brushed Bree's face, and he kissed her lightly.

Ewan, the spitting image of him with the same dark hair and a chunk of a body, smacked his palm to his mouth and gave it a loud, squishy kiss. "Muah."

Colin couldn't stop his smile and kissed his son's forehead. Evie frowned, the image of her mother, with brown wavy hair and a pale little face. He leaned toward her and kissed her, too. Mrs. A. returned and handed Colin a towel. As he dried himself off, Ewan wiggled in his arms, but Colin's strong grip held the fidgety toddler, who giggled at his wrestling game.

Mrs. A. made a tsking noise. "M'Laird, dry him off too."

Colin took the towel and dried off Ewan, who fought against his father's actions and made Colin chuckle.

Mrs. A. shuffled off to the kitchen and shook her

head.

He turned to Bree. "I told ye not to come here, Bree. I don't like it when ye are close to the chapel and the stones."

Bree strode past him toward the study, and he eyed her as she walked away, her hips swaying. They rounded out quite nicely after the twins' birth, but she still kept her fit shape. Her brunette hair bounced as she walked, and the color reminded him of the first day he met her when she stood next to the study window with the sun shining behind her hair, casting a halo around her head. *My soulmate,* his heart said. She looked like the image of his soul mate from the Fae Fable story, The Stone of Love.

She stopped and glanced over her shoulder. "Nonsense, Colin. I'm perfectly safe, and what's the fun of staying away?"

Colin shook off the vision and followed. "Lord, Bree, ye sound like Brigid."

Bree glanced at him as they entered the study. "Did ye see her? Did John make it through the portal, okay? What about Marie? Which stone are they going after?" She set Evie on the couch before the fireplace and stood with her arms crossed.

Colin shook his head. "Bree, this is not a game." He set Ewan next to Evie, and the fireplace cheerfully lit the room. The kids chattered in baby talk, which sounded like little birds.

Colin gathered Bree in his arms as they stood behind the couch. "I am *not* happy ye are here, but I am happy ye are in my arms." Colin kissed her deeply, and she responded with a moan.

Bree spoke between kisses. "One night away from

you is one too many." She brushed his lips. "I couldn't stay away, no matter what." She touched them again. "And it's storming tonight." Bree ran her finger along the collar of his shirt.

Colin rubbed her back to comfort her. "I thought I chased all yer storms away. Plus, ye made up with yer brother, Dominic, for locking ye away in the shed. Shouldn't things be okay for ye now?"

Bree snuggled into his embrace. "Yes, I did make up with Dom, but it's not the same. I like to be in your arms during every storm. And Dom's in the States, and you are here, with me."

The twins pealed into laughter. Colin glanced over the back of the couch at his children, and together they glanced at the mantel.

Bree shrugged. "Twin speak. They started it recently." Bree kissed him, pushed him away, and strode to the whisky. "So, update me."

She poured two glasses as he settled in a chair before the desk. Bree sauntered toward him and handed him a drink. She sat beside him and curled her feet under her.

Colin didn't want to talk about the Fae or the Stones. It bothered him to have her here again, so close to the chapel, the Stones, and the *Fae Fable Book*, which sat in the same room. He didn't want anything to happen like before when the Fae whisked her away to another time. It was hard enough to keep her safe, but now they had the twins to think of. God, if anything happened to his wee babes…

He needed to get them out of there, so he came quickly to the point. "Fifteenth century, the Stone of Fear, Marie finds it, and they'll make it back."

Bree sipped her whisky. "That's it? What about the *Fae Fable Book*?"

The twins pealed into laughter again, and Colin glanced over at the couch. He couldn't see them but sensed they were okay.

"That's the confusing part. The fable has nothing to do with John. It's about a man bargaining with the Fae to be with his dead wife. Makes no sense."

Evie's face popped up from the rear of the couch and stared at them. Colin smiled and winked at his daughter, who smiled back with a saliva-covered grin. Her face turned to the mantel and disappeared behind the couch. He sipped his whisky as he and Bree sat silently for a moment. Colin set his glass on the desk, took Bree's glass from her hand, and placed it next to his.

He gathered her in his lap as he cradled her in his embrace. "I am glad to see ye." He kissed her once.

Bree grinned. "You are? I am glad to see me too." She kissed him and giggled.

His fingers caressed her face, and he deepened the kiss. "I can't wait to get ye alone in my bed."

Bree sighed and kissed him.

He glanced down at her chest to unbutton her shirt, and a movement in the corner of his eye caught his attention. He glanced at the *Fae Fable Book*, and Evie crawled across the study past them and held onto the wall as she reached for the *Fae Fable Book*. How the hell did she get there so fast?

Colin's heart stopped because the glass case had disappeared. His daughter pulled herself to a wobbly stand, held onto the book casement, and nearly touched the magical Fae book.

Colin dumped Bree on the floor and, in two long strides, made it to Evie. As he whisked her into his arms, he spun away from the book and elicited a peal of laughter from Evie.

When Colin glanced back at the book, the glass case came back. He turned, and Bree blinked at them from the floor. His gaze traveled to the couch, and Ewan stood on the sofa as he stared over the rear and smiled at them.

Bree glanced at Ewan and back at Colin. "I think our kids just met Brigid, Colin."

Colin growled, "This is why I didn't want ye and the kids here. Let's get them to bed."

Bree stood and swept Ewan into her arms. "Colin, they must learn about the Fae, the stones. Don't you think sooner is better than later, especially after your experience?"

Colin headed out the door. "That damn sprite."

****

Colin lay in bed, the covers pulled to his waist. So much ran through his mind now the Fae were active again.

Bree emerged from the bathroom, rubbing her face with cream. "Exactly where I wanted you, naked and in my bed."

Colin smiled and lifted the sheet inviting Bree to join him. She slid into the covers, and he gathered her in his arms, thankful for the distraction.

He glared at the wall opposite them. Bree pouted. He still didn't respond.

Bree straddled him and placed both hands on either side of his face. "There's nothing more you can do to protect them. The twins will learn when the time is right, and everything will be okay. I promise."

Colin gathered her in his arms. "I need to keep my family safe. It's too early. They are just babies."

Bree kissed him. "It will be okay. You can't dwell on it all the time. You would miss life."

Bree smirked devilishly. "I have a surprise for you, Colin."

He rubbed his hands up and down her back and shifted his hips, so he rubbed against her. "Mm, yer surprises I like."

She slid down his body and kissed a path down his chest.

Colin growled as his fingers threaded through her hair, all golden brown as the waves formed a halo around her beautiful face. She kissed his stomach, and his muscles contracted as desire shot through him.

She peeked at him from under her lashes and giggled. Is she…before he formed the idea in his mind, she licked the end of him.

Colin sat up and held her shoulders. "Bree, ye do not have to do this. Only when ye are ready and only when ye will enjoy this will ye do that kind of loving. I'll not force anything on ye, ever."

Bree smiled and caressed his face as her other hand grasped him. "Colin, you said you'd never ask again, and you haven't. You said it was my choice, and I choose now. I want to please you like you please me. A favor returned, remember? Please…let me please you."

Colin kissed her deeply as he gripped her tightly.

She pushed him back and lowered her head to him. She giggled and peeked at him.

He allowed her to take the lead. She needed to feel confident and in control. This type of play went badly for her with an ex, and he hoped she had conquered her fear. Colin wanted her to enjoy herself, to gift her control so she understood how much he loved her. His hand shifted to her head, and the other rested behind his pillow. He smiled, for he planned to enjoy his wife's new game.

She licked the tip, and heat shot to his toes. His stomach flexed with the rest of him, which provoked a groan. She grabbed the base and licked the tip slower, then placed the end on her lips and sucked lightly.

Overcome with desire, Colin threw his head back as he gripped her hair. He immediately released his grip. He must be careful and not force her. She might slip into an unbearable memory, and he wanted her mind on him.

Colin shifted his hand from her head and gripped the sheets beside him. Colin didn't want to grab her or startle her. He allowed her to set their pace.

She sucked a little more, then slowly lowered her mouth to his base. The heat of her mouth and tongue swirl spread warmth over his body. She had done this before but never to him. He would have to admit, she was skilled, and damn, she had just started.

She increased the suction and swirled her tongue again. Pleasure shot through him, and he concentrated on stopping himself from grabbing her. Unable to touch her, he feared she would drive him to insanity or kill him with her skills.

She released the suction and slid her mouth up to the tip, then glided his shaft into the back of her throat and almost swallowed the end. He gripped the sheets harder as his hips involuntarily bucked. Her throat seized his tip, and the pressure sent shockwaves through him. Bree bobbed once, and his hips jumped again.

She took the cue and bobbed her mouth faster, her lips rode up and down his shaft faster and faster.

Colin panted loudly. With each movement, she glided down his shaft, and she buried him deeper down her throat. At the end, she closed her muscles around the tip and intensified the pressure.

She sped up the pace, and he groaned louder as he panted harder. Her hard breathing through her nose pulsed against him. She moaned, and the vibration shot sparks from his groin to his skull. The pressure built, his sacs tightened, and his lower back contracted. Bree didn't slow her motions. He tried to grab her shoulder, but she batted him away, and pounded her mouth on him repeatedly.

"Bree, if ye don't stop, I can't…"

She moaned and pummeled her mouth relentlessly.

He threw his head back as both hands gripped the sheets, twisting them as he tried to secure himself. He held out; the ecstasy of his release became mind-numbing. She kept up her pace, and his groin tightened then a bolt shot through his back.

Unable to hold back, he released with a roar.

Colin almost forgot who he was. He tried to catch his breath. Sweat dripped from his chest as he lay on the sheets and panted. His skin, a little red from the exertion, flashed heat, then cooled. He lay still for a moment; his blood pounded, and his head spun. His breath slowed when his ears stopped ringing, and he returned to earth.

He opened his eyes and gazed at his wife, who rested her chin on his chest with a satisfied smirk. She trailed her finger in a circle through the hair on his chest, which sent chills over his body.

She glanced at her finger, then back into his eyes. "So, would you consider this a favor returned?"

Colin smiled widely, grabbed her by the shoulders, and quickly flipped their position, so she fell beneath him.

"Come here, ye wee minx. Revenge shall be mine." She giggled as Colin planned a long night of thorough seduction of his wife.

****

Late into the night, Colin lay wide awake. So much ran through his mind. He didn't want Bree and the kids close to the chapel and the stones. It was enough that he must ensure John and Marie returned in one piece with the Stone of Fear. But his heart nearly stopped when Evie reached for the *Fae Fable Book*. The Stones may be part of the family's responsibility, but he needed to figure out how to keep Bree and the kids safe.

He would die if anything happened to Bree. He would go insane if anything happened to his wee babes. *Keep them safe, keep them safe*. He chanted it over and over in his mind.

Chapter 6

Dunstaffnage Castle 1498

John sipped whisky and studied Colin's ancestor, Laird John Alexander McDougall, as they sat in the study. His fifth great-grandfather, Douglas MacArthur, stood by the fireplace and stared at John as he took a slow mouthful of whisky. Douglas resembled John's grandfather, an exact spitting image. He laughed out loud.

Laird Alexander raised an eyebrow as they sat in the chairs before the desk. John glanced at Alexander, who looked more like Colin's father than Colin. Colin remained the identical replica of Laird Roderick MacDougall from the seventeenth century. John became a little dizzy.

John shook his head. "It's surreal, that's all. I'm sitting here with an ancestor in the same room I stood in, in the twenty-first century."

Alexander smiled. "So, the clan survives until the twenty-first century. Good to know we are the powerhouse then that we are now."

John's eyebrows shot up. He covered the reaction as he took a pull on his whisky. He couldn't tell them what became of their future. John glanced into his glass and recalled Scottish history, the clan's wars, the Jacobite rising, and the fall of the Scottish people. They needed to live this out on their own, without future knowledge.

Time, that was the irony. Colin traveled from the future to right the past. John jumped to the past to bring Marie back and right the future. What did the future hold for him and Marie? Fortunately, both ancestors received some exposure to the Fae and the stones and vowed to help. At least Brigid and Morrigan were here. Well, not in this room, but around somewhere. Laird Alexander and Douglas mentioned they met them.

Laird Alexander shifted in his chair. "Glad I canceled me trip. Someone stole our horses last night. It's good I remained here when ye arrived." He sipped his whisky. "I sent me wife Anabelle on ahead anyway. We were te visit her family. I should thank ye for saving me a trip te me in-laws." He chuckled.

The men laughed, and Alexander leveled his gaze at John. "So, we'll connect ye with Douglas MacArthur, our main boat captain. The best sailor on the seas. We'll get yer Marie back."

John glanced at Douglas by the fireplace, who frowned. "Not me, ye dafty." He pointed to his chest. "I'm Douglas John, the captain of the castle. Our cousin Douglas *James* is the boat captain." *Douglas James, the same as his da, who went missing.* A chill snaked down John's spine, and he shook it off. The males in the family were all named after each other. Maybe they named his da after this one.

Alexander rubbed his chin. "I had planned to send him to Islay to negotiate the new partnership with the whisky distillery. They make it, we ship it for a share of profit, and"—he held his glass up—"the best whisky in Scotland."

Douglas held his glass. "I'll drink to that."

Alexander laughed. "Ye'll drink to anything."

Both men raised their glasses and said in unison, "Slainte!" and sipped their whisky.

Alexander turned back to John. "We'll send ye down to see him. He's just returned from a run and sailed around the western coast. He sees and talks to many on his travels. I'll bet he's got news of where yer woman is."

John nodded. "I'm grateful for yer help. We'll track her down, and I'll be back before ye know it." He came closer to her now, and he needed to find her. It took all John's willpower as he sat there and drank, but he needed their help. Hell, he needed all the help he could get. He wanted to get out of there now. John exhaled and chugged his whisky. Aye, he needed Marie.

Alexander stood. "Douglas, get him down to the dock before he drinks all me whisky while pining for his woman."

John stood and set his glass on the desk. "Thank ye, Laird. I appreciate all ye are doing."

Douglas led him out of the study through the hall and into the bailey. They strode to the dock at the castle's rear and passed through the village that became Marie's next project. John took stock of all around him, the rows of huts, the smithy, the tanner. Heck, even the boat house in the distance looked just as Marie described. God, she would love this, a peek into history and the project she would work on in the future.

Douglas kept glancing at John every few steps and then back to the trail. "Are ye sure ye are me relation? Ye don't look much like me?"

John smiled. "Ye are the spitting image of my grandda. We're related, I promise ye."

Douglas stopped and gazed into the distance. "Twenty-first century? What's it like?"

John rubbed his neck. Of all people sent to the past, a previous physics major understood the ramifications of sharing information from the future with someone from the past. Even accidentally mentioning any outcome of an event that influenced history changed the future, and harmed those he loved—hell, even affected the world. He couldn't share much, or the future would change, and he couldn't allow that to happen. *Keep it simple and vague, yet always stick to the truth.* That's what his da always said.

John shrugged, "Faster, easier, less nature. Enjoy what ye got now." He clapped Douglas on the shoulder and proceeded to the dock.

John gazed at the dock and the largest ship he had ever seen. Today became the first time John had seen a galleon so close. He witnessed a replica sail the loch once, but it wasn't near the size of this vessel. The old boat reminded him of his father, an avid mariner who spent many hours sailing on the family-owned antique sailboat with Colin's da, Laird Ronald MacDougall. His da's voice echoed as he described the parts of the ship, and John's gaze roamed the ship.

"The most distinguishing feature of a galleon is the long, prominent beak which formed the bulkhead, followed by a foremast and mainmast, the centermost tall columns the sails hung on. Both foremasts were taller than the single lateen-rigged mizzenmasts closer to the rear, which also held sails. Below those, the square quarter gallery at the stern was a place to stand

and captain the ship."

Douglas clapped him hard on the back, and John stumbled as Douglas yelled to the ship. "Ahoy, Captain, got an addition to yer voyage this trip. Come on down, Dougie."

John glanced at Douglas as he raised an eyebrow and mouthed *Dougie*?

Douglas smiled. "Ye'll like the captain. Everyone likes Dougie." A tall man with hair the color of John's made his way down the plank from the boat to the dock. His face remained down, but his movements looked familiar.

As the man drew near, Douglas said, "John, meet yer cousin, Douglas James MacArthur." When introduced, the man raised his face and gaped at John. John nearly stumbled as he grabbed Douglas' arm. The man on the plank stopped and stared for a moment. *It can't be.* He stood in the fifteenth century, for crying out loud. *How the hell is this possible, and how the hell did this happen*?

John became the first to recover—his breath expelled in a whoosh. "Da?"

Douglas John glanced between them both and scratched his head. "Dougie, I thought ye said ye was from Oban."

His da smiled widely. "It's a long story, Douglas, but right now, I'm going to catch up with my son."

Douglas shrugged and strolled away as he mumbled. "He said he was from Oban. Now his son is from the future. Damned Morrigan's Fae tricks again."

John's father strode to him and gathered him in an enormous hug. "God, John, I've missed ye."

His father's voice hitched a little as John's eyes

watered and his nose itched. His arms slowly wrapped around his father. He hadn't had a hug from him in so many years. He believed he stayed in a dream but stood and held his da.

John held back tears and barely breathed. "Da?" was all he managed to say. Tears streamed down his da's face as they gazed at each other in stunned silence.

Finally, his da wrapped an arm around his shoulder as he steered him to the plank. "Come on, and I'll show ye the boat."

They climbed the plank, and his father yelled over his shoulder. "Hugh, go run and get the missus from my cottage. Tell her it's time, our son is here for his visit, and she's only got till dusk to see him. We set sail tonight."

John tripped and almost fell off the plank. "Ma? Mom is here."

His dad clapped him. "Ye haven't been reading the *Fae Fable Book* as I told ye. I thought Granny was there to help ye."

He strode ahead of John as he muttered, "Can no one do anything right?"

****

As the boat sailed away, John watched the castle fade in the dusky light. His parents, ma, da, lived here in the fifteenth century. After all these years, he visited his parents. Hell, he hugged them both and touched them in real life.

His ma, God, he hadn't seen her in years. Not since she died when he was thirteen. When she stepped into the captain's cabin, John's heart dropped to his feet. At first, they stood and stared. Then he stepped into her arms and felt like a little boy again.

He openly sobbed as she said, "My son, my sweet grown son."

John stood and held her, then smelled her hair, light wildflowers. He embraced her longer as he allowed her love to encircle him. The three of them sat close, always touching—a pat on the knee, a touch to the arm, a grasp of a hand, not wanting to let any moment go.

John couldn't stop himself from asking, "So how did ye end up in the fifteenth century, and what is this bargain with the Fae, Da?"

His da exchanged a glance with his ma, who glanced down as his da patted his knee. "Nothing ye should worry over, something between Morrigan and myself."

His ma touched his leg. "Ye have met her, Morrigan yer Fae?"

John ran his hand through his hair. "Aye, first in a dream, then yesterday in real life."

His da nodded. "That's how they always start, son. Ye need to be wary of the Fae, John. They may seem to help, but it's mostly tricks and games for them. What they do with humans, that is." His ma and da exchanged another glance.

John tried to ask more questions, but they inquired about him as they skimmed over their time in the past. They spent all their time catching up on John's life, the castle. He spoke about Marie and how they fell in love while Colin and Bree recovered a Stone of Iona in the seventeenth century.

Before he realized it, it became time to set sail. What would happen now? Now he had found his parents in the past. As he stood there and the castle grew smaller in the dusk, he figured his parents didn't want him to know, and perhaps he remained better off not knowing.

His eyes teared up again. John didn't think he would ever get over the overwhelming emotion of seeing his parents again. The shock of the moment shook him, and he held on to the rail to steady himself.

His da joined him and patted his back. John stared at him. He still couldn't believe it, his da.

His da smiled. "Ye did read the story, didn't ye?"

The Fae Fable wasn't about Colin and Bree. Hell, the story wasn't even about John and Marie.

A man who bargained with the Fae to return his dead wife so they could spend time together. Damn, if it wasn't about his ma and da.

Morrigan's words at the portal returned to him in startling clarity. *"Blood was already spilt for ye."*

His da somehow bargained with the Fae so he stayed with his ma. They spilled his da's blood, was what Morrigan meant.

But what did she mean when she said, "Ye must remember the Fae Fable Story of The Stone of Fear; without it, ye are doomed as yer father?"

He hadn't bargained with the Fae as his da had. How could he make the same mistake?

John nodded. "Aye, it makes some sense now. At first, Colin and I couldn't figure it out."

His father's voice rose as his eyes opened wide. "Colin, what about Ron?"

John sighed. "Died last year in a car accident, Emily, too."

His da bowed his head and nodded. "God rest their souls."

John tapped his fingers on the rail. "Aye, the evil Fae did it."

His da rocked back. "So, they are at it again? The Fae fighting never amounts to anything good. I figured as much when you mentioned Colin had to travel in time."

John's gaze snapped to his da. "This has happened before?"

He laughed. "Before? Try all the time. The battle of good against evil is ongoing. There is no end."

John gazed out across the water.

His da leaned on the railing and clenched his hands before him. "How many stones have ye recovered?"

John shook his head. "Just one, the Stone of Love."

Douglas frowned. "Then we are in for a battle, son."

John sighed as his da tapped his arm. "The good news is, I know where yer Marie is."

John grabbed his da's arm as his da nodded. "Stood out like a fart in church. The man who has her is stupid. He's still wearing modern clothing and has an English accent to boot. I knew he was from the future but wasn't sure what it meant. Now I know."

John breathed deeply. "So she's okay? We thought a Fae possessed him. That happened when Colin traveled back in time for the Stone of Love."

His da shook his head. "No way this lad possessed. The Fae are smarter than that and better at blending in. Na, he's probably just a fanatic chasing power."

John gaped at him. How did his da know all this, and what exactly had his da done with the Fae, the stones? Many years ago, when his da told him about his duty to protect the rocks, John believed it a myth, the same as Colin. As his father stood beside him, he wondered what all his da knew.

Douglas returned his stare and shrugged. "This isn't my first time dealing with the Fae, and it won't be my last. We'll find yer Marie and the stone. I'll get ye back to yer time. I promise ye that." He hugged John, who held his da a little longer. They stepped back and gazed at each other. His da patted his cheek and strode away.

John stared out over the ocean. *Marie, she is okay.*

He took a deep breath, then another. He should have seen the Fae coming, should've seen the warning signs. Granny said the Fae played with humans and told him he needed to be aware of what the Fae showed them, catch it, and realize what the sign meant.

He gazed across the water. Darkness met his stare, and his mind returned to when the first sign happened. It occurred the day he and Colin worked with the Medieval broad swords before Colin traveled back to the seventeenth century.

****

John picked up his sword and eyed Colin. "Disarm only, no blood. I recall ye like to draw blood."

Colin smiled widely at his recollection of their practices in their youth. *Oh, so this was how it would be. Well, let's see what the lazy solicitor has in him.*

They took a ready stance, and soon the clang of metal rang loudly in the yard.

Colin advanced on John, who stepped left and parried right. After John's block, he rebounded and answered with a swing toward Colin's left, forcing Colin to shift to the right to block his left side. The swords locked in fierce tension, and Colin's gaze connected with his.

John smirked back at him. *Old man, what do ye have in ye?*

Colin returned the expression with a raised eyebrow, and the fight was now on.

Colin broke free and started toward him. Colin swung his attack on each side and pushed John toward the old stable arch ruin. Was Colin's goal to back him into the wall and take advantage of the lack of space John would have? If so, Colin would corner him, disarm him, and win this round. Well, John hadn't sat on his arse all day like Colin and remained ready for a fight.

Swing after swing, Colin worked side to side as he advanced hard on John.

Colin swung right again, then blocked another left advance from John. John rounded on him, struck from overhead, and Colin had to backstep and stop the blow. Colin blocked the blow and slid his sword to the side as John forced his sword off Colin's. Colin didn't pause but struck again to maintain his advance and backed John closer to the archway.

I can't let him best me.

John swung for Colin's legs and forced him to jump to avoid getting hit.

Colin continued his assault that pushed John closer to the wall. The faint voices of women floated over the wall. Colin shifted his attack as he glanced at the archway; that's when John recognized Marie's voice.

"Is that metal?" *Why are the women here?*

Bree crossed between him and Colin, and Colin was already in a full-force downward swing at John.

John stopped, frozen. His block stuck in place as time slowed. Colin threw all his weight to the side. With a roar, he twisted, threw his blade out of line, and his momentum sent him stumbling. His sword missed her, but his body knocked into her. She hit the stone archway and cried out. Off balance, Colin lurched into the wall as his back scraped against it.

Marie ran into the yard. "Bree!"

Colin rounded on Bree and yelled at the top of his lungs, "Good God, woman, never walk into a sword fight! Ye damn near got yer head taken off!"

Bree crumpled into a ball and covered her head with her hands.

Everyone went still.

Bree shook as she softly cried.

"Oh, God, Bree." Colin touched her shoulder.

As his hand made contact, she screamed, "Please don't hit me. Please don't hit me." She crawled farther down the wall on her hands and knees. She curled into a ball, rocking back and forth as she whimpered.

John took a deep breath as he lowered his sword, and his heart turned cold. Marie mentioned Bree's ex beat her, but he didn't know how bad or the toll it took.

Next to him, Marie cried softly, and he took her in his arms. "Shush, it will be all right." He kissed her head and squeezed her.

Colin stared at Bree as he spoke. "John, come take my sword. Take it away."

Colin stood still. "Ye and Marie head into the castle. Go on; we'll be along soon."

John disengaged himself from Marie, who still tried to grip him. Her crying tore his heart. Carefully, he took the sword from Colin.

John leaned toward Colin. "Ye sure ye want us to go? Maybe we need to stay. Help or something."

Colin shook his head. "No, I've got this."

John gathered the bags and handed them to a sniffling Marie. He picked up the swords, sheathed each, and slipped them over one shoulder. He placed his arm around Marie and guided her toward the castle.

John and Marie rounded the corner. John dropped the swords, sat by the castle's rock foundation, and ran both hands through his hair. He glanced at Marie, and she cried again. He rose and strode to her.

She dropped the bags, launched into his arms, and gripped his shoulder tightly. "Oh God, John. He almost took her head off."

John sat back on the rock and cradled Marie, grateful for her warmth and comfort. He held her tightly for a moment. Her tears soaked through his shirt. He closed his eyes and inhaled—*lilies*.

From the woman's side, they were blind to the sword work he and Colin did. If Marie walked into the fight, Colin might not have been able to change direction soon enough. God, he might have lost Marie today.

"*M'eudail, my darling*, God, I don't know what I would've done if ye crossed in Colin's blade." John held her tight as he slid down the rock, sat on the ground, and cradled Marie in his lap. He kept her close, didn't want to let her go. He rested as he rubbed her back as her tears subsided.

Marie glanced into his eyes. "I never knew." She sighed. "…I mean, I never realized how bad Bree's ex was to her. Did ye see her reaction?"

John cupped her cheek. "Aye, I did, and it made

my heart cold. I've seen nothing like her fear and the physical reaction."

Marie nodded. "It makes me rethink everything she's told me. Initially, I thought she acted dramatically. Like exaggerating to make a point." She glanced away. "Now I rethink it all. Everything."

Marie shivered, and John gathered her close in his arms. "I don't want ye thinking of such things. Yer thoughts bring them to yer door whether or not ye want them."

Marie gazed into the distance, silent in her reflection.

John tried to read her expression. Had something like this happened to her? John cupped her cheek and turned her face to his.

He swallowed and gazed at her. "Marie, has something like this happened to ye?" He brushed her hair off her face. "I want ye to be honest. I need to know."

Marie's eyes went wide, and she swallowed hard. "No, it hasn't happened to me, but I had a dream." She shook her head. "No, nothing."

John grabbed both her shoulders. "There is no nothing to it. I see something in yer eyes. What is it ye saw?"

Marie stared off toward the loch.

Her voice sounded far away when she spoke, yet she stayed in his arms. "A dream, a dream I had after I arrived at the castle. I remained tied up. In an old boat in the rain." She tried to draw her breath, and it hitched.

John squeezed her.

"A priest stood over me, screaming. He seemed so real." She shook her head. "It's nothing, just a reaction to Bree's situation." She smiled at John and kissed him quickly. "Just stupid imagination. It's nothing."

Nothing echoed in John's mind.

****

"Nothing here, Captain," a man yelled near him.

John blinked and fell out of his memory to the sound of the men loosening the mizzenmast's sails as they called orders to each other. John knew now he should have paid better attention back when his da tried to teach him.

He and Colin realized the Fae were at work, that the evil Fae targeted those close to the stones. People close to those who guarded them, to him and Colin. It was naïve to think the evil Fae only pursued the MacDougall family. Now he understood, and he wished he would've listened then. John should have protected her and done something to stop the Fae from coming for her.

He glanced back at his da and understood a greater sense of failure. His parents—could their situation be a product of the evil Fae as well? His da seemed at peace with their choices, a dangerous bargain with the Fae for extra time spent with a dead wife.

Marie's kidnapping, the Fae, the stones. Could John have prevented this all from happening? Either way, he must find Marie. For now, he feared her life depended on it.

Chapter 7

Father Clarke dragged her back to the St Martin's Cross at Iona. The monastery came into view as they came up the hill from the port. Smaller and newer, the building seemed similar yet different.

Nuns walked around the building and stopped when they spotted them.

The priest drew up short, quickly turned, and cut her bindings. "Damn, I didn't think anyone would occupy the place. You will do what I tell you, or I will cut you."

Marie smirked at his bent head. He became stupider by the minute. How could he think nuns wouldn't inhabit a *nun's* priory. What an idiot. His mistake became her good fortune. She would somehow signal the nuns, get free, find a boat, sail back to Dunstaffnage, the chapel with the portal, and back to John. Far-fetched but possible if she only put her mind to it. One step at a time. Signal nuns and get free.

Father Clarke grabbed her hand and approached the two nuns. "My fair clergy, how fortunate we are to come to this holy place."

Marie pulled back and glared at the nuns.

Father Clarke dragged her beside him. "*My wife* and I are on a pilgrimage and wish to pray before the great cross, St Martin's cross."

Marie tripped when he yanked her forward. When

her head came up, she caught the eye of one nun and slightly shook her head. Surely, they would recognize a distressed woman, one taken against her will. Marie needed help.

The nuns exchanged a look, and the taller of the two stepped forward. "Any pilgrim wishing to find solace with the lord is welcomed at Iona Abbey. The cross is in the main yard on the other side of the monastery." As she walked on, she waved with her hand for them to follow.

Father Clarke grabbed her arm hard.

Marie jolted as they stepped forward.

The second nun followed behind as the group progressed through the property. "So nice that a married couple comes to pray together. Yers must be a love match."

Marie turned and shook her head, but Father Clarke yanked on her arm, forcing her to face forward. "Yes, my *wife* and I truly love one another. We must pray before St. Martin's cross for our new beginning, a match made in heaven and blessed by God."

They rounded the corner, and the cross came into view. New in this time, it shone brightly in the afternoon sun. Drawing closer, Marie needed to take advantage of the nuns' presence before she lost her opportunity to escape.

She twisted back to the nun again. "Sister, would it be possible to freshen up in the monastery? I am dry and dirty from our travels. Maybe I may find *sanctuary* with the walls while *my husband* prays."

The priest wiped her around to face him and raised his eyebrow as he spoke through clenched teeth. "Now, wife, you know we are on a mission from God. He has spoken, and we must follow his command. The stone, remember the stone and what not finding it threatens."

Both nuns stopped and glared.

The first nun stepped forward and placed her hand on Marie's arm. "Kind woman, ye must heed yer husband's good advice. A pilgrimage is a trip taken for the lord. Ye give sacrifices as God sacrificed himself on the cross for our sins." She patted her arm before she turned to continue to the cross. "A dutiful wife obeys her husband in all."

Father Clarke twisted his hand on her arm, the sting bringing tears to her eyes. "Yes, *wife*, be dutiful and *obey* your husband."

Marie couldn't believe her ears. Be dutiful. What had the world come to? But then again, they were in the fifteenth century, and this was all a woman's value was back then. A shell of a woman defined by what man wanted her to be. As they neared the cross, Marie thanked God she lived in the future.

Father Clarke stopped them before the cross and stared with an open mouth.

The first nun bowed. "I shall leave ye both in peace and prayer. Come to the monastery for a meal before ye leave."

He waved without taking his eyes from the cross. "It will not be necessary. We will pray and leave to catch our ship back to the mainland."

Both nuns bowed, and Marie stepped forward only to be dragged to the ground scraping her hands on the bottom of the cross.

When the nuns cleared the corner and were out of view, he hissed in her ear, "The stone, get me the stone, you bitch."

She ignored him and studied St. Martin's Cross instead. It was a beautiful cross, complete and unharmed in this time. The front resembled the Irish high crosses, with biblical scenes on the shaft, and the cross's very center design represented the Virgin and Child. She sat there as she took in the completed cross. In her time, the cross sat broken and lacking.

He shoved her shoulder. "Concentrate. Get the stone."

Marie righted herself and closed her eyes. She concentrated on what he commanded but not on what he wanted. No, Marie prayed with all her might. *Please, God, hear me. I must get back to John and the future. I love him and all I want is to be back in the future. I serve you well and am devoted to my beliefs. Please hear me. All I've ever wanted is to remodel a holy building.*

****

The day John took her to see the priory ruin, Ardchattan Priory came to her clear and bright as the cross before her.

Marie and John walked down the dock toward the marina and pub as they left Brielle and Colin for their day of sailing on Loch Etive.

John stopped at the end of the pier. "So, today's a day off from the chapel work. Care to spend a day taking in some scenery of the glen?"

Marie blushed. "Well, I haven't planned how to spend my day off, so I am free. What did ye have in mind?"

John took Marie's hand in his. "Well, there's a priory, Ardchattan Priory, close to here." Marie's pulse sped at the mention of the old priory ruins. She meant

92

to take a day off and explore them, and this was the perfect chance.

"Ardchattan Priory. I'd love to see it. But we'll need to grab lunch. It's far from here, and I'll want to examine the layout and buildings. Oh, and I'll need to take notes. I've got my cell for pictures. We'll need to go back to the castle…"

John kissed her hand. "No need. I've prepared for this day just as we prepared Brielle and Colin's day."

Marie blinked. "Ye did?"

John nodded and kissed her hand again. "I knew the best way to convince ye to join me was to promise ye a trip to see some old rocks."

Marie pulled her hands from his. "They are more than just some old rocks."

John took both her hands back into his. "I know. I was teasing. The church is what's important to ye, so it's important to me. Who knows, I may learn something new today."

Marie didn't spend the day alone. John always came to her rescue. He smiled as she peered into his eyes.

He turned and escorted her to the car. "Why can't minerals lie?"

Marie shrugged as John laughed. "Because they're in their pure form."

Marie danced like a child as they approached Ardchattan Priory from the parking lot. The grounds lay in an idyllic location that overlooked Loch Etive.

Marie researched the property before she arrived at Dunstaffnage. Years had passed since the modernization. Her eyes roamed the building, and she noted the updated sections held an aged look. The old abbey remained her lifelong dream—to remodel a historic religious structure. Between Ardchattan Priory and the chapel, this one was in sore need.

She frowned as she examined the chapel ruins near the priory. The chapel here was in even worse condition than the one she and Bree worked on at Dunstaffnage. This one had lost three walls, yet portions of the altar remained.

John led her around the property. The rear area opened into the garden with a picturesque view of Loch Etive. Beyond the loch, the shadows of the Ben Cruachan mountain range stretched for eons. Layers of green highlands lapped over one another, slipped into the loch, and reflected like a mirror in the tranquil waters.

She sighed, and John took her hand then kissed the back of it. "I knew ye'd like this."

"Aye, I thought I might spend my day off working alone in the chapel, but when ye suggested exploring the priory ruin…"

John's hand caressed her face and stopped her speech as he smiled. "I know."

They continued along the garden paths, which honored the site's monastic origins, with names such as Monk's Walk and Priory's Walk. The main house patch included a rock garden and extensive herbaceous and rose borders, all with excellent views of Loch Etive. To the west of the house sat rows of shrub borders surrounded by a wild garden of roses and floral displays. Marie stopped to take in the scenery, and John held her hand between his. His constant touch became a welcome reminder that she wasn't alone.

She led them farther along the path until they

encountered a display marker. Marie read the text aloud. "Duncan MacDougall, Lord of Lorn and builder of Dunstaffnage Castle near Oban founded the priory dedicated to St Modan in 1231. Kings of Scotland and Norway fought to control Argyll and the Inner Hebrides. Robert the Bruce held a parliament here in 1309."

Marie shifted to read the rest. "The MacDougalls dominated the priory throughout most of its existence. Indeed, by the end of the fifteenth century, the family monopolized the prior position."

She looked at John. "So, the MacDougalls built and developed the property."

He tapped the marker. "Aye, they founded this entire area of Scotland with my family alongside."

John squeezed her hand as he led her away. "I knew ye'd want a closer look at the chapel here."

Marie squeezed his hand back and smiled.

Like her first trip to the ruins at the Chapel in the Woods of Dunstaffnage, Marie examined the area as John followed behind.

She traced her finger over the small piscina near the altar where three bowl-like stone carvings sat. She sensed the people who made the old stone as she touched it, felt closer to the monks who worked here centuries ago. She gazed around her and took in the ambiance while she read each marker. She revealed what each represented—the impact each person had on the property, on history.

Marie crossed to areas of the chapel yard, where they crammed tombs into burial rows. She kept her feet perfectly parallel as she walked between the graves. Some were so close, she couldn't step between them, but she bent over and studied them to read each grave marker as she noted each person entombed for all time.

John stood by patiently and allowed her the time to examine each part of the ruin.

Marie strode from the grave area. John stretched his hand out and helped her. When she stepped up, she stumbled and fell into his arms.

He steadied her against his chest. "I got ye, Marie." They stood there momentarily, gazed into each other's eyes, and John brushed a hair from her face. He took her hand and guided them to the other side of the ruins. In this area, old grave markers sat upright so visitors got a closer look.

John cleared his throat and read from the display. "Among the many fine grave markers and carved stones on display, the greatest is the MacDougall Cross. Commissioned by Prior Eugenius MacDougall in 1400 and carved by John Ó Brolchán, a stone carver from Iona. This is one of the few examples of West Highland carving and a fine example of detailed work."

Next to the display sat the large cross with portions of the design cracked off. Marie strode around the cross as she looked closer. On one side, the cross bore a crucifixion scene. On the other, an image of the Virgin and Child sat incomplete.

She sighed, "Cromwell's Clearances is probably responsible for the damage. Damn shame, the clearances ruined so many Christian monuments."

John glanced at the marker again and gasped. "This is something I didn't know. The ghost of a nun haunts the priory ruins. It says she was the lover of a monk and hid beneath the floor of his room so that she visited her lover at night. But the prior found her and, as punishment for her sins, buried her alive."

A chill shot up Marie's spine. She shivered and rubbed her arms.

John's hands took her shoulders and rubbed them. She shivered again, and he hugged her in his arms. His warmth and his care chased away her chill.

He kissed her forehead. "Hungry yet?"

Marie nodded, ready for a distraction.

John led her to the grassy area near the loch, a place the priory reserved for picnicking. He touched her face. "Ye wait here. I'll get the picnic basket. Mrs. A. packed it, insisting we enjoy ourselves."

Marie stood there as she waited for John to return.

Every so often, a sailboat passed by, and she wondered if Bree's day became as lovely as hers. She smirked. Bree deserved a nice day sailing on the loch with Colin. She and John set up the MacDougall hunting cabin with candles and flowers and included a cooked dinner from Mrs. A. for them both and an overnight bag for Bree. Bree certainly had a better day but was due for an even better night.

She giggled, then laughed out loud.

John approached from behind her. "What's so funny?"

She turned, and he held a large basket in both hands. The wind ruffled his hair as a smile rose on his face. A fluttering grew in her chest as she took a breath. He was such a handsome man.

Marie grinned and kissed him quickly. "Nothing."

John set the basket down and spread a blanket. He shifted the fabric once as he ensured they overlooked both Loch Etive and the priory.

Marie sat and dug into the basket. "Look, Mrs. A.

sent sandwiches and fresh fruit with wine. Merlot, my favorite."

John sat next to her, and her face heated in a blush as they set out the food and lounged side by side in comfortable silence as they ate.

Her gaze roamed the priory building. Taking note of the structure's dilapidated state she wished someone would restore the building like she and Bree had worked on Dunstaffnage's Chapel in the Woods. She sighed at the idea of what an enormous undertaking this type of project took.

John nudged her shoulder with his. "What's wrong?"

Marie glanced at him, then back at the priory. "Oh, nothing."

He picked up his wine glass, swirled it. "Really? That was an awful big sigh for nothing."

Her gaze returned to the building. "The priory, it's such a beautiful place. Someone should take better care of it, fix it up."

John sipped his wine and waved his glass at the building. "Tell me, what would ye do with this place?"

Marie sipped her wine as she studied the grounds. Her gaze roamed the buildings and took stock of what she wanted repaired first if this were hers to renovate. After the Jacobite rising and the fall of Scotland, almost all historic buildings were destroyed or abandoned. Hope spread in her, a renovation project of a historical worship house in Scotland.

She shook her head. "Aw, this would take too much money to fix this place up right, do the dwelling justice. No one would put that kind of money into it. It's why so many Scottish buildings sit in disrepair. Too expensive."

John sat up. He rested his arm on his knee, the wine glass dangling from his fingers. "Suppose ye got a grant from the Historical Society, maybe added private funds. Found someone who was willing to put money into this place. What would ye do?"

Her gaze roamed the priory. "Frist, the foundation likely needs a lift. Then repair the cracks in the walls, double-check them for rot." Her eyes roamed to an area in the wall with significant water damage. "Most of the walls must be torn down and redone. That will be expensive as I would want them built historically accurate, stone wall and hand mixed plaster inside, not the synthetic crap people use today." She shook her head. "The cost would be astronomical, an amount impossible to gain any return on from mere tourists." When her eyes shifted to the roof, she shook her head and glanced back at John. "The roof and the archways need replacing as well."

John glanced at the priory then back at her. "Ye know the MacDougalls own this place. The chapel ruins, the graveyard, and gardens are now under the care of the Historic Environment of Scotland who opens them to tourists, but the priory is a private residence."

She sipped her wine and huffed. "I'm surprised someone is living in it now. I bet rainy days make for wet nights."

John laughed. "Aye, they do. The tenant complains about putting out over a dozen pots and bowls."

Marie sat up. "Ye mean, this place is a property ye manage as well."

John sat up and faced her. "Aye, it is. And it's

something I've been meaning to discuss with Colin. The place needs work."

Hope flared in her. Would Colin take on the cost and allow her to oversee it? "Oh, what I wouldn't give to restore Ardchattan Priory. It's been my all-time dream to lead the renovation of a historical religious site, but the cost."

John's hand caressed her face. "Would ye like to help me with the proposal? Maybe suggest ye oversee it?"

She set her glass down as her heart raced. She breathed out and as she tried to calm herself, her gaze returned to John. "Ye mean it?"

John nodded as Marie launched herself into his arms and spilled his wine into the grass.

She kissed him as he rolled to his back and held her against him. "If I had known asking ye about this old place would make ye jump into my arms, I would've done this the first day ye arrived." She kissed him again, and his hand wove through her hair. He tilted her head, deepening the kiss as their tongues swirled together.

She sat back and disengaged from him. "Wait, I have to get back. We have so much planning to do."

John lay still and glared at her. "That wasn't the reaction I wanted after kissing ye."

She crawled over to him, pecking a light kiss on his lips. "I promise more after we finish the proposal." Marie shoved each item into the basket as she hastily packed the food.

John sat up. "Lord, woman, that could take weeks. How about a kiss after each planning session?"

She leaned over and kissed his cheek. "Deal!"

****

Father Clarke shoved her again. "That's long enough. Where's my stone. God demands the stone, and I must deliver it or suffer his wrath."

She glared up at him. "It's not here. The stone wasn't in the future and it's not the *past*." She yelled the last word, and "past" echoed in the yard.

A nun came around the corner and stared at them. Another chance at escape!

Marie bent forward and moaned. When nothing happened, she moaned louder.

Footfalls came near. "Sir, is something wrong with her?"

Marie lifted her head and spoke, but Father Clarke grabbed her. "Nothing, just overcome with the lord's presence." He dragged her to stand and strode away as he held her arm.

Marie resisted but the priest kept a fast pace. "Try anything and I'll cut you here."

He made fast work of getting to the dock and loaded them on the ship. Marie stood at the bow and tears fell as the ship sailed. The view of Iona Abbey faded as did her hope for rescue and escape.

Later Marie stood at the ship's bow. A cold light rain started and reminded her of the night John held her during the storm, the one after the priory visit.

****

She couldn't reach the opening. The hole seemed barely large enough to turn around in. Her fingers grazed the dirt as more dropped upon her face. She clawed the walls repeatedly as the soil packed under her nails, but she didn't care. Grime landed on her head, stuck in her hair. She leaned back and tried to find fresh air, but more dirt fell. *No, this could not be happening*. As she tilted her head back for air, the monk's red, sweaty face appeared at the top of the pit.

She stretched toward the opening again, like a lost soul who reached for heaven, but a shout answered. "Women are the temptation placed on the earth to foul men. You shall pay the price of the priest's sin. Die, whore!"

Debris fell continuously now and covered her legs. She cried for help, but none came. The monk shuffled around at the top. The dirt fell in large clumps and piled up as it gathered around her body. *Please, God, don't let my life end, not this way, not without John. Please let me see him one last time.*

It covered her chest, pressed in, and she struggled for air. She couldn't stop the dirt's fall and the mound trapped her arms. She couldn't touch her face. Earth piled around and covered her. She tried to draw in a breath but couldn't. Left suspended, her lungs burned desperately as she tried to breathe.

Marie screamed. She glanced from side to side and sat in her bed. She inhaled, and it hitched. The door burst open, and John came beside her before she drew her next breath.

He pulled her into his arms and hugged her. "What is it? What has scared ye so?"

She drew in a shaky breath, released it, and then another. A tear dropped on her cheek. John sat back and wiped the tear away.

He kissed her lightly. "Ye are safe. Ye are dreaming, that's all *m'eudail, my darling*." John eased her back so she lay down as he helped her untangle the bedclothes. He brushed her hair aside and studied her face.

"What is it?" She shook her head and said nothing.

John gazed at her for a moment, then tucked her in bed and kissed her softly.

He rose, but she grabbed his arm and stopped him. "Will ye stay till I fall back asleep?"

John nodded, climbed into bed, and took her into his arms and carefully wrapped himself around her in a protective cocoon.

His voice came soft as he spoke. The timbre of his voice was clear and haunting as he nearly whispered in the poem's rhythm.

The sea fairy swam fast away,
Safely over the wave and sea.
Gave her heart to her human love,
Will she ne'er come back to me.

His chest rumbled a little with his breath but the way his voice softly echoed in the room reached her.

Will ye no come back again?
Will ye no come back again?
Better loved ye canna be,
Will ye no come back again?

He paused and rubbed her back.

She tilted her head till her eyes connected with his. "Please don't stop; it's soothing. Did ye make that up?"

He smiled. "Aye, after our first dinner together."

She sighed. "Yer sea nymph."

He whispered the poem again as he brushed his fingers over her back.

The sea fairy swam fast away,
Safely over the wave and sea.
Gave her heart to her human love,
Will she ne'er come back to me.

Will ye come back to me?
Will ye come back to me?
Better loved ye canna be,
Will ye come back to me?

He kissed her head and held her. Nothing more, nothing less, and she never felt so safe before.

She lay awake deep into the night, unable to fall back asleep. A light rain started and pattered on the window. The rain trailed down the window, and the light cast rippling shadows over their embraced bodies. The rain reminded Marie of their night in the kitchen when the power cut out. She snuggled closer to John, resting her head against his chest. With the lulling sound of the rain, and the light shadow of trickling water over their bodies, Marie fell asleep to John's heartbeat.

****

Rain drops jolted Marie out of her memory. She stood on the ship's deck and gazed at the ocean. The vessel, new in this age, left Marie a little off kilter. She believed this was a galleon ship, the three sails with a main tall mast in the center. Large ropes crowded near the edge, yet she found a place and stood at the rail as she gazed out over the sea.

She remained wet and cold. But she stood and stared across the water toward Dunstaffnage. She couldn't see the castle but sensed the building's presence—*home*. She wanted to be home again, home in John's arms. A tear trailed down her cheek, and she wiped at it hard.

Father Clarke probably slept warmly in the small cabin. She didn't want to be anywhere near him and, for once in her life, she enjoyed being alone. Father Clarke commanded her to study his book the previous night in hopes she would provide him with directions to find an Iona Stone. But her goal remained to find a way forward in time, back home to John. She sighed. She found no way which took her back to John. She thumped her fist on the railing. There had to be something.

Marie closed her eyes and ran the book images through her mind. Something had to be there. There were chorales, drawings of various crosses across Scotland, and descriptions of the Stones of Iona, but no list of them individually or their locations. The book described how the stones held the ability to rule the world. She recalled the pages which displayed the Dunstaffnage Chapel in the Wood. The book led Father Clarke to believe she drew power from the mosaic floor she renovated.

While the volume didn't specifically reference any power, it spoke about magic from the floor, the same theory Emily MacDougall, Colin's mother, had about the chapel. A page referenced Fae portals and listed a few which included the chapel door. That must be the page where he learned the chant to open the chapel portal. From what Bree told Marie, a Fae must be present to open a portal. However, he used a simple chant.

Other biblical-type quotes were inside, and one page spoke about the consequences if a human died on the holy ground without being shriven. The book gave him only a portion of what he needed to locate any of the Iona stones, and she sure as hell wouldn't help him.

When Father Clarke asked her what she found in the book, she told him she viewed nothing more than what he had. He looked like he wanted to slap her, but he didn't. From what Marie figured, he pieced together a part of the book and filled in the rest from his demented imagination, *the power of God, to power the stones*. Bree mentioned human emotions powered the rocks. She used her love for Colin and powered the Stone of Love which returned him from purgatory.

She gazed out over the water and wished she existed someplace else. The next cross listed in the book led them to Islay isle. They caught the same ship that took them to Iona as it headed to Islay, the capital for the whisky trade. She smirked. She needed a drink about now. She was wet, cold, and alone, and a shot could warm her inside and ease her headache.

She stared at the ocean for lack of anything else to do. In the distance, she spied another ship, one like hers. She sighed. If only John stood on that ship as he searched for her. She wrapped herself tighter in her plaid and prayed he came for her.

Chapter 8

"Ship ahoy, Captain!" a lad called from the ship's crow's nest.

John barely viewed the outline of another ship as it sailed in the rainy distance. God, how he wished Marie traveled this close, so he could reach out, grab her, and take her to safety.

His father stood next to him with a spyglass. "Too far to tell, and in this rain. I don't know, son."

John closed his eyes. He sensed her call him, and while his logical mind told him this was nothing more than his yearning, his heart told him differently. They sailed close to Iona and might catch up with the priest and Marie. He feared they missed them altogether.

His father spoke softly. "Ye know, John, fear—it's a good and bad feeling."

John opened his eyes and gazed at the ship across the sea as his father's voice calmed him. "Fear can apply to many different areas of yer life."

Douglas leaned on the railing. "At times ye fear losing yer friends, or ye fear for yer children's health." Had his da feared for him when he chose to leave the future? John would have.

"Ye fear for loved ones, especially the one closest to yer heart." His father was right. His fear for Marie was so high at times he couldn't think straight, but other times, so clearly.

His da huffed a laugh. "Fear of losing yer quick wit—" Douglas took a deep breath. "—and so much more."

John turned to his father, who tapped his arm. "What defines ye is how ye deal and cope with fear." His father made a fist. "The emotion can either eat ye up inside or ye use it to fuel yer actions to help ye steer to a better outcome." His da released the fist and waved his hand out over the ocean. "Whether by fate or choice."

They stood silent momentarily, the waves lapping against the ship as the rigging creaked.

Fate or choice echoed in John's mind. Fate acted on people. Yet choice, well, that was what someone made of a situation—choose to sit back or decide to act.

He glanced at his da, who winked at him. "Facing yer fears, John, it's what defines ye as a man."

His father clapped him on the back. "Have no fear, son. We'll find her soon."

John nodded as his father walked away.

He closed his eyes trying to find peace and remembering the kayak trip they took together on Loch Etive rolled into his mind.

****

Marie wobbled in the small craft as she adjusted her seat for the tenth time. "John, I am not as experienced a kayaker as ye. Ye will have to help me if things get rough."

John smiled at her. "Ye will be fine. We are in the same kayak, and I'm in the back so I can control it all the time. Just do as I say and follow my lead."

They steered out of the marina in the two-man kayak. John sat behind Marie, and she kept glancing back at him.

He grinned and winked. "What do ye call a rock that bunks school?"

Marie laughed out loud. "Wait, I know this one. A skipping stone."

John grunted. "Aw, now she's on to me."

John steered them toward the Falls of Lora. The time neared, the change in tides, and the rapids churned as they created a rushing set of waves. He enjoyed the falls every spring and wanted to share this with Marie. He hoped Marie remained up for the challenge.

Marie looked around. "John, we aren't going to the falls, are we?" She glanced back at him; her voice faltered. "John, I am not skilled enough for the falls."

John lifted his paddle and rested it across his lap. "Marie, I am skilled enough. I run the falls all the time. They are light this time of year and I promise, ye will be safe with me."

John picked up his paddle, and they continued to the falls as she spoke. "The Falls of Lora is a narrow gap hemmed in Loch Etive and a shallow underwater cill."

John switched his paddle to the other side of the boat. "Depending upon the tide, the level of the loch can vary by several feet from the sea level. As the ocean level outside the loch rises or falls, vast amounts of water spills into or out of the body of water. The resulting conditions range from a strong current or a rough rapid forming midstream."

Marie turned and gazed into his eyes. He looked back with the affection in his heart. He wanted her to see he would always be there for her.

He set his paddle in his lap as they freely drifted.

"The falls are a law unto themselves. But don't fear, this is a mild time, and we'll have a good ride."

As they neared the falls, Marie tensed when the roar of the waves reached them.

John needed her relaxed, ready as he shouted commands, so they would make it through the rapids safely. "Marie, listen, all ye need to do is keep yer paddle in the water with the edge out to help guide us. When I say switch sides, just change sides of the boat. I'll do the rest from back here. Keep yer weight in the center and I'll rock the boat to the sides. Okay?"

Marie peeked back at him and nodded.

She smiled. "If ye can control it, I think it'll be fun to ride the waves."

John guided them into the falls, and they rolled a little to the right. "Change sides," John yelled.

Marie flipped her paddle. They rolled to the other side and rushed out of the falls. Marie yelped as John laughed.

Marie panted and peered back at John. "I did it. We didn't die."

John laughed out loud. "Want to try again?"

Marie nodded as her grin went wide. They rode the waves for an hour before the tide changed and they paddled back to the marina.

John maneuvered the small craft near the dock, caught the side, and tied his end to the cleat. "Marie, stay in the boat. I'll get out first then help ye out so ye don't dunk in the loch."

He stood and the boat wobbled as he stepped out.

Marie cried out. "John!"

Her end of the boat drifted from the dock. He quickly bent and grabbed the side of the ship.

He pulled the vessel closer, took the rope, and secured her end of the kayak. "Nothing to worry about *m'eudail.*"

John helped her out of the boat, she stumbled, and John caught her in his arms.

She huffed. "John, my body feels like a noodle."

He smiled. "Aye, my goal all along. To make ye so tired ye will fall into my arms."

Marie smiled and righted herself. "John, if ye wanted me in yer arms, all ye had to do was ask."

John held her closer and kissed her deeply. He slowly finished the kiss and gazed into her eyes. "Why was the geologist never hungry?"

Marie shook her head.

John kissed her nose, "Because he lost his apatite. Let's go get a fish 'n chips and a beer at the pub. I'm starved."

****

Rain fell on his face as it carried him out of his memory. He recalled the night she experienced the nightmare, and he held her as she slept. He reached her in time then; he hoped he would get to her in time now.

He stared out at the ship crossing the opposite direction and prayed he hadn't made a mistake and possibly cost Marie her life. "Please don't let me be too late."

****

"Ye just missed 'em." John's heart sank. "Awful strange fellow, he was, too, dressed funny and a Sassenach at that. The lady with him, though, fine stock and a lovely woman."

John grabbed him by his collar. "The woman, was she okay? Had he hurt her?"

111

His da pried him from the harbor master, who brushed his coat off and stepped back from them.

"Come on, son, no need to attack Mac here. He's just telling the news, that's all."

Mac straightened his collar. "Nay, Dougie, it's fine. I can see a lovesick pup for what he is." He scratched his chin. "Strange, though, she wasn't going against her will. I mean, she went with him willingly."

He nodded, then raised his head. "Well, she didn't look happy, though, and she had a roughed-up look about her as if someone punched her a few times, but the bruises are fading."

John shook his da's hands free and ran both hands through his hair. "I'll kill him. Priest or not, I'll kill the son of a bitch."

His da sighed. "Thanks, Mac. We'll dock for now and head out with the tide. Would ye know where they might have headed?"

Mac looked at John briefly, then at his da, and shrugged his shoulders. "Islay, they headed to a chapel in Islay. The damn man kept muttering it and something about a stone."

His da clapped Mac on the back. "Well, isn't fortune smiling upon me? I must head that way anyhow. Need to complete the whisky partnership for the laird."

Mac grinned. "Ye get a hold of an extra cask, ye send it my way."

John walked down the dock and left the two men to their chatter. He wanted to kick himself a hundred times and again for good measure. She stood on the ship they passed, just within his sight but out of his grasp. He sensed her and should've listened to his heart. She probably stared at him as he gazed across the rain-swept sea. God, he failed her. The priest hurt her, maybe abused her in God knows how many ways, and he couldn't get to her soon enough.

He shoved his hands in his pockets as his imagination drove him mad. His right hand hit his Iona stone. He gripped the gem, and it warmed in his hand. He hadn't thought of the charm this whole trip.

He pulled the stone from his pocket, held it tight, and prayed, "Marie, if ye have yer stone, feel me; feel my love. I'm coming."

Chapter 9

Marie's professor's voice from the university rang clearly in her head. The image on the projected screen was much smaller than what stood in front of her now. A tall, thin cross in gray stone with moss that grew around the base, some green, some gray.

Today the sun shone brightly from behind the cross. The relic seemed like it descended from the heavens through a sunbeam.

The professor's highland lilt lent to the historical moment as she examined the historical cross. "Kildalton High Cross remained Scotland's only surviving complete Celtic cross, and the only Celtic cross still in its original position. The cross sits next to the church in Kildalton, Islay. In eight hundred A.D., the carver made it in gray-green chlorite schist, a local hard rock. The cross remained very difficult to work because of the dense rock they made it from, but due to the rock's durability it's in an excellent state of preservation. Fine carvings covered much of the cross's surface, which became more impressive given the stone's hardness."

Marie sighed as her hand touched the old cross before her. Her fingers rippled over the grooves of the design. Being tied up and dragged across Scotland's islands wasn't how a history major wanted to visit Scotland's greatest religious landmarks. She and her girlfriends talked about a weekend trip to this island to see this cross, stay a night in an old inn, and tour the whisky distilleries.

A shadow passed over the stone. She glanced up, and Father Clarke glared at her.

She turned to Kildalton Chapel, which sat near the cross, and her gaze traveled through the beautiful woodland with old, mossy oaks and birch trees. A quaint cottage sat beyond, likely the resident priest's home. It would've been convenient if he popped up and she cried for help, but the priest serving the chapel wasn't there. As she looked around, she figured this would've made a nice romantic trip. She and John could wander through the woods and tour the distilleries. End the day together, drunk off whisky, life, and love.

The priest yanked on her ties, and her hands ached at the tug. Father Clarke yelled in her face again, but she refused to pay attention. She grew tired of this total arse. She liked to think of him that way. She kept herself amused at his expense and that became the only thing that made the days bearable.

He yelled at her again. "I've tried the chant, and it's not working. You need to get me the Stone of Iona. It *is* here, and you have to find it. God demands a stone." Marie rolled her eyes, and they landed on the delicate patterns on the cross that crisscrossed, like in his book. *If I examined the text, then I'd know the next cross.*

A plan formed quickly in Marie's mind. "Well, this cross has many depictions. It's hard to interpret them all without looking at yer notebook. Let me look at the book and compare it to the cross. Maybe something will line up."

Father Clarke shook his head. "No, you can't look at the book. Just tell me where the stone is."

Marie shrugged. "I can't help when I don't know what I am looking at or what I am even looking for. If ye claim the book ye hold has all the clues, then I need to study them both together." Father Clarke looked at the book, then at the cross. He flipped a couple of pages and glanced at Marie. He tilted his head and studied her for a moment.

She looked away, hating the glint in his eye.

He shoved the book under her nose. "Fine, see what you can make of it, but I am not uniting you."

Marie took the book in her hands and rose. It took a few attempts as she held the text and turned the pages with both hands tied, but she did it. She recognized some depictions on the cross but not all. If he were following the list, this would be the most decorated they visited. She might as well try something, especially if she gained an edge against the priest. She needed a plan to get back to the chapel, the portal, and back to John.

Since she stood on the west side, she started there. The cross depicted geometric designs comprising two roundels of "snake-and-boss" decoration, a prominent boss set in a ring of smaller bosses and paired snakes in the center of the west face, and four inward-facing lions, symbolizing Christ as the Lion of Judah. She flipped through the book—nothing to note.

She crossed to the other side. On the east face, rich spiral work wove around five open roundels on what appeared to be peacocks that feasted on grapes—a detail she found in some scrollwork border in the book but nothing notable related to stones. The cross depicted the Virgin and Child on the crosshead, typical of most all crosses of the time.

She continued her stroll as she turned the pages of the book. She pretended to note the arms of the cross and compare them to the book, but really, she read the book. Now that she held it, she studied the pages and translated the Latin. The Latin disclosed information about the Fae that was a jumbled mess compared to what she learned from John. On the bottom of the page was a quote in Latin, and as she studied the page, the sunlight hit the section,

The fear of man brings a snare: but who so put his trust in God shall be safe.

She memorized the line, and it echoed in her mind. *Who so put his trust in God shall be safe.* She interpreted the quote as a message from the Fae. *Ye'll get through this. Just have faith.* She smirked—faith— and a plan.

She turned to the cross page, and the next cross on the list showed the MacDougall Cross at Ardchattan Priory. If he followed the book, their next stop occurred near Dunstaffnage and the chapel portal. *The chapel portal, the next cross. This is my plan!*

She wanted to memorize the chant the priest used to open the portal so if she got close to the chapel door, she would use the chant and jump time. She turned back to the book as she searched for the chant. The priest's fingers gripped the book and yanked it from her hands.

She glanced up, and Father Clarke held it to his chest. "Enough. What have you figured out? Is the stone here? Can I have it now?"

Marie jerked her hands back purposefully, pulling

on the fabric. The father stumbled and almost dropped his book. Her wrists hurt from his abuse, but as he fell, she dreamed she tied his hands and dragged him around Scotland. She dropped her gaze and hid her face as she smiled to herself.

Now to her plan. It had to work. She just needed to drop the right hints, so they traveled back to the chapel and the portal.

Her eyes rose and met his. "No, it's not this cross. The next one. The MacDougall Cross. It's new at this time and likely the place a monk would've hidden a stone of power."

She held her breath. Had he bought this half-lie? Would he take the bait so she got back to the portal? Father Clarke opened the book to the cross page.

He turned it this way and that. "Are you sure? I thought for certain it stood on Iona, the center of Christian power."

Marie shrugged. "We were already there. It's not there at this time or another."

Father Clarke grabbed her ties and pulled her as he strode away. "Fine, back to the mainland it is. We'll stay in Islay till the ship departs. I've already spent one ruby for our passage here. Considering the size of the gem, that captain should cart us back as well."

****

On this morning's tide, they sailed into Port Ellen, Islay, a nice fishing village on the island and the major port used for commerce, or what there was of business, in the fifteenth century. In the future, Islay would become the highest producer of Scottish whisky and a tourist trap for people who visited the distilleries.

None of that remained in this time. Grassland, peat

bogs, livestock, and fishing made up the village which overlooked the ocean. It looked like a beautiful island filled with wooded meadows and rolling hills. This would've made a perfect romantic getaway in the twenty-first century. A cozy stay in a seaside inn, dinner before the fireplace, smooth whisky on the deck, as they gazed upon the sunset over the ocean, then she and John as they made love...

He pulled her hands again and interrupted her daydream. Clarke untied her when they entered the village, Port Ellen, but refused to let go of her wrist for anything. His grip rubbed the already chafed skin. After conferring with the ship's captain and negotiating that they'd travel on back to Loch Etive near Dunstaffnage tomorrow morning, Clarke secured them a room at Islay Inn.

He stopped and pried another ruby from the relic cross as payment for the room. "Damn stone doesn't want to come free."

Marie would give the entire cross, stones and all, for her freedom. He told the inn keeper his wife remained deaf and mute and glared at her while he fingered his dagger. Fine, she would wait for another chance to escape. She just needed to be patient.

Once inside their room, she looked around—one bed, a table with a chair, and a fireplace made up the room's entirety. She strode to the fireplace. She placed the leaves in a pile and flicked some flint together. She thanked a youth group for her camping skills as the flame took. After positioning twigs and a small log, she set her hand before it, her fingers numb from the rope and the cold. For the fifteenth century, this room seemed lavish.

Clarke ordered dinner delivered to the room. A luxury she hadn't expected and one he didn't comment on. Once she finished eating, maybe she would wash away the day's travel with the pitcher of water on the dresser. The screen in the corner for the privy could offer some privacy.

Clarke rummaged around in his bag when a knock rapped at the door. He looked at her and waved her away.

He whispered loud enough she was certain whoever stood on the other side of the door overheard. "Stand by the other wall, away from the door."

Clarke pulled his dagger, then hid it in his pants. "Move, and I'll cut you."

He opened the door, and a maid carried in a tray of fish, vegetables, and soup. The accompanying pitcher of ale gave off a heavy scent of hops and barley.

Marie's stomach growled. The maid glanced at her, then back at Clarke.

He shooed the maid out, locked the door, then quickly sat. "I am famished."

He prayed and crossed himself. Marie stood there, the moment at odds. To her, he wasn't a priest anymore. Why Marie still called him father remained beyond her. In her mind, he was only Clarke. He shed his robes in the twenty-first century and didn't possess the honorable, quiet manner typical of a priest, even in the modern time they were from. His zealous greed and thirst for power were not traits of a devout follower of God.

Her gaze traveled over him as he sat and stuffed food in his soiled face. His clothes remained nothing more than a dirty white shirt and black pants. He stole a coat some time back. To her, he now seemed more like a greedy, selfish peasant than an honorable member of the clergy. From now on, she wouldn't think of him as *father anything.*

She sat, took a moment of prayer, and eyed him from under her lashes. He observed her keenly since their arrival in Islay. She sensed a change in his demeanor that put her instincts on edge.

Between bites, she spoke, "I don't understand something."

He peered at her over his cup. "There's a lot you don't understand, Scottish trash."

She let the insult slide. "If ye don't like Scots, why are ye serving as a priest in Scotland?"

He barked a laugh. "Punishment. I insulted a Scottish nobleman in England and as a lesson, they sent me here to learn to *love the great people of Scotland.*"

He huffed. "Great people. Bullshit, if they were so great, how come the English destroyed their entire way of life?"

He gulped the rest of his ale and poured another then belched and sat back in his chair.

Marie sipped her ale. The brew tasted very potent, more so than anything they consumed in modern times. He made tonight's plan so easy.

She sat forward and poured more ale into his cup as she spoke. "But certainly, serving in Iona was a good assignment for a priest. The start of Christianity in Scotland began on the island and the village ye served seemed small. I'm sure they were religious and smart people."

He gulped his ale then waved his cup. "No, dumb as dirt. Not a higher educated one in the bunch.

Farmers, peasant's lowlife Scot scum."

Marie scrunched her nose. Maybe he confused the past with the present. She let that slide and kept him drinking, the plan for tonight already in motion. She poured the rest of the ale.

He smiled over the rim as he drank deeply.

She picked at her food and glanced away.

Clarke shook himself and sprang out of his chair. "I'm going to the bar. I'll lock you in. No funny stuff or I'll tie you up."

Marie stared open-mouthed but closed it.

He stood, took the utensils, and placed the dagger in his belt. Nodding at her, he wavered, then made his way to the door. He teetered a bit, a cup of ale still in his hand. He awkwardly made his way through the door almost falling as he held too long on the handle, then slammed it shut. The key clicked in the lock.

His heavy footfalls meandered down the stairway in groups of three. She imagined he veered from side to side, the wall keeping him upright. A final group of thuds told her he tripped at the end. *Finally, alone.*

Marie jumped up and rattled the door. Locked. She rushed to the window. They were on the second floor and the wall dropped directly to the ocean shore, rocky and forbidding, as enormous waves crashed against the rocks. If she jumped, she would at the very least suffer a broken leg.

She searched the room for anything to pry the lock. He took the dagger, left no utensils, but his bag sat on the floor. She smiled. The drunken fool got lazy.

She rushed to the bag and dug through it. Nothing of use, but she found the golden cross. He used two of the four rubies, one for the ship and one for the room and a meal. Two red rubies and the deep purple stone remained.

She held the cross and studied it closely as the gold warmed in her hands. Something familiar pulled at her memory, but she couldn't place what it was. She flipped the relic one way, examined the markings, and then the other. Nothing noteworthy, but the cross grew warm, and the purple stone glinted in the remaining light from the window as dusk settled on the port village.

As she studied the purple stone, she swore she viewed a man inside of it, a man in priest's robes. *The dream!* Her heart slammed against her chest, and she flung the cross back into the bag.

The dirt and grime from travel scratched. She stood and crossed to the pitcher of water. Stripping only her shirt, Marie grabbed the cloth and washed as much as she could. She hoped the key's rattle in the lock warned her and gave her time to cover herself before Clarke entered the room. The cold of the cloth and the scent of the soap rejuvenated her. Finally clean, she felt like a new woman.

She finished her meager bath and shifted the soup bowl close to the fire to keep it warm. She sat cross-legged before the fire and stared into the flames. Marie sensed a warmth in her chest, and her hand went there. Her Iona stone hung from its necklace.

She lifted the necklace from her bodice. Her grandmother claimed she picked the rock off a beach on Iona as a child.

The year before her passing, she gave the stone to Marie. "Marie, my dear, ye will need it one day. I feel it in me bones."

She stared into the fireplace. Orange, yellow, and red flames danced like the sunsets on Loch Etive. Marie sighed and wrapped her hand around the stone. Her mind drifted away in a welcome, numbed trance as a memory wafted into her mind.

****

The masons finished setting stones for the windows. Bree already ran off for lunch and left Marie as she contemplated—late lunch in the kitchen with Mrs. A. or hang out with the wharf lads? She never consumed lunch alone. She turned to the chapel doorway, and John stood there as he leaned against it, the same way he did the first day she examined the chapel. The first time they kissed.

He smiled. "Hello, ye."

She strolled closer. "Hello."

His hand rose to her cheek and brushed some dust off with his thumb. His gaze traveled over her face as if he took inventory of her features.

She took a moment and studied John's eyes. They looked greener today. As they flicked between her features, flecks of gold shimmered in them.

His hand held her cheek, and he leaned in and kissed her lightly on the lips. He savored each kiss as if he suckled a delicate piece of candy. This close, his aftershave filled her nose. His scent, a light musk always made her heart flutter.

He breathed against her lips, "I have a surprise for ye."

He kissed her lightly as she kept her eyes closed. "Ye do?"

He kissed her again. "Aye." They slowly parted and opened their eyes, and then they smiled together.

He led her away from the Chapel. "Ye must promise to close yer eyes, or ye'll ruin my surprise."

She kept her eyes closed but recognized they traveled toward the loch. "John, if this is some silly prank and ye dump me in the loch, I'll get ye back."

John laughed from in front of her as he held her hands. "No peeking, and yes we are going closer to the loch but no, I won't take ye for a dip." He finally stopped and turned her facing away from him as he gathered her in his arms.

He leaned down whispering in her ear, "Open yer eyes, Marie." Opening them, she looked out over the loch, then out to the ocean. He stopped them on the hilltop between the dock and the castle. The pier remained in her line of sight, but beyond stayed the complete panorama of the loch and mountain landscape. Different boats slowly sailed from the loch's ford to the ocean.

He whispered in her ear again, his breath against her ear sending tingles to her toes. "Ye have to look down."

She did, and there sat a picnic setup. The MacArthur plaid, green and blue with a small yellow stripe, sat under a full spread of various foods. Wine chilled in a bucket with ice and extra plaids laid out to ward off the wind's chill. The scene seemed right out of a movie.

Marie turned in his arms. "This is for us?"

John nodded. "Aye, I convinced Bree to give ye the afternoon off. She and Colin picnicked here the other day. I figured ye might enjoy it. Kind of like the priory picnic."

She squealed in delight, launched herself into his

arms, and kissed him.

He kissed her and set her on her feet slowly as he ended the kiss. "While I could kiss ye all day, I'm starved." He waved his hand, and she sat. He joined her as he picked up the wine bottle and poured them each a glass.

As they lounged together, they dined on bits of roast beef, cheese, and bread. Plus, a fruit bowl and assorted desserts completed the feast. Mrs. A. cut each item to a finger size, which made it easy as they ate with their hands.

Marie picked up a piece of cake and offered it to John, who bit into the sweet and nipped at her fingers. She squeaked and jolted, but John held her firm in his arms. He picked up a bit of chocolate and fed it to her, but as the treat neared her open mouth, he leaned in and kissed her.

They shared a bite here and there as they nipped at each other's fingers, kissing between bites, and laughing as they played.

John traced his hand up and down her arm as he held her in his embrace. "So, ye almost finished with the priory proposal?" He wiggled his eyebrows at her, reminding her of her promise to kiss him after each plan, then more when she finished.

Marie smiled. "Aye, I am, and I recall my kissing promise. The priory is just the beginning of my aspirations." She glanced at him. "What about ye? What are yer grand plans?"

John frowned into his wineglass. "I had grand plans, but my da disappeared while I was in college."

Marie turned in his arms. "So, he up and vanished one day, not a trace?"

John gazed out over the loch. "Aye, I was young. Not yet ready to take on the position of the Captain of the Castle, but I had little choice." He huffed. "It took me away from my studies. I wanted to finish my physics degree, but I didn't have time after being thrust into the captain's position."

Marie sipped her wine and sighed. "I'm sorry to hear that. It must have been hard not knowing what happened to him."

John glanced at her with a small smile. "I had Granny. She kept me going. She understood an awful lot about the captain's position. It seemed strange. She said she always knew she would be needed one day, and she was. I couldn't have done any of my duty without her."

John set his glass aside and took Marie's glass as well.

He cupped her face as he kissed her softly. She smiled into the kiss, then returned his kiss fully. John rotated her beneath him and deepened the kiss. Her arms slid around his neck, and she ran her fingers through his hair. She returned his kisses, measure by measure.

His hands roamed her body, and his knee slid between her legs as he parted them slightly.

He cupped a breast, and she moaned lightly. "John, we are out in the open. Ye naughty devil."

John laughed. "God, Marie, ye tempt me so. I want to feel yer body." Marie giggled, ran her hands down his back, cupped both butt cheeks, and gripped them.

John moaned deeply and rubbed against her leg while he rubbed her breast. He squeezed it a little, and she arched into his hand. They continued to kiss each other as their hands roamed over each of their bodies. She put each curve and crevice into memory.

John slid his knee farther up and slipped his hand down and cupped her over her pants. She moaned, and he rubbed her in a rhythm that sent her into a panting frenzy. He kissed her deeply and rubbed a few more times until her legs closed and gripped his hand. He kissed her softly until her legs relaxed.

John gathered her in his arms, and they lay together as the sun set over the loch in rich orange and yellow streaks across the sky, which melted into the purple mountain range.

****

The key rattled in the lock, shocking her out of her trance. *Clarke!* She jumped up and backed to the far wall.

Clarke stumbled into the room and practically fell on his face. If he hadn't caught himself on the bed frame, he would've fallen on the floor.

Marie sucked in her breath and smelled him from across the room. Whisky, strong and potent, wafted off him in aromatic waves. The stench became so intense she covered her nose.

He tried to level his gaze upon her but wavered as if he couldn't pick which one of her he tried to focus on. He slammed the door, locked it, and pocketed the key.

He took a deep breath and nodded once. "I'm tired of watching you." He grabbed her. "I'm tired of smelling you."

She sidestepped and easily avoided him.

He grabbed her arm and pulled her to his chest. His whisky fumes made her dizzy.

His speech came slurred. "I'm tir'd of be'ng a pri'st. A man of God."

He grabbed her around her chest and trapped her arms in his. He backed her into the wall. She hit it hard and whimpered. He rubbed himself against her, and his stiff shaft bumped her stomach. Bile rose in her throat, and she swallowed as she kept it down.

He smiled at her like a starved man eyed at a juicy steak. "I'm tired of being chaste."

Marie gasped and struggled. "Ye gave me yer word. If I helped ye, ye wouldn't do anything. Ye promised ye wouldn't hurt me."

He barked a laugh. "A promise from a fallen priest. You *are* a fool."

He leaned forward and tried to kiss her. She struggled with him as she turned her head from side to side. "I thought ye hated Scottish women!" Her voice rose. "Ye said ye found us disgusting!"

She fought in earnest, tried to kick him, but his grip was too strong. He dragged her to the bed and grabbed the ties he used before. The fact he held them in his state spoke to his determination. He tied her hands to the top post. She pulled, and they only tightened, cutting off her circulation, but she didn't care.

He picked up her legs and swung them on the bed. She tried to pull away as he unbuttoned his shirt. He swayed again and almost fell on top of her. He blinked slowly and rocked again, then fell over on Marie.

She shrieked but stopped. Clarke lay unmoving. His heavy weight almost suffocated her. She twisted her body once, twice, and he flopped to the floor with a loud thud. She peeked at him and spied his legs. She sat back and closed her eyes.

Tears escaped and trailed down her cheeks. No man had ever tried anything like that. Her mind immediately went to Bree as she remembered her stories about her ex. She blinked, and more tears fell. She closed her eyes and thanked God Clarke couldn't handle his drink.

As she tried the ties again, she found the knots were out of her reach. Here she sat trapped, tied to the bed, and a drunk man passed out on the floor. The quote from the book echoed.

The fear of man brings a snare: but who so put his trust in God shall be safe.

She prayed. "Thank ye, God. I am safe."

Chapter 10

John sipped his whisky and held the glass near the candle in the inn's bar. The light reflected off the golden liquid. This tasted better than whisky in the future. Was it the old organic farming versus the new agricultural technology or possibly the pollution in the future? Either way, this he savored.

John and his da had arrived in Islay a day ago. They met with an ecstatic Torquil McDonald and inspected his whisky business located at the head of Loch Laphroaig situated on the south coast of the island. As John viewed the vast landscape, purely nature as God made, he pictured what the place would become in the future—one of the largest whisky distilleries in Scotland. What was Torquil's small farm became a thriving village, tourist stop for many coming to Scotland over summer break. He and Marie had discussed a trip themselves but hadn't taken the time to go.

Torquil stepped into his first building, the largest on the property, as he led them on a tour. "Pot still distillation is a batch process and I need more stills and a bigger warehouse to make more to ship for sale. Demands have gone up. Some distilleries use double-distillation, while mine is special—distilled three times."

He walked past the first large copper pot with a

narrowed end, pointing to the top. "The wash goes into the first still, called the low wines still, where it's heated up. Alcohol boils at a lower temperature than water, so the alcohol vapors rise off the liquid and into the still neck or lyne arm, eventually reaching the condenser, which turns them to liquid once again."

He strode to the next copper pot. "The resulting liquid goes into the second still, or spirit still, where the process is repeated. The spirit still, that's where the spirit of the whisky is born."

Torquil glanced back and winked. "And this is when my magic happens, a third distillation." He waved to the large copper still. "We throw out a certain amount of spirit from the beginning and end of the run, known as the head and tail, due to their unwanted flavors and aromas. Some we reuse as starter for the next batch which produces our richer flavors."

He moved on to another copper tank. "The rest, well that's yer treasure—known as the heart—goes into barrels." He touched his hand to his heart. " 'Tis why I call it the Heart of Scotland."

They walked out and into the next small building, his warehouse. Wooden barrels stacked from floor to ceiling filled the space. Upon entering, the liquor scent overpowered John's nose and he imagined if anyone lit a match, the place would go up in flames.

Torquil patted the nearest barrel, pride clear in his voice as he spoke. "All my whiskies are aged in oak barrels I make, stored in my warehouse. As the whisky matures, the angels visit."

He placed his hand over his heart as he gazed at the heavens. "A bit disappears from each cask. Tis known as the 'angels' share' when the angels come to bless each barrel."

His gaze came back as he smirked. "It creates a distinct and lovely smell in the warehouse." Torquil sniffed for a long time then blew out his nose. "So, do we have a deal? Yer investment for my expansion, traded as shares of ownership, as well as yer fee for shipping services?"

Torquil had given John a cask from his first batch of whisky, already aged three years, for Laird MacDougall forming a long-standing partnership between the distillery and the family. Honored to be a part of such an important moment in the history of Dunstaffnage Castle, John wondered if this was how Colin felt when he traveled back in time and became a part of a tradition formed.

"Angel's share." Torquil truly believed angels blessing his whisky was basic science. The vanishing liquid was evaporation over time.

My angel, Marie. John set his glass down. She never remained far from his mind.

His da clapped John on the back and sat next to him at the bar. "I found out what's up with yer Marie and the priest."

John raised an eyebrow. "So, what have ye learned?"

John shook his head as he gaped at his father. He still couldn't believe he sat there with his da.

His da grinned wide as he spoke. "Small talk in the other pub says the night before a priest boasted about receiving riches when he found a stone on a cross. He drank heavily, and it seems the weasel can't hold his drink."

His da laughed out loud. "A priest who can't hold

his drink. That's a joke if I ever heard one." He caught his breath. "Must not be a very good priest."

John sucked in a breath. "What else ye learn, Da?"

His da took another sip of his whisky and smacked his lips. "Their ship left yesterday morning." He laughed again. "Ye're not gonna believe where the ship is headed back to."

John grabbed his da's shoulder. "Dunstaffnage?"

"Aye, Dunstaffnage. If we sail with the evening tide, we'll arrive just after it." His da toasted his whisky and chugged the rest.

John's breath stuck in his chest. Dunstaffnage. He would catch up with her, finally have her in his arms.

With each step he took closer to Marie, the priest took her one step farther away. *So close, yet so far away.* He ran his hand through his hair and chugged the last of his whisky. The situation was fitting. This began at Dunstaffnage castle, and this time he damn well made sure this ended there and soon.

He closed his eyes and concentrated on Marie, hoped and prayed she sensed him. *Hold on, Marie, I'm coming.*

****

Late that afternoon, John was half asleep, rocked by the motion of the ship. He couldn't take his mind off Marie. He imagined he might sense if she became truly in danger. His heart might know. But he was so unsure. All he thought of was his love for her and he worried she may not know how much he cared. His mind drifted to the night he first tried to tell her he loved her.

****

In the Great Hall, the fireplace burned low and kept a warm radiant circle around the sitting area.

John stood in the shadows, as Marie sat in the soft glow. Her profile was smooth as she stared into the flames.

Over the past few months, she had come to mean so much to him. First as they corresponded over the chapel renovation project, then spent more time together when she arrived to work on the chapel—the moments he spent with her meant more to him than most other memories he experienced in his entire life. He woke needing to see her smiling face and fell asleep dreaming of her kind heart.

Only moments ago, he had sent Colin through the chapel portal back in time to find the Stone of Love. Colin's concerns to keep Bree and Marie away from the chapel, so they wouldn't become entangled in the Fae duty were real. Hell, John felt the same. He doubted he could keep Marie from learning about the portal and the stones. She remained smarter than she let on, and he recognized she would eventually figure everything out.

God, he would do anything to keep her safe. All he wanted to do right now was gather her in his arms and show her how much she meant to him.

John found himself next to the couch and next to Marie. He didn't even realize he had crossed close to her. The thought of her drew him to her like a moth to the flame.

She turned and rose. John waved telling her to sit as he slid onto the couch beside her. She held a glass of wine, still full. He took it from her, and their fingers brushed and tingled where they caressed. John sat next to her, she shifted, and their hips touched. He wrapped his arm around her, and she snuggled into his embrace, a perfect fit beside his body. He took a sip from the wine glass then stared into it and took a larger sip as he prayed for strength. He wanted to tell her everything that existed in his heart. As he set the glass on the table, Marie sat forward and gazed at him. He took a deep breath and released it. He wanted to say so much, share his heart with her, and he didn't know where to begin.

He took her hands in his and kissed each one. "Marie, I need to be honest with ye."

Marie nodded as she looked over his face.

John smiled and hoped he reassured her. He meant to make her happy, them both happy. "Ye have come to mean so much to me, especially over these last few weeks. We've got to know each other better."

Marie smiled. "Ye have come to mean a lot to me too, John."

John gazed at her; the curve of her cheek was soft in the firelight. His eyes shifted to her lips, smooth and ripe. His hand rose and brushed her cheek.

She tilted her chin down and her gaze traveled to his eyes then his lips. She licked her lips and that became the only invitation John needed.

He bent and brushed his lips against hers. She returned the kiss and sighed as their tongues tangled in a heated dance. He shifted closer, gathered her in his arms, and she moaned as his lips trailed kisses down her neck. He returned to her lips, slowed the kiss, and caught his breath.

He desired to share his feelings for her, revealing all that pulsed in his heart. He wanted to take her to his room and make love to her to show her how much she mattered to him. But he needed to tell her first.

He stared for a moment. Within her eyes, he saw his love for her reflected. It reached into his heart, making him speechless. He tried to say something, but he stopped. His breath caught as he attempted a second time. He leaned toward her and brushed his lips softly on hers.

"I've wanted to show ye how I have felt for so long." He kissed her again. "Words fail me." He tilted his head and kissed her again. With his face still close to hers, their mouths so close their breaths mingled. "Can I show ye, Marie? Can I show ye how much ye mean to me?"

Marie sighed. "Yes, please." And kissed him deeply.

He gathered her in his embrace, kissed her lips once, then again. He stopped and gazed at her, as the flames' shadows danced across her face.

She gazed at him with such love, his heart skipped.

He kissed her as he shifted her under him on the couch. He had wanted her for so long and she made him as nervous as a schoolboy. As he kissed her, she moaned softly, igniting his desire and making his heart race. His hands roamed her body as he molded her form in his mind's eye.

She shifted and returned his kisses equally.

His hand progressed over her tee shirt, massaged her breast. She arched and he trailed kisses down her neck. Her arms trailed up his back, encircled his neck, pulled him deeper into their kisses. His hand slid under her shirt, then bra, and cupped her naked breast. She arched and moaned as she nibbled his earlobe which made him jerk. God, he couldn't stand it anymore. She drove him crazy. He needed to ask her. He wanted her to know how much she mattered and what this moment meant to him.

"*M'eudail, my darling,* I've enjoyed this. I don't want this to end here." He kissed her gently.

"I've wanted to ask so many times but wasn't certain if ye were ready. If ye aren't, I'll wait. I'll wait forever for ye if I had to." He gazed at her face again as he searched for a sign.

She smiled as she spoke. "What is it?"

John smiled and kissed her again. "Please come to bed with me. Please let me make love to ye."

Marie kissed him deeply. "I'd like that, John." He smiled widely, stood, swept her in his arms, and headed for the stairs. Marie placed her hand on his chest over his heart.

****

A hard shove woke him, and John startled awake to his da's face. He jolted again, not used to his da in real life as he stood over him. John shook himself as he tried to fully wake.

"Come on, sleepy head. We've already cleared the pass and are docking." His da strode out of the cabin. John jumped up, grabbed his bag, and followed. Out on the deck, men rushed around as they set the boat to rights after a long voyage. His da stood beside the plank and waved to him.

John and his father stepped off the dock at Dunstaffnage late into the night.

The castle captain stood there and held a lantern to greet them.

Before the castle captain got a word out, John grabbed his shirt. "Have they arrived yet? The priest and the woman, are they here?"

Douglas MacArthur, the Captain of the Castle, shook his head. "Aye, the boat arrived, but they weren't on it."

Where the hell were they?

****

As the early sun's rays shined through the window, Marie lay tied to the bed while Clarke snoozed on the floor.

She whispered loudly and hoped she didn't wake the other guests. "Clarke, ye must get up."

His snoring met her request.

She spoke louder regardless of who overheard. "Damn it, Clarke, wake up!"

He snorted and shifted.

Marie held her breath in a moment of silence as she waited for a sound signaling he woke.

Snores filled the room again. The bastard was too drunk to arise.

Last night she tried to grab his dagger that knocked to his side when he fell. She eyed it now as she wished she could shift objects with her mind. *If I got that dagger...* But the blade lay there and winked in the sunlight.

Not to dwell too much on her current state, she focused on John—visions of him always carried her away.

She remembered the first time they made love.

****

He came to her in the great hall. He kissed her and stopped. He seemed he wanted to say something but had trouble. When he did speak, he touched her heart.

"*M'eudail, my darling,* I've enjoyed this. I don't want this to end here." He kissed her gently.

"I've wanted to ask so many times but wasn't certain if ye were ready. If ye aren't, I'll wait. I'll wait forever for ye if I had to." Marie gasped. What he said touched her heart. He looked her face over again. She gazed into his eyes and knew she wanted him.

She smiled. "What is it?"

John smiled and kissed her again. "Please come to bed with me. Please let me make love to ye."

Marie kissed him deeply, "I'd like that, John." He smiled widely, stood, swept her in his arms and headed for the stairs. Marie placed her hand on his chest over his heart.

He shouldered his way into his room and lowered her along his body. John reached behind him and closed the door.

When he bent and kissed her, Marie avoided the kiss and stepped back as she gave him her best "devil take care" expression. She turned around and stripped her shirt off. She glanced behind her as John leaned against the door. Marie hoped he appreciated her little show. She giggled as he smiled. So, he enjoyed it when she took control. Little did he know she liked foreplay, a lot, and planned to tease him until he couldn't stand it anymore. She reached behind her, undid her bra, and slipped it off as she glanced over her shoulder at him.

He slid against the door frame and gripped the edge as his breaths came faster.

She slowly turned with her hands over her breasts. She gave him that "devil take care" look again and lowered her hands. He gazed at her for a moment not moving.

She covered them again and turned around.

He took her in his arms. "Please *m'eudail, my darling* I love looking at ye."

Marie smiled. Her little show worked. He finally

approached her.

He kissed her deeply and turned her into his embrace.

Not wanting to wait, Marie reached for his shirt and stripped it off in one motion. She rubbed her hands through his chest hair as she whimpered softly. Marie wrapped her arms around his neck and caressed her breasts against his chest. Her nipples hardened against his springy hair. He bent and his mouth covered her nipple as she sucked in a breath. Her body slid against his as she moaned again, and his mouth returned to hers with a more demanding kiss. She squeezed her body against his. She wasn't sure who started what or if they just responded to each other. She never felt this way with a man before, so open and natural.

His mouth continued to play with hers as her hand slid to his rear, gripped it, and pulled him closer. He grasped her rear in response.

She practically climbed up his body as she tried to kiss him deeper. His hand shifted to her front as he cupped her. She moaned and gripped his shoulders. He rubbed her, which made her squirm.

John unbuttoned her pants.

Smiling, she lowered them to the floor, undies and all. She giggled and he kissed her.

With a growl, he swept her in his arms and carried her to the bed. He gently lowered her upon the soft covers. So, he was as impatient as she—good. She wiggled and settled on the soft cushion.

John stood back. His gaze slid over her in the pale moonlight. Under his heated glare, she felt sexy, all woman, his woman. She wanted this man like no other, and she wouldn't allow him to leave her wanting. She sat up and reached for him, needing him closer. John approached her, and she rose to her knees, stroked his shoulders, and kissed him deeper. Her hands wandered down his sides, tickled him a little, and he chuckled into their kisses. His fingers trailed to her breasts, circled them with his fingertips, and tickled her in return. In a growl, he cupped both breasts as he kissed her harder.

He was as playful as she. She loved everything about him and wanted to show him time and time again. Her hands shifted to the front of his pants. As she kissed him, she undid them and giggled again. He smiled, stripped them off, climbed on the bed, and he fell on top of her in one motion that made her laugh.

He rolled close and took her into his arms with renewed kisses. John cupped her breast as her head dropped back. He kissed her neck and ran his tongue to her breast. He slid between her legs, and he pinched her nipple. The tingle sent jolts of heat through her. He suckled the nipple, and she arched as she moaned, loving his aggressive play. He sucked the other, slid up a little, and rubbed against her. She wiggled as he flexed against her. John stopped, took a deep breath, and shifted to her side. It seemed he wanted to take his time. She lay back and placed her hands above her head—a signal she gave him full access and permission, curious to know what John had in mind for his play.

He bent and kissed her as he trailed his hand up her leg while he suckled her lips. He cupped her and she sucked his bottom lip. As he rubbed his fingers against her nub, her hands gripped the bed covers.

He slid a finger inside, and she sighed in ecstasy. He shifted back a little and settled into a lounge as his finger pushed inside her. He licked her nipple as he increased the pace, the sensations sending tingles through her. The tension built inside her as his speed increased, the movement striking her nub on each thrust. She closed her eyes and arched as her hands gripped the fabric harder. He continued his onslaught, her hips bucked, and her nub pulsed.

He chuckled and slowed. Her eyes opened and found he gazed at her. She pouted knowing he teased her. He smiled and slid in another finger as her head fell back, and a moan escaped. He quickened his pace and elicited a groan from her. He drove harder as he quickened the pace even further.

She panted, and her walls gripped him as her hands fisted the covers. Heat built in her and flashed over her body. The intense pressure built again, and she climbed with it as she reached for her release. Stars burst behind her eyelids, and she screamed as her world fell apart. She panted and slowly became aware of the world around her. Her hands let go of the covers, and John rose over her and kissed her softly.

"God, Marie, ye are so beautiful." She smiled into his kiss, her hands dipped, and she gripped his hardness as she pumped a perfect rhythm. He shifted over her and slid against her and she jolted, still sensitive from his play. Her body arched, and she threw her head back in one long moan. He kissed her neck, then nibbled her ear.

He pushed close to her entrance but stopped and whispered in her ear, "I've dreamed of this…"

She cupped his cheek as she gazed into his eyes. "Me as well. Make me yers."

His gaze locked with hers as he slid into her slowly

and strained as he entered her. They looked into each other's eyes as he made them one whole and joined. He seated himself fully and stopped.

He caressed her cheek. "Marie, I am yers." This moment, this connection she wanted to capture forever, lock away, and keep for all eternity. He remained the man she wanted, the man she loved.

She smiled, "John, I am yers."

He rocked, slowly at first, as he kissed her. He quickened his pace as his tongue caressed hers. His kisses became more demanding. Her body gripped him tight and sent sparks through her as he glided in and out. He created the friction she craved since their first kiss.

As their bodies danced together in the art of making love, he pulled her knee higher to slide in deeper. Deeper into her and deeper into her soul. John claimed her for his own. He moaned as he glided in repeatedly, going deeper, faster. She gripped his shoulders harder and pulled him closer. Her being closer to him took him closer to her heart. She sensed her passion build as her body squeezed his. She arched and shouted his name as he continued his onslaught to her senses. He made her pant and screamed his name again. He swelled inside her and grew stiff. He slammed into her once and then again. He arched and roared his release. John stayed there for a moment, then another, unable to breathe. In one long sigh, John rested his forehead against hers and stared into her eyes as his hand caressed her face.

"Marie, ye make me whole." He kissed her, and a tear dropped from her eye.

His thumb caught it as she sighed. "John, ye are

my everything."

He rolled to her side, gathered her into his arms, caressed her face, and shifted until he held her close. She nestled her cheek against his chest and took a deep breath. She lay for a while as the moonlit shadows shifted. She drifted off to sleep against his heart.

****

Father Clarke moaned and rolled over on the dusty, hard wooden floor.

He's up?

She called his name again. "Clarke, get up!" Marie, still tied to the bed, yelled this time. "Damn it, Clarke, get up!"

He scuffled around with a moan, sat up, rubbed his eyes, and looked around. "What time is it?"

Marie struggled against her bonds. "It's morning, and untie me now before I pee on the bed."

Clarke slowly rose as he rubbed his head.

He yawned and tried to untie Marie. "What have you done to the knots? They're too tight, and I can't get them undone."

Marie gripped her legs together to hold it in. "Can ye just cut them? I really have to, ye know."

Clarke eyed her. He glanced around, grabbed the knife, and cut her fabric ties.

Marie ran behind the screen. After a moment and a long sigh, she stepped from behind the screen as Clarke splashed water on his face.

He moaned again and wiped his face with the cloth. "What time do you think it is?"

Marie glanced out the window. "Midmorning, I think."

He gasped and slammed his fist on the chest of

145

drawers. "Damn, we were supposed to sail at dawn."

Marie rolled her eyes, put her hands on her hips, and yelled loudly, knowing she irritated his obvious headache. "Ye got drunk and passed out!" She rubbed her wrists as she stepped back and spoke softer. "Ye don't remember last night, do ye?"

Clarke rubbed his head again. "No, I don't."

Marie stood still. If he did not remember that he attacked her, he hopefully wouldn't try it again. She sure as hell wouldn't bring it up.

Clarke scanned the room and gathered his bag. "We'll have to book another boat. Get your things."

Marie barked a laugh. "What things?"

He startled. "Come on."

Chapter 11

Dunstaffnage Castle 1498

John placed a scroll in the bolt hole at the bottom of the mantel, knowing Colin received it in the twenty-first century, just as he had exchanged letters from the seventeenth century with Colin. He sighed, grabbed his whisky, and stared into the dancing flames of the fire.

He remembered when Marie caught him as he retrieved a letter from Colin. John smiled. That happened when Marie learned about the stones and the Fae. It didn't shock her, as he suspected. No, she was understanding.

****

John bent over near the fireplace mantel and opened the box hole. He pulled an ancient scroll from the hole and stood up just as Marie opened the door. He shoved the document in his vest and tried to appear indifferent.

Marie stopped in the doorway, stunned. "John, what are ye doing?"

John stepped to the desk and sat, folding his arms over his chest. "Nothing, Marie." The crackling of paper followed his statement.

Marie closed the door and approached the desk. "Mrs. A. said I would find ye in here working."

She pointed to his chest. "What do ye have there?"

147

John shrugged, and a slight crinkle followed his movement. "Nothing."

Marie looked at John's chest, then at his face. "I know ye told me that Brielle had to pick up supplies, but it's been a week. I can't even get her on her cell." Marie sat in the chair opposite the desk. "I'm worried, John. That isn't like her."

John shrugged again, keeping his arms folded to hold the document inside his vest.

"Have ye heard from her? It's been a week since she disappeared."

John nodded. "Yes, I have. Said she got delayed getting some stones."

Marie glanced at her hands and glanced up at John. "John, they've delivered all the stones from the quarry. We don't need any more stones."

John leaned forward and rested his elbows on the desk. The scroll, forgotten, fell to the floor.

Marie rose from her chair and picked up the parchment.

John reached across the desk and grabbed the roll.

Marie shifted backward, avoided his hand, and held the scroll to her chest. "What is this?"

John strode around the desk and tried to grab the document from Marie's hands, but she stepped away and half-turned her body.

"It's nothing, Marie. Ye need to give me the scroll. It's castle business and something ye shouldn't see."

Marie glanced at the parchment crumpled to her chest. She looked at the fireplace mantel, and John followed her gaze. The box hole door stood open.

She stared at it for a moment, then slowly turned to John. "John, what is going on? Where's Bree?"

John ran his hand through his hair and raised his voice. "It's nothing, damn ye, now hand over the scroll."

Marie jumped slightly, blinked, and slowly handed John the scroll.

John snatched the document, stormed to the fireplace, closed the box hole, and returned to the desk. He placed the letter on the desk and rested his head in his hands.

Marie slowly walked to the chair and sat in her seat. "John, I'm really worried. If something is happening and ye cannot tell me, that is okay. Just please tell me Brielle is okay."

John shook his head. "Oh God, Marie. That's just it. I don't know if she's okay. Colin's gonna kill me. I hoped this message would inform me. I can't tell ye how or why or even where. None of this makes sense."

John peered into Marie's eyes. "It's been such a burden to carry the worry alone. Ye don't understand how crazy I've gone, not knowing what has happened. I suspected I realized, but I'm not for certain." He ran both hands through his hair. "Damn, if I tell ye all of it, ye would call me bat shit crazy." John glanced around the room and then slashed his hand down. "Ye can't mention it to anyone that ye've seen even this much. I can't tell ye. I'm not allowed."

Marie jumped from the chair, rounded the desk, and took John's hand in hers. "John, whatever it is, it will be okay. We'll get through this together." Marie stared into John's eyes and nodded. "Just share with me what ye can. We'll go from there."

John nodded, picked up the scroll, stood, and broke the seal. As he unrolled it, he walked to the mantel, not sure what Colin's first message from the past would be.

22 March 1720

J-

I made it here in good time. My work has begun. Archie is a big help.

He has your nose.

Something has blown through the chapel doors. If you're missing a storm back there. She's here.

She was injured slightly but safe—no word from Brigid and no idea how I'll get us both back.

Following note in a few days.

Stay vigilant

-C

John reread the note. He sighed and rested his hand on the mantel. "Thank God. She's with him."

"Bree, she's with whom?"

John whirled around. He was so relieved to hear about Bree he forgot Marie remained in the room. He hadn't planned to say anything in front of her. It was bad enough that she harassed him about Brielle's unexplained absence. And he ran out of excuses. But now she caught him opening the box hole and observed the scroll. He didn't know how much more he could keep hidden from her.

Colin was right. Marie was too smart, the same as Bree. They both would be on to them soon, and John didn't know what might happen then. He must tell Marie about the Fae and his duty to the stone. He hoped she would help him, help him figure out what to do next, and keep him from going crazy. John made a short mental prayer to Morrigan. *Please forgive me.* He drew a deep breath and caught it in his head. *It'll be okay; she can help.*

John turned and gazed at Marie, her presence a soothing balm to the stress he had experienced these last weeks. He strode to the desk, set the scroll down, took Marie's hands, and sat in the chair. John took a deep breath and told Marie about his duty to the Stones as captain of the castle. He detailed the dreams he and Colin shared with their Fae and explained how Colin returned in time and his task.

He expected Marie to be shocked and angry, maybe believe he went nuts at such an absurd explanation, but she didn't. She sat and studied his face with each answer. John finished with the description of the purpose of the box hole, then picked up and handed Marie the parchment. "This is the first letter from Colin from the past."

Marie read the note and bounced out of her chair. "Bree is in the past?"

John nodded. "Apparently so, and with Colin. Who is pretending to be Roderick. Oh, he looks just like him."

Marie paced behind the chairs as she waved the scroll. "How'd she get there, and when's she coming back?"

John took the old paper from her and carefully put it on the desk.

John eyed Marie as she paced. "Ye don't seem to be surprised by any of this. Why?"

Marie stopped and shot a sharp glance at John. "John, I study churches and religion, ancient religion. With ancient spiritual buildings, stories like this occur all the time." She glanced to the floor, chewing on her nail, something John saw her do when she focused on a task. "I've read some accounts of spiritual encounters, but nothing like this. Emily mentioned she believed there was magic in the chapel." Marie chewed her nail, "Had me look into the two stained-glass windows at each end of the chapel, but I found nothing." She resumed her pacing and stopped again. "Who is Archie, and why does he have yer nose?"

John laughed. "He's my ancestor, the Captain of the Castle in 1720. His name is Archibald." John shrugged. "I guess Colin calls him Archie. This makes him seem real. Like I got a new relative I didn't know I had."

Marie sat in her chair and lifted John's hands into hers. "John, we'll get through this. I can look some things up at the university and maybe shed some light on the chapel." They both startled. *"…shed some light on the chapel."* She sounded like one of John's rock jokes.

They both laughed, and John squeezed her hand. "We'll pull through this, Marie, together."

****

John sighed, sipped his whisky again, and recalled her nightmare just a few nights before the priest kidnapped her. She had suffered them since her arrival at the castle, and they got worse the past month. They always woke her at night. They disturbed her so badly she couldn't catch her breath and sometimes screamed.

She refused to discuss them except on one occasion. After the sword accident where Colin almost took Bree's head off, Bree experienced a breakdown that scared them all. Marie admitted a priest tied her to a boat and yelled at her in her dream. The other visions were different, though. She couldn't catch her breath each time she woke like someone had suffocated her in her dream. That night she spoke aloud before she woke, and John couldn't get it out of his head. He ran the incident over for the hundredth time.

****

Something struck him, and he jolted awake. Marie thrashed about on the bed as she mumbled. He tried to grab her, but she rolled too fast.

"Please, it's not what ye think. I am not a real nun. It's not me."

John grabbed her and caught her by the shoulders.

"No, Father, please stop. I'm not guilty. It's not me."

John shook her once. "Marie, wake up. *m'eudail, my darling,* it's just a dream." She thrashed and clipped John on the chin. He grunted as he rolled her over and covered her so she couldn't hurt him or herself.

He whispered in her ear, "Marie, please wake up. It's John. Ye're here at the castle. Ye're safe." She calmed down but still panted. John rose a little, peering at her face as he brushed her hair aside. She opened her eyes and stared at the ceiling. Marie gasped as she tried to catch her breath.

John caressed her face. "Marie, what dream is scaring ye so?" He kissed her lightly, but she didn't respond, just stared at the ceiling.

"Marie, *m'eudail.* Talk to me." A tear ran down her face into her hair. John placed both hands on her face and shifted his eyes even with hers.

He shook her head slightly. "Marie, look at me."

She blinked and looked into his eyes.

She shook her head and tried to turn away, but John wouldn't let her. "No, ye tell me what has sacred ye so much. Ye talk about a priest and it not being ye.

Tell me. I want to help."

Marie gazed at him and silently cried.

At a loss, John rolled to his side and gathered her in his arms as he held her close. "Doesn't matter. Ye have nothing to fear. I promise." He kissed her head and held her tight until she finally relaxed and fell asleep in his arms. He lay awake and promised himself he would do anything to keep her safe.

****

John's da clapped him on the back. "It's a good partnership, and we were the ones to make this happen for the MacDougalls. What a great day in history, eh, son?"

John smiled. "Yea, Da." They stood in the study with Laird John MacDougall and the Captain of the Castle, Douglas MacArthur, their ancestor. When John spotted his father next to their ancestor, John still did a double take. The expression looked like he saw a ghost. He glanced back at his da and witnessed his da do the same.

John squinted at Laird MacDougall. "Ye sure yer cousin is okay with yer guards swarming the priory? I mean, we are going to be on holy ground."

Laird MacDougall waved him off. "Aye, he's not only fine with it. What this priest has done has disgusted him, saying it's a sin above all sins. Lust for power and using a helpless woman to boot. His only stipulation, no killing on holy ground, says it damns the soul to eternity."

John rubbed his head and shook it.

His da glanced at him. "What is it, John?"

John looked at his da and shrugged. "Well, I'm puzzled, is all."

All three men stared at him. He looked from his da to Captain Douglas to Laird MacDougall. They all carried the same questioning expression, and John chuckled.

He scratched his chin as he spoke. "Well, Morrigan said Marie became part of the plan to retrieve the Stone of Fear."

Laird MacDougall nodded. "Aye, and what of it?"

John glanced at him. "Well, that's it. There's nothing we've seen or heard about the stone. If she's the plan the Fae made to retrieve the stone, where is it?"

All four men sat in silence.

His da broke the quiet. "If we have seen no sign of it, then she already possesses it."

John paced in front of the fireplace. His kilt swung as he crossed back and forth. "But if she has it, why hasn't she used it? I mean, on priest to escape or to travel back in time?"

His da barked a laugh. "First, ye have to know how to use it, but I suspect she has it and doesn't even know what she possesses."

John shook his head. "No, Da, she's a historian; plus Bree saw the Stone of Fear, described it for us all. She would know what she held if it stayed in Marie's hands. But I agree she may not know how the stone works."

John stopped, and his gaze went to his da. "What if the priest knows what he has? What if he has used it?"

His da shook his head. "No, ye'd hear from yer Fae Morrigan if he had. I haven't heard from her since…" He glanced around the room and cleared his throat. "…in a long time."

John peered closer at his da. "I haven't seen our

Fae, and ye haven't seen her. Where the hell is she?" He huffed a sigh. "Damn Fae."

Laird MacDougall chimed in. "Either way, we'll know no later than tomorrow. The sailor who spotted them said their ship docks in the morning. Before sunrise, we'll go to the monastery and lay out our plan."

Douglas raised his glass. "To saving Marie."

They all raised their glasses and clinked them as they said together, "To saving Marie."

John sipped his whisky and stared into the flames. The Fae Fable came true. He just prayed her dreams weren't coming true as well. If they were, he needed to get to Marie before the priest found the stone and gained control of both realms or, worse, hurt Marie. And if the madman already had—holy ground or not, John would kill the priest.

Chapter 12

After Father Clarke found and settled payment with a new boat captain, he stood beside Marie on the deck. "Damn you, I used another ruby to buy passage back to Dunstaffnage. It's your fault."

She gaped at him as they strode into the cabin. "Ye are the one who got drunk. It's yer fault ye slept late." A priest who can't hold his liquor—Clarke proved a horrible priest.

Later, Marie huddled in the boat's cabin since it remained cold to be outside. She didn't know where Clarke stayed and remained happy. He wasn't in the room. He got more and more careless and left her alone and untied. This time he left the place unlocked, but out in the ocean, where could she go without drowning or freezing first?

He left his bag behind in the cabin this time. Marie smiled. *He's not a good priest nor a good criminal either.*

Marie slid the bag into her lap, hoping he became sloppy enough and left the knife behind. She rummaged through the pack and shifted past a shirt and a watch as she tried to find the knife. Marie tilted the bag into the candlelight, and nope, no knife. She lowered the bag in defeat. Marie wanted that knife for her escape. She glanced into the bag again. Well, he might not be as thoughtless as she hoped, but careless enough he left his book behind.

Marie examined the book again. She turned the pages, but this time they appeared in a different order. Maybe she didn't recall them correctly, but she believed the Chorales page was first and now the crosses page came first. Marie tried to make sense of what Clarke saw in the pages that she didn't, what made him think the Fae stones held power.

The jeweled cross sat half out of the bag. She picked it up, studied the cross again, and remembered her last vision from it—the priest in the stone, the priest in her dream. She shivered, shoved it in the bag away from her view.

She curled up on the bed and held the book as she tried to read it, and eventually lost interest in that as well. Marie stared at the candle, and it blurred, unfocused. The blob reminded her of a sunset, like the orange and yellow sunsets in the loch.

****

Marie strolled on the trail from the castle to the dock. As the time neared sunset, the views from the pier progressed back onto Loch Etive, where the mountain range formed a backdrop.

She carried a plaid wrap to keep her warm against the chill and held it tighter around her as she hoped tonight wouldn't get so cold to chase them into the castle. The dock appeared as she descended the small hill and rounded the last turn. Marie stopped at the sight before her.

The setup John arranged was impressive. A small table with a white tablecloth and two chairs sat with portable lights positioned so they viewed the evening but not too bright to block out the sunset. Gas heaters kept the area warm. A silver box sat near, and there were a couple of lads from the pub dressed in black pants and white shirts with jackets, like servers. Candles lit the table. Next to that, they built a firepit ready with a log for a seat. A motorboat floated at the dock but set farther back to not obstruct their view of the loch and the sunset beyond.

She sighed and a breath blew gently against her ear. "I hoped ye would like it." So caught up in the sight before her, Marie didn't notice John's approach.

His arms wrapped around her and held her for a moment. "Ye know, ye look beautiful in the dusk light." He turned her in his arms and kissed her.

She shivered and John's fingers trailed to her hands. "Ye are cold. Come, let us get under the heaters."

Marie nodded as he led her to the table and chairs. "John, ye didn't have to go to all this trouble."

He held a chair out for her. As she sat and looked out over the dock, she experienced the best view of the loch at sunset.

He joined her and poured wine for them both. At this time of year, the sunsets were the most spectacular colors of crimson and marigold, casting the mountains in various hues of indigo and juniper. She looked forward to what promised to be a special evening. Marie peeked at John and knew she wanted not just dinner but what to do with him for dessert.

He chuckled. "I've always wanted to do this. Dinner on the dock at sunset." He glanced at her. "I just had to wait for the perfect woman to come along to share it with."

Marie sensed her face heat and sipped her wine—

Merlot, her favorite. "I'm surprised ye are drinking wine. Beer is yer usual."

John smiled after he sipped his wine. "Aye, but this 'tis yer favorite. Are ye ready to eat?"

She nodded as John signaled the two attendants to serve dinner. His gaze roamed her body; she held the plaid wrap around her for warmth. Under she wore a low-cut blouse on hopes to entice John this evening. Would he find her outfit sexy? After all the work he put into this evening, she should reward him. Marie smiled to herself as the server set her plate down. She planned to enjoy tonight.

After the servers stepped away, Marie took a bite of her meat, steak, medium well with peppercorn sauce. She hummed as she chewed.

John tilted his head as he took a bite. "Tell me about yer studies at university."

She sipped her wine. "Well, the chapel project is the last part of my graduate work. Once I complete the flooring and turn in my final paper, my grad work is complete."

John sat back. "Done, so soon? It was only last fall we started talking about the chapel."

Marie set her wine glass down. "Yes, well Bree and I discussed the Chapel Hill project, but we didn't discuss it more before she left. Well, went."

Bree and Colin stuck back in time.

Marie set down her fork and faced John. "So, she's back in time with Colin now. Ye think everything is going okay?"

John nodded and set his wine glass down. "Aye, I'm sure if there's an issue, I would've heard by now." Bree accidentally followed Colin back in time on his quest to find the Stone of Love and return Roderick, his ancestor, to his proper time.

Marie sipped her wine. " 'Tis good to have the notes from Colin via a bolt hole in the mantel. I wish we could send messages back in time."

John took another bite, chewed, and swallowed. "Aye, well either way, it seems good to know how things were in the past. She's there and they both are fine."

Marie took his hand in hers. "John, I am worried. What if they do not make it back to our time? What if they do not find the stone? What will we do then?"

John smiled as his thumb stroked her hand. "I have faith in Colin. He's a lot like his da—he'll have a plan, a backup plan, and then another plan. The MacDougalls tend to get through challenges and come out on top."

Marie sighed and gazed at the sunset. John was okay with the stone and time travel, which to her seemed surreal. She guessed she should put her faith in Colin and John as well.

John squeezed her hand, and she glanced back at him. The warm dusk light shone on his face as he smiled at her again. She gazed into his eyes, and there she found comfort, safety. With John she realized everything would be okay.

As they ate dinner, the sunset transitioned from bright shades of daffodil and tangerine to deeper shades of sandstone blended with mulberry wine. Each time Marie scanned out across the loch, the view changed. She stayed silent as she marveled at the artistry of God's work before her. Then the scenery would remind her of something she wanted to share with John, and she would jump back into a lively conversation. The night became so magical like God made this one sunset just for the two of them to share.

After dinner, the lads from the pub packed everything away and loaded the boat. John rose, took Marie's hand in his, and drew her to the fire ring. The lads lit the logs as Marie and John settled with the wine and plaids. The pub lads then shifted the heaters around the firepit. Before she realized it, the guys waved to them and motored out to the pub.

Marie peeked at John. "Ye planned this evening well. I'm impressed."

John smiled into his wineglass. "I wanted it to be perfect for ye, for us."

Marie snuggled under the plaids and sipped her wine. The Merlot made her mellow and she relaxed in his embrace.

John set his wine beside him and took hers and set it aside. He turned to face her as they lounged on the log under the plaids. John took her hands in his and kissed them then took a deep breath and gazed into her eyes.

"Marie, what ye said about wanting to do more work with Bree after the chapel project? Did ye mean that?" Marie blinked then smiled. The future. He asked about the future. Her heart fluttered.

She took a deep breath. "Aye, after the artifacts we found, we know there's more to discover than just what we found at the chapel renovation, and I would very much like to continue to explore the area."

John smiled and brushed his fingers on her cheek. "Did ye know Bree made plans to ask the Historic Environment of Scotland for another grant to excavate the grounds?"

Marie smiled; the next project meant a future here with him. "Aye, I do. We discussed it at length. The Chapel Hill, a rocky ridge a where a village was."

John nodded and lowered his head to hers. "Aye, so if ye work on that, then ye'll have to stay at the castle much longer than the chapel renovation project."

Marie nodded and tilted her head back. They gazed into each other's eyes and their mouths were so close their breaths mixed and made her head light. She hoped they continued their play—last night stayed magical for them both and she enjoyed John's playful lovemaking. She remembered last night well and hoped tonight ended the same. Desire built inside her and her pulse beat and fluttered in her throat. She hitched her breath and looked at John, his gaze intent on her.

John smiled. "I'd like it very much if ye stayed here at the castle for a long time." He leaned in and kissed her on the lips.

Between kisses, John whispered, "A very—" He kissed her. "—long time." And he deepened the kiss.

Marie's heart skipped at his declaration. They experienced a whirlwind start of a romance, and they made love once. But she remained uncertain till this moment how deeply John felt. She fell in love with John with their first kiss in the chapel and now he asked for a future, more time.

Marie slid her hands around his neck and as he deepened the kiss, she rolled him onto his back. Their lips danced with each kiss as John's hands roamed her body. Her hands traveled up and down his chest. John slipped his hand under her shirt, tickled her side, and he slid up and captured her breast in his palm. Marie wiggled, and the wrap fell off her shoulders and exposed her low-cut blouse. John's eyes shot to her cleavage, and she smiled, then sighed as he massaged her breast. As he shifted both hands under her shirt, the fabric tightened, and between kisses, she whipped off her shirt and then her bra.

John laughed lightly. "Inpatient?"

She grasped his shirt, and he sat up and helped her pull it over his head.

He smiled. "I guess so."

She lowered her chest to his and as they kissed the hairs of his chest rubbed against her bare breast. The hair teased her nipples and sent shivers over her body. John kissed her and turned them till they lay side by side. His hand slid up her skirt, cupped her, and made her squirm. He rubbed her slit causing heat to shoot up her spine, and she grew damp. She felt the heat from his play and remained exactly where she wanted to be. Between kisses, she stripped her skirt off and then her thong.

She smiled at him and whispered, "Better."

John gazed into her eyes and smiled even wider. "I knew ye were a perfect match for me."

She smiled back as she undid his pants and helped him strip them off, boxers and all. Under the plaid, beneath the moonlight, they were as God created them. When they came together, they fit perfectly, like they were made for each other.

Marie's hands roamed John's body, from his shoulders to his chest. She spread her fingers through his chest hairs and delighted in the wiry spring. Her hand drifted lower, molded around him. He groaned and she pumped him once, then again, and he grunted in response. She milked him and a drop came on the tip.

Her thumb rubbed over it, and he threw his head back in a groan. She enjoyed his play, but to be able to play with him intoxicated her. Marie became overcome with desire, and she wanted to feel all of him.

John bent forward and kissed her lightly. "Marie, God, I want ye something fierce. Should we head into the castle?"

Marie shook her head. "John, I've got ye right where I want ye. And I want ye now." Marie positioned herself over him and slid him over her folds. She was already damp. She slid him over her wetness a few times then shifted, and he glided slowly inside. Marie moaned and arched her back as he filled her. He jumped when she hit the base.

John caressed her breasts and suckled one nipple as he glided in and out of her passage. Marie kissed him and rocked her hips in time with his. He sucked the other breast, and she moaned. Marie picked up the pace and his arms slid down her back and gripped her rear like he asked for her to go even faster.

John grunted and she flipped them, so he came over her. On top, he gained better leverage for the hectic pace she desired. As he pumped into her, she arched her back again and moaned while her hands ran up and down his back. He kissed her and continued his drive as he got a little faster each time. Her desire quickly built, and her release came rapidly.

Marie threw her head back and cried his name as she exploded. Her release sent her to the heavens. When she returned to her senses, John still rocked in her. She took control and flipped him under her.

John laughed as he leaned up and kissed her.

As she straddled him, she braced her hands behind

her on his thighs to get better leverage.

John picked up the pace making Marie arch her back and moan louder. He grabbed her hips as he sat on his knees and continued his assault. Marie sensed the pressure build again and John pushed once, twice, and on the third roared her name as his release hit him.

Marie moaned his name, and her legs gripped his hips as they jerked twice.

John gathered her in his arms, and they lay by the fire as they stared at the stars. He trailed his fingers up and down her arm as her head rested against his chest. His heart raced as he wrapped the surrounding plaids around them and formed a cocoon. They lay in comfortable silence for a while as each caught their breath and relaxed comfortably.

Marie giggled. "Ye think anyone at the castle heard us?"

John smiled. "Castle? There is a castle near here?" Marie chuckled as John sighed. "Damn, woman, I forgot everything but ye. That was amazing."

Marie smiled and glanced into his eyes. "Aye, that was amazing."

After the fire burned down and the gas heaters ran out, the chill eventually forced them back to the castle. Wrapped in the plaids, they carried their clothing. Both tiptoed their way to the upper levels like two naughty teenagers out after curfew.

Marie giggled as she turned to her room, and John gathered her in his arms.

His hand caressed her cheek. "Marie, sleep beside me. I want to wake in yer arms and see the sunrise on yer face just as I viewed the sunset upon yer face tonight."

Marie's eyes watered, and she blinked. "Aye, John, I'd love that."

He picked her up in his arms and carried her to his bed.

****

The cabin door burst open startling Marie from a near sleep.

Clarke stumbled into the room. "Get off the bed, wench. I'm tired."

As Marie jumped up, the book fell to the floor, but Clarke did not notice. In his drunken stupor, he climbed into bed and rolled over with his back to her. She shuffled trying to get as far away from him as possible. She glanced at the book, and the candlelight lit a quote.

Be not afraid of sudden fear, neither of the desolation of the wicked, when it comes.

She glared at Clarke as his snoring filled the room. She thanked God for liquor and his susceptibility to strong spirits. Marie bent, picked up the book, and returned it to the bag. She grabbed a blanket and curled up on the floor. She wouldn't risk being next to him as he slept. Before she closed her eyes and tried to sleep, she offered a silent prayer to God. *Please, God, let John be close.*

Chapter 13

Dunstaffnage, present day

Bree curled up on the study couch, sipping from her wineglass as Colin wrapped her in his arms. There was no place she would rather be on a rainy night at Dunstaffnage. She remembered the first stormy night Bree stayed at Dunstaffnage. She'd snuck down here during a storm to pass the night and fell into Colin's arms. She smiled remembering as she literally fell off the bookshelf into his arms.

That occurred the first time she recognized she became attracted to him. After that night, their romance blossomed into love. Thunder boomed.

She jolted slightly.

Colin wrapped her in a tighter embrace. "Storms still bug ye, *mo chridhe*? Ye should know I'm here to chase yer storms away."

Bree hugged his arms and replied in her best Scots accent, "Aye, ye big, sexy Scot."

Colin chuckled and kissed her.

She cuddled back into his arms and sipped her wine. A moment of silence passed, then another. She couldn't get Marie off her mind. A priest took her, traveled back in time with her, and John followed. The same as she and Colin—taken for an Iona Stone. This time they searched for the Stone of Fear. Was her friend okay? Had John found her yet? Would they return to the present, if at all?

Colin grunted, "I can hear yer mind churning from here." He kissed her head. "What's bumping around in that head of yers?"

Bree sighed. "Marie and John. I'm worried about them."

Colin took her wineglass, set it on the table, and turned her in his arms. He caressed her face and kissed her. She grinned into his kiss, and he growled, then deepened the kiss. Their tongues danced. Marie and John flitted into her mind.

Bree sat up. "I know you are only trying to distract me."

Colin growled, "Damnit, woman, I was just beginning to enjoy myself."

Bree swatted his chest. "I mean it, Colin. I am really worried."

Colin sighed. He gazed at her from the side. "If I put yer fears at ease, can I have my way with ye?"

Bree raised an eyebrow. "*Ye* can't put my fear at ease. They are back in time. It's not like you can call them on their cell phones."

Colin's smile widened. "Ease yer fears, and I get me way with ye. Deal?"

Bree grabbed her wineglass and took a sip. "Challenge accepted, but if you lose, I get to have my way with you."

Colin leaned toward her and kissed her so hard the hairs on her arms rose.

He sat back. "Ye got yerself a deal, woman, but be prepared because I'm coming for ye."

Bree barked a laugh.

Colin rose and strode to the fireplace. He glanced over his shoulder, raised an eyebrow, and smiled. He stood there momentarily, and Bree shrugged her shoulders, uncertain what game he played tonight.

He smirked at her. "Woman, ye should know me better than that by now. I always have a trick up my sleeve."

He bent down to the left side of the mantel and opened the bolt hole.

Bree sucked in her breath. "Damn!"

Colin pulled out a scroll, turned, waved it, and chuckled. "Ye have such little faith in me, wife. I'll always have a way to make ye happy."

Bree gulped her wine and folded her arms as she huffed. Clearly, she lost the bet.

"Yes, I forgot about the bolt hole, but obviously, you and John didn't."

Colin sat beside her, holding the scroll up as he stared at the rolled paper.

Bree adjusted her seat and leaned close. "Well, open it."

Colin sighed. "Bree, ye need to be prepared. This may not be good news. It may be something ye don't wish to know."

Bree's brows crossed, and she gave him her best pout. "It must be good news. I can feel it."

Colin stood, crossed to the fireplace, then opened the scroll. He didn't want her to see it until he read it—always the protector. Colin took a while reading it, and the words made a long letter from where she sat. Much longer than other scrolls the men exchanged between times before. Colin's expression shifted from concern to shock, and he abruptly laughed out loud.

Bree about jumped off the lounge and tackled him. "Well?"

Colin glanced at her, then back at the scroll, and laughed again. "Ye will not believe me when I tell ye."

Unable to wait any longer, Bree jumped up and crossed to Colin. "What, is Marie hurt? What's happened?"

Colin shook his head. "The priest still has Marie, and they've chased him all around the western coast of Scotland. They plan an ambush at Ardchattan Nunnery. But that's not the shocking part."

Bree grabbed the scroll from Colin, and he still laughed, almost out of breath.

Bree read frantically. "His father? He found his father. Wait, didn't his father disappear years ago?"

Colin laughed. "Aye, and he's been living in the past. Do ye know what this means?"

Bree looked at him and shrugged.

Colin smiled. "The Fae Fable isn't about John and Marie, or even ye or me. It's his da." the *Fae Fable Book* thumped across the room and startled Colin. Curious. The book stayed the same since Marie went missing. What would the Fae want now?

Bree strode toward the book, but Colin caught her arm. "No, I don't want ye near that damn book. I prefer nothing happening to ye."

Bree smiled at her husband and patted his arm. "Colin, it's just a book. No harm ever came from reading a book."

Colin wouldn't let go of her arm. "She says after the last time ye read from a poem book, ye fell back in time. I don't want ye reading it."

She turned and kissed him. "It'll be fine. The Fae

wouldn't move the book if they didn't want us to see what it says. You can hold me while I read if it makes you feel better."

Colin growled and took the scroll from her. As they walked past the desk, he set the paper down. When they neared the *Fae Fable Book*, Colin gathered Bree in his arms and gripped her tightly. He shifted her almost behind him.

She squirmed and tried to move around him to view the book. "Colin, how can I read the book this way? You brute."

Colin growled, "I'll read the book. Ye stay here."

He leaned over, peeked at the book, and then slammed his hand on the glass case.

Bree jumped in his arms. "Careful, Colin, that is glass."

He growled again. "It's not glass. It's a damn Fae spell. I won't have ye touching it."

Bree sighed. "Okay, but what does it say?"

He heavily sighed as he rolled his eyes. "The page is blank."

Bree giggled. "Colin, Brigid is playing with you again. She wants me to read it, not you."

Colin groaned as Bree patted his shoulder. "You sound like a bear tonight."

She turned in his embrace and leaned over the glass case. The words appeared, but only one line. She read it aloud. "The father thanked God, for our best blessings are often the least appreciated."

Bree smiled as she glanced at Colin. "See, that wasn't so bad. It's the end of the fable. Brigid says the end is near, and we must appreciate our blessings."

Colin swept her up in his arms, carried her to the

couch, and laid her on it.

He slid over her. "Aye, our best blessings. Ye, Bree, ye and the kids are my best blessings." He kissed her again. "And I thank ye."

She slid her arms around his neck as he kissed her. He slid his tongue in and connected with hers as he deepened the kiss. She moaned lightly. Colin's hands roamed her body, down her sides to her hips as he rubbed against them. She wiggled her hips in delight.

Colin trailed kisses down her neck and back up to her ear. "Ye know, I've dreamt of taking ye on this couch since that night of the rainstorm."

Bree smiled and arched her neck in an invitation, so he kissed it again. "You have? Well, your wish is my command, husband." She grabbed his shirt and stripped it off, then ran her hand through his chest hair as he helped her by tossing his shirt aside.

Colin growled and kissed her deeply, then grabbed her shirt. As she sat forward on the couch, he stripped it off, and she hoped he liked her surprise.

When his gaze roamed her body, he chuckled. "No bra? Were ye planning this, wife?"

Bree smiled. "Maybe. You always said this was the best place to pass the time during a storm."

Colin sat up and gaped at her. "What about the kids?"

Bree smiled as she took hold of his neck and pulled him to her. "Already asleep. I checked on them before coming down."

She guided his head to her chest, and he sucked on a nipple as she arched her back.

He repeated the same for the other and nibbled on the nipple. His hand cupped it and squeezed the tip, sending sharp tingles to her toes. Bree shifted and arched, begging him to do the same to the other.

His chuckle let her know he understood what she wanted, and he complied with the other making it tingle as well. Grabbing both, he squeezed them together, suckling both tips in his mouth as Bree arched, and the sharp tingles shot across her chest. He released her and slid farther down the couch as he kissed his path toward her navel. The tickle of his unshaven chin caused her to suck in as his tongue against her lower abdomen spread heat.

She rubbed her hands through his thick black hair as he undid her pants and revealed her second surprise.

Colin sat back and stripped her pants off, and when his eyes fell upon her, he smirked. "No knickers. Why, Mrs. MacDougall, ye are becoming a naughty wife."

She wiggled as he stared at her body. "Your naughty wife enjoys her naughty Scot."

Colin bent and spread her legs. She allowed one to dangle off the edge. He blew on her curls, then ran his finger over her as he spread her juice. He hummed as he licked her nub.

She arched and moaned.

He licked it again and glanced up. This remained one of Bree's favorite forms of play.

He smiled as he teased her. She liked it when he tormented her with his mouth. His tongue flicked again, then he wrapped his mouth over her nub and sucked.

Bree gasped. "Oh, Colin."

He sucked a few more times and licked her nub as it grew hard under his torture. Colin stood, stripped off his pants, and his hand stroked him.

He slid up her body and kissed her hard. "God,

Bree, I can't take it anymore. I must have ye now." He entered her swiftly, and she yelped. He kissed her hard again, pumped once, then stopped, seated fully in her.

He panted. "Woman, I can't ever get enough of ye. Every time I touch ye, I can't stop myself. I must have ye, over and over."

Colin rocked slowly within Bree as she caressed his face. "I know. It's like an obsession. Please take me, Colin. Make me fly."

He kissed her in a promise to make sweet, hard love to his wife.

She slowly responded as she wanted this to last. She waited till they were back at Dunstaffnage, waited for a rainstorm so she could make love to him here where their attraction started. Her fantasy of taking him to the study came true, and she wanted to savor it.

Taking her cue, Colin started again, slowly, the friction enhanced by the sensitivity of his earlier play. He bumped into her nub and sent tingles through her as she moaned. He bent and kissed her as he slid in a little harder.

He read her needs and desires and shifted as his hand traveled from her hip to her knee. He drew it up against his hip, allowing him better access, and he went deeper on the next thrust.

She sensed his desire build, felt him swell in her. She arched in the next push.

He grunted as he increased his pace. He rose a little on his hands, shifted again, and gained better mobility. Colin liked his loving hard and fast. She grabbed his shoulders and held on for the ride as Colin increased the pace, building pressure inside her.

Colin continued to push and drove the force of love

that became part of their lives. All their passion poured into each stroke and thrust and rose in anticipation. Bree became the first to find release as she cried out his name. Colin followed quickly, slammed into her, and shouted her name with his release. He still shook when he shifted her to his side as they snuggled on the couch.

As Colin still tried to catch his breath, Bree giggled. "I won. I had my way with you."

Colin huffed. "No, I won. I had my way with ye."

Bree ran her hands up and down his back. "I appreciate you, Colin."

Colin kissed her once and then again with each word he said. "God, woman, I appreciated ye yesterday, today, tomorrow, last year, and next year."

Bree laughed. "I love you."

Colin finally caught his breath as his hand caressed her face. "Aye, *mo chridhe*, I love ye too."

Chapter 14

Ardchattan Priory, 1498

"Well, lads, that's it, the MacDougall Cross. Made to honor our King and the MacDougalls buried here." Father Egan MacDougall, Prior at Ardchattan, strolled along the walkway in the gardens outside the chapel.

John and his da strolled with Father MacDougall, who shrugged. "I still don't understand how any priest believed a stone could appear from our cross. It may be, as you say, he's gone mad."

John glanced back at the cross, whole in this century. He still remembered the future version clearly in his mind—several areas cracked, and portions had broken off. John blinked, and the cross in front of him was new.

John turned to his da, who shook his head. He stayed quiet—say nothing. If he told them any facts about the future, too many parts of history might change. He and his da were not there to change history, only to retrieve the stone and rescue Marie.

Behind his da, John Douglas MacDougall, the captain of the castle, positioned a group of highland warriors around the garden area to lie in wait for when Marie and the priest arrived.

Prior MacDougall spoke and took John out of his musings. "Ye say he kidnapped yer woman?" The prior shook his head. "Such a shame. He's had her for how long now?"

John stared in the distance across Loch Etive. *Marie.* "Five days—five long days."

John's da patted him on the back.

Prior MacDougall folded his arms into his robes. "Such a shame. She's likely compromised. Now he's ruined her. We can make a place for her here as a nun."

John's gaze snapped to the prior. "No, she won't become a nun."

The prior stopped and glared at John. "Why, my son, certainly if he compromised her, ye will want a different bride?"

John grabbed the man by his robes. "She will come home with me. I love her, and I will marry her. She will never be a nun."

John's da grabbed him from behind and yanked him off the clergy. "Now, son, no need to get angry at the man. He's just doing his duty."

Prior MacDougall shook himself and scowled at John.

John didn't care if he offended the clergyman. Marie remained his love, and they would go home together.

"I see ye have powerful feelings for her. As ye wish."

They strolled along the walkway, the lush gardens in spring a stark contrast to the cold settled in John's heart. *Marie.* He sent a silent prayer to God. *Please let her be okay.* He didn't care what the damned insane priest did to her. He would do whatever she needed to see her healed. He just wanted Marie back.

A monk approached Prior MacDougall. "Father,

the couple ye are waiting for has arrived."

John advanced toward the monk and quickly spoke. "The woman, is she okay?"

The monk nodded. "The woman is unharmed."

The monk turned back to the prior. "But the man is impatient and demanding. Refused to wait in yer study."

Thank God she remained unharmed. John stood there a moment and gained control of his breathing to calm himself.

His father tapped his arm and nodded to the bushes.

John strode toward his hiding place, but Prior MacDougall stopped them with his hand. "I'll try to see if I can separate them. Get her in my study so we can have her out of harm's way. Remember, no killing on holy ground."

John nodded. "Try if ye can, but if not, we'll take it from here."

The prior made the sign of the cross before John, then his father. "God go with ye, my son. Trust in Him."

John nodded, and the prior strode back to the main building, his robes flapping in his haste.

John settled near a wall area close to the walkway, with a clear view of the MacDougall cross. He glanced around. The warriors were all in place. Their plan must succeed without harming Marie. He glimpsed behind him at his da, who nodded. He nodded in return. All was ready. Now they waited.

He took a deep breath. Marie came so close he almost felt her. John closed his eyes, and a memory slid into his mind, the night before the maniac kidnapped her, the night he professed his love.

****

"A brooch? Complete except for the stones," Marie exclaimed. They sat in the kitchen for a casual, quiet dinner.

Marie filled him in on her most recent find. "I'm so glad Bree and I agreed to start a small excavation site to find historical items where we surmised the small village rested. It seems our work paid off, and our goal is to get the next project for the castle, Chapel Hill, 'quick listed' by the Historic Environment of Scotland, a success!"

Over dinner, they discussed a new, fascinating item, and Marie's excitement became evident. "Aye, an old brooch. I believe it's The Brooch of Lorne. We found it in a rotted chest, but the pin being gold was well preserved."

John smiled as Marie's eyes lit up when she spoke. Bree did the same thing, but when they were together, they chatted like magpies.

"The brooch is one of three West Highland sixteenth-century silver turreted brooches centered on charm stones. However, historians believe the brooches to be a resetting of magic stones already possessing reputations. The others are the Lochbuie Brooch in the British Museum and the Lossit Brooch, still in private hands."

Marie grew animated as she discussed her find. Her arm went wide and waved in the air. "Here's what's interesting. This pin not only holds one stone but two. The other brooches have compartments to hide sacred items behind the gemstone, but this one holds a heart-shaped stone on the back and an oval stone on top, layering the stones together."

Marie shifted her hands and placed them one over the other as she showed the different layers.

John smiled; she loved history and became so caught up in it.

"Bree and I believe the heart-shaped stone is the Stone of Love, but we cannot figure out which of the Stones of Iona the top stone might be or if they are interchangeable."

John nodded. "I will send the brooch to the Historical Society of Scotland and see what they can tell ye of it."

Marie smiled. "I already called them. Bree took it to Edinburgh when she left. We are both so excited about this find."

Marie sat back in her chair. "We looked it up, then cataloged the item for the society. The Brooch of Lorne, it's a MacDougall brooch lost after 1306. The Battle of Dalrigh occurred when John of Argyll, chief of the Clan MacDougall, ambushed Robert the Bruce of Scotland, where he ripped Bruce's cloak off and kept the brooch for the family. Gosh, it would be so cool to see that."

Time travel again?

John laughed. "No, it wouldn't. We won't see any more time travel. The one-time of Colin and Bree's remained enough of a strain on us all. Plus, the Fae haven't been active, and the *Fae Fable Book* sits back in its case. All is well and good."

Marie glanced down, unexpectedly quiet. Why had she gone quiet? Was she worried about the find? Bree shared all the credit with her for every discovery thus far.

John lifted her chin till her eyes met his. "It's a wonderful find, and ye will get credit for it." He kissed her and then rose to gather the dishes.

Marie quietly sat while John cleared the dishes. Every so often, he peeked at her. Her behavior this evening seemed unusual, especially for a typically very chatty woman.

He grabbed his wine and kissed her softly. "Come, let's sit before the fire in the Hall. Relax for a while."

Marie took her glass as John led her to their favored spot in the Great Hall. They settled into the couch. John pulled Marie into his arms as they sipped wine, and the flames danced, casting shadows around the room.

Things between them grew into a routine over the past few months. She chose to live at the castle halfway through the last project, and he insisted she stay, knowing the new project started soon. While they had few long-term conversations, they hadn't cemented any firm plans. John tried to devise a way to speak about it, a more permanent arrangement for them, and he became tongue-tied.

Marie opened her mouth, then stopped. She sighed and sipped her wine. This wasn't his outspoken Marie at all.

He leaned over. "Ye look like a fish out of water. Do ye have something to say, Marie?"

She sat back and spoke softly. "John, if something were to happen. Um, something like what happened to Bree. Would ye come for me?"

John barked a laugh and turned his answer into a joke. "Well, now, would I? A trip in time, that's an awfully long way, sweetie." John sipped his wine.

Nothing had happened with the Fae. Certainly, she joked.

She paused and took a deep breath, then glanced at him. "W-well, if it were to happen, for real. Would ye come and get me?"

John choked on his wine. "What do ye mean by that? Nothing like that is going to happen."

Marie bit her nail and gazed into the flames.

John set his glass on the table, took her glass, and set it down.

He took her hands into his. "Marie, there's been no Fae activity since Colin and Bree returned. The *Fae Fable Book* is back on the Corinthians quote. Nothing is going to happen. I won't let it."

Marie glanced away, then back at him. "What if something did happen? Would ye come for me?"

John caressed her cheek. "Aye, I'd come for ye."

He kissed her softly and gazed into her eyes. "I'd go anywhere, overcome any obstacle, go to any time. All for ye."

Marie smiled and kissed him back. John deepened the kiss and rested his forehead against hers. *Now is the time. Tell her now.*

He took a deep breath. In for a farthing, in for a pound. "I've been trying to find a way to ask ye, but words sometimes fail me."

Marie gazed at him. "Aye, John?"

He wanted to say something poetic, something romantic. He wasn't always good with words and wanted to make this memorable for Marie. He chastised himself for not planning this better, but emotions always got the best of him.

He struggled to find romantic words of love which

swept her off her feet, but what came out was, "Marie, what did the infatuated boy volcano say to the beautiful girl volcano?"

Marie giggled and replied. "It's a sediment?"

John huffed a laugh, but that wasn't what he wanted to say. "Nice try."

He took a deep breath and tried again. "I lava ye."

Marie sat for a moment as John held his breath. Maybe she didn't realize what he tried to say. She mouthed the words, and when she got to lava, she mouthed love. Her gaze snapped to his.

Marie laughed and threw her arms around him. "I lava ye too, John."

He fell back on the couch and held her in his arms. "I want ye to stay here forever, Marie. I want ye to be my wife."

Marie stopped and gaped into his eyes. "Ye mean it? Marry ye?"

John nodded. "I don't have a ring yet. I wanted to allow ye to pick out yer ring as ye are so specific about rocks. I wanted to let ye pick yer stone."

Marie's eyes teared up. "Oh, John, I love ye."

He gathered her in his arms, "I love ye too."

****

Yelling roused John from his memory. Abbott MacDougall approached with another man who shouted his demands. The priest and Marie had arrived.

Soon he would have her in his arms.

Chapter 15

Marie skipped alongside Father Clarke, who hastily marched as he stopped every few feet. At the same time, he waited for Prior MacDougall, who walked at a plodding, steady pace.

Clarke waved his hand as he spoke. "No, thank you. I do not want to have a respite in your quarters. My wife"—Father Clarke pulled Marie beside him—"and I want to see the cross. *Now!*"

Marie stumbled alongside Clarke and winced. She tried to walk slower and stray behind Clarke as she hoped to signal the prior. She even made a face at Prior MacDougall, then raised her eyebrow as she signaled to him.

Father MacDougall folded his hands in his robes and nodded at her. "Maybe the lass would like to freshen up. She looks—a little road worn."

Marie nodded as she strode toward Prior MacDougall. Clarke grabbed her arm and snatched her back behind him.

When she cried in alarm, Prior MacDougall reached out to her.

Clarke stood his ground. "My *wife* stays with me."

Marie shook her head behind Clarke.

Prior MacDougall's gaze slid to the side of the monastery.

Marie's gaze followed, and a kilted highlander

with a sword shifted behind the wall's corner. His plaid flashed the MacDougall pattern. Was he a guard?

Prior MacDougall nodded. "This way, my son." He stepped in measured steps toward an outer courtyard.

Now that they walked slower, Marie examined the area and searched for other men. She peered out across the garden area toward Loch Etive. Everything was so lush and green. The grounds were just as spectacular in the fifteenth century as in the twenty-first century, likely more so. There were just as wide varieties of flowers, trees, and shrubbery, although placed in varying different locales. She viewed the other priory buildings as they passed through an archway to another garden area.

They exited a garden into a courtyard that seemed to sit where the car park existed in the future but now held a circle of trees that lined the area where the large cross sat.

The prior stopped.

Clarke stopped behind him, and Marie startled as she almost ran into Clarke.

"The MacDougall Cross." Priory MacDougall waved at the large stone cross. "Just recently delivered to the grounds and placed in its place of honor. We had this garden created with its tribute to our devoted dedication and *duty to God*."

Marie peered at the cross but did a double take back to Prior MacDougall as he emphasized "duty to God." Marie sensed an undercurrent of energy about her like it encircled the garden.

The prior glanced at a tree behind her and widened his eyes, but when Marie turned, nothing stood there. She glanced at Clarke.

He stared at the cross. "Thank you, Father, that will be all." Clarke waved his hand as he still gazed at the cross.

Prior MacDougall glared down his nose at Clarke. "Excuse me, my son."

Clarke yelled, "You may leave. My wife and I need to pray *in private*."

Prior MacDougall stepped back.

Marie doubted anyone took that tone with him, let alone shouted.

The prior stepped forward as he spoke. "I believe I shall stay and pray with ye."

She wanted to scream yes but only jostled when Clarke shifted her as he slashed his hand. "That won't be necessary. We will pray alone."

Prior MacDougall glared at Marie, then Clarke. He nodded and slowly walked away as he folded his hands in his robes.

As he left, dread seeped into her heart. As he glanced back, he made the sign of the cross and nodded to the bushes. She turned her head and scanned them as another highlander ducked and hid. She sensed that something was about to happen.

When the prior cleared the wall and went out of sight, Clarke grabbed her arm and yanked her hard toward the cross. "Find it now, you bitch. Bring forth the stone."

Marie cried out as he dragged her to the cross and flung her to the ground. She crashed to her knees as her hands caught her fall, and her palms scraped the gravel.

She looked over her shoulder at Clarke. "I don't know what ye mean."

He slapped her hard. Stars danced across her

vision, but she kept her head down and pretended to pray. Truthfully, she kept her head down and prayed for John.

****

John crouched behind a tree next to his da and witnessed everything. His blood boiled. The heat within him rose when the mangy excuse for a priest grabbed Marie's arm and made her cry out. He started toward her when the bastard slapped her.

His da grabbed his arm. "Wait, son, I know it's hard, but we must see if he'll produce the stone. Ye and Marie need it to travel back to the future."

John nodded at his da's wisdom and didn't question how he came by it. As difficult as it was, he sat back and observed.

Marie seemed to have gathered herself, took full breaths while she kneeled before the cross, and slid her gaze sideways to Clarke. "I'll need the cross. The one ye took from yer church in Iona. The cross will help me call the stone."

Clarke huffed, looked at the MacDougall Cross, and then at her. He shrugged, pulled the cross out of his bag, and handed it to her.

When the priest revealed the cross, John's da jolted beside him. The lone, deep purple stone glinted in the sunlight.

His da gasped. "Of course. How could I have been so blind?"

John glanced at his da, who smiled at him. "John, of all the things we have been through, ye know I love ye. I love ye and yer mother with all me heart."

John nodded and returned his da's gaze—something he grew used to being in the past with him,

188

only now to realize he missed. "Of course, Da."

His da smiled and patted his face. "Ye have faith in me, faith in my love for ye."

John nodded as his eyes watered, and his voice cracked as he spoke. "Aye, Da, always."

If he and Marie returned to the future, he would leave his parents behind in the past and lose them all over again.

His da nodded once and placed his hand on John's shoulder. "Know what I do is for ye and yer love. My fate was determined long before ye traveled through the portal. A bargain made and a promise kept."

John didn't know what his da meant but nodded all the same.

His da smiled as he looked over John's face like he tried to commit it to memory. "Follow my lead, son. We go to save yer true love."

****

Marie gripped the cross and prayed with all her might for John to save her.

Clarke kicked her once. "Where's my damn stone, bitch?"

Marie grunted but kept her head lowered, eyes closed, and prayed for John's arrival. "Please send him to me. I have faith in ye, God. I have no fear in ye."

Marie opened her eyes, and before her stood the MacDougall Cross, whole and not broken. She wished he would allow her to study the cross at her leisure. Marie faced the side damaged in the twentieth century but whole now in the past. What little she viewed of the base looked exquisite.

So intent on her attention on the cross and that of Clarke, she didn't notice anyone approach until they were almost upon them. "Hello there, sir."

Clarke jerked at the voice.

Marie slid her gaze back to see who approached behind them. Two men stood directly behind her and Clarke, not but four feet away. It took her a moment to recognize John MacArthur, and the other looked like an older version of John. *It's John, and he's here. He's come for me in the past. I'm saved!*

She gasped and rose as she strode toward John. Only to have Clarke grab her arm and snatch her in front of him. She cried out and tried to say John, but she only yelped.

Clarke drew his dagger and held it under her chin.

John and the man drew swords. Behind them, the yard filled with armed highlanders that encircled the group.

Clarke gathered her tighter against him and raised the dagger. He nicked her throat, causing her to whimper in pain.

She shifted in his arms, and blood dripped down her neck.

Everyone froze.

John stepped toward her. His eyes pleaded as he gazed upon her.

The priest shifted her in his arms as he yelled, "Do not come closer. I'll kill her."

John shouted, "Marie, don't move, love."

Clarke's menacing laugh rang in her ear. "Love, is it?"

The older man slashed his arm. "John, ye are not following *my lead*."

"Aye, Douglas," a warrior nearby said.

So, his name is Douglas. isn't that John's da's

name?

Clarke shifted from around Marie's head. "Drop your swords, or I'll cut her again." Father Clarke moved his dagger.

She lurched from another nick to her throat as more blood trailed down.

Everyone dropped their sword except John, who jolted when the priest cut her the second time.

Clarke nodded in John's direction. "Him especially."

Marie's eyes connected with John's as she shook her head slightly.

John glared at her, not dropping his weapon.

A warrior near him took the sword from his arm and lowered it to the ground.

Douglas nodded at both and returned his gaze to the priest who held her.

Marie shook in the madman's arms, helpless as they all stood there and waited. She held the cross to her chest as if it gave her hope.

Douglas didn't budge but stood waiting, but for what?

John glanced at the priest, then at the man before her. Something seemed amiss, but she couldn't put her finger on it. The wind shifted and blew around them as something ethereal stirred in the yard. Douglas folded his hands before him and waited.

The priest glanced from warrior to warrior and back at Douglas, who spoke. "So, ye're a priest from the future—" He looked the priest up and down. "—find what ye come for, then?"

From the corner of her eye, the priest's eyes widened and then narrowed on him. "What business is it of yours?"

Douglas took a step toward the madman. "I'm Douglas MacArthur, and ye are holding my future daughter-in-law. But I think ye are more interested in a stone than a pretty lass. How about ye release the girl, and we'll discuss the stone. The one ye are after?"

Marie's eyes widened and shot to John. *Douglas was his father, who went missing in the future.* Her eyes connected with John's, and her shock must have been apparent.

John gazed back at her and nodded as if to say, *Aye, he's my father.*

Clarke gripped her tighter. "No, I'll hold on to my insurance. But you can tell me of the stone, the Stone of Iona."

John's father sighed and took another step toward them. "Aw, son, there are many a stone from the isle of Iona. Yet only three make a difference. Which one are ye searching for?"

The priest stood frozen.

John's father laughed and took another step as he approached Marie and the priest. "Aye, I see it now. Ye don't know which stone ye seek."

Step by step, as John's father spoke smoothly, he crept closer to the priest and Marie. She glanced at John, who stood near his sword on the ground. The rest of the yard stayed frozen, maybe by sheer shock or another force. Marie wasn't sure.

John's father still spoke softly. "Ye see, son, to find what ye seek, ye must know what it is ye are looking for. If not, then ye are doing nothing but chasing yer lost mind."

As John's father approached Marie, the cross

warmed in her hands. At first, she assumed it might be nerves, but the closer John's father came, the warmer the cross grew.

Someone whispered in her mind. *Be not afraid of sudden fear, neither of the desolation of the wicked, when it comes.*

She peeked at John, who stared intently at her. John's eyes slowly tracked to his father, who watched her. When her eyes connected with John's father, he winked. Had he heard the voice as well? The priest mustn't have. He didn't move.

As Douglas spoke to the madman, his eyes shifted to the cross. Then slowly up at her.

He nodded. His eyes traveled to the priest who held her and then back to her with wider eyes. "The mystery of the stones of Iona is a long and tragic tale... *The stone in the cross*, powered by emotions, can give or take life, depending on how ye use it."

John's father's voice faded as the cross grew warmer, hot in her hands. She glanced down, and a purple glow emanated from the front.

What John's father said, the words whispered in her mind, *the stone in the cross*. She held the Stone of Fear, and John's father wanted her to use it. Her eyes darted to his, and she smiled widely.

****

John paused, rooted in the ground. He sensed out of his body like he had no way to move, only an ability to witness—time slowed as he stood in stunned silence.

Marie twisted and turned in the priest's arms. She cut her arm as it passed the blade. His da took a deep breath as Marie pressed the cross to the priest's face. The cross sizzled and burned the priest. His da lunged as the priest shoved Marie away. Douglas caught her in his arms and shifted her behind him. She held the cross close to her chest.

The priest cried out and grabbed his face. He scowled at John's da and lunged with his knife.

His da stood his ground and didn't block the strike, turn, or back away. Douglas took the stab directly to the heart and shuddered as the blade struck true.

Marie screamed.

John ran forward and caught his da as he fell. The yard erupted into chaos. Guards swarmed the priest and captured him as he bellowed.

Marie ran to John and kneeled across from him—time sped up.

John breathed hard as he held and rocked his da. "Da, God, Da." John cried over and over.

His da opened his eyes and gazed at John. "My son, I love ye with all my heart. A bargain made and a bargain kept. Just as it should be."

John stared at his da.

Marie gasped a sob.

His da grabbed his shirt. "It's always as it should have been, son. I made a bargain with this Fae. I wanted to be with my wife, yer mom. And I got that. But they asked for a high price, too high a price. So, I took a chance and haggled."

Marie ripped fabric from her skirt and tried to stop the blood flow.

His da kept a tight grip on him as if he held on to the last threads of connection between father and son. "Heed me, boy. This happened as it should, and one day ye will understand. My time with yer mom had a price, but I couldn't lose ye."

He drew a deep breath and winced. John's heart broke at his da in pain. "They wanted yer life in exchange for my time with my love. So, I made that damn Fae Morrigan promise. If I delivered a Stone of Iona back to the Fae, they'd spare both yer lives, ye and yer true love's, by taking mine and yer mom's instead."

John's sob broke free, and he cried openly. "No! Not now that I found ye, found ye both only to lose ye all over again." His da sacrificed himself and his ma for him and Marie.

Douglas smiled and patted his cheek. "Don't worry, son. Yer mom and I will always be with ye. We have fulfilled our oath. We both may now rest in peace together in our eternal love." He took a shaky breath. "It's how we wanted it. Ye go home and reread the Fae Fable. Then it will make sense."

His da jolted, drew a shuddered breath, and glanced at Marie. "Such a pretty wife ye picked, son. Ye'll have bonnie kids."

His da took a short gasp and shook. "I love ye." With those words, Douglas James MacArthur drew his last breath, a smile for his son frozen on his face.

John sat there long, holding his da in his arms. Sounds reached him in the silence as people surrounded him, then shifted away. Marie softly sobbed as she stroked his da's head.

She glanced up and cried as she crawled beside him and took him in her arms.

The prior approached and faced them solemnly.

Marie shifted and tucked the cross into the folds of her skirt.

The prior sighed and made the sign of the cross over them.

He gazed around the yard. It had cleared. The madman was gone, and the guards were with them.

John glanced up at Prior MacDougall and started to speak, but the prior held his hand up. "We took the man to a cell and locked him away. He will stand before fellow priests for judgment, which I expect will be harsh."

The father slid his gaze to Marie. "My lady, are ye well?"

Marie glanced at John and then at the prior. "Aye, I am well, thank ye."

The father's gaze dropped to John's da, held still in John's arms. "A shame to die on holy ground. It will cast his soul into purgatory." John gasped.

The clergyman turned, his robes flared at the movement as he strode away.

Marie dropped her arms and huffed. "Wait, Father, that's not necessarily true."

Prior, MacDougall turned, raised his eyebrow, and glared down at Marie. "Excuse me, my child?"

Marie folded her arms and drew herself up and sat taller. "Is it not that the spirit of a virtuous human who dies on holy ground, God shall give the seven gifts of the Holy Spirit, which are—" She counted her fingers as she listed them. "—wisdom, understanding, counsel, fortitude, knowledge, piety, and the last, fear of the Lord."

The Father's eyebrows shot into his hairline. "Mm, why yes, that is true."

She snorted. "And isn't it true an evil person who dies on holy ground becomes stripped of these same gifts, except the fear in the Lord?" The clergy nodded and stared off.

John gazed at her, smiled, and leaned over and kissed her.

Prior MacDougall glanced back at them. "Bless ye, my son. Ye have a very courageous and knowledgeable woman as yer future wife." He signaled the monks behind him, who glided forward. "They will take the body and prepare him for burial." He made the sign of the cross over them, turned with a flare of his robes, and left the yard.

John carefully set his father on the ground and rose. He pulled Marie up with him and held her in his arms. As John and Marie stood solemnly, the monks gently lifted his da and carried him away.

When they had gone, John squeezed her. She returned his embrace, and they remained there momentarily as they held each other tightly.

John stepped back and gazed into Marie's eyes. "God, woman, ye gave me a sure fright."

Marie gazed into his eyes as tears filled them. "Ye came, ye came for me."

John blew out a snort. "Hell yes, I came for ye, ye daft woman. Made me jump time and chase ye all over western Scotland."

Marie laughed and twinged as her hand went to her neck.

John grabbed his handkerchief, wiped the blood, and pressed it on her cuts. "Ye okay, *mo ghràdh*?"

Marie nodded. "John, I am so sorry about yer father and mother."

"Aye, I am too. But it seems something my da planned all along."

He jolted and took Marie by the shoulders. "The stone. He said he recovered a stone."

Marie smiled and glanced around the yard before she revealed what she hid in her skirts. "I suspected this was it, but it wasn't until yer da started talking that I realized what I held."

She pulled the cross from her skirt and held it for John. The purple stone no longer glowed, and the one ruby stone glinted in the light.

John gasped. "The purple one, the Stone of Fear?"

Marie nodded. "Aye, yer da signaled me. I understood what to do. I don't know how; I just did. Father Clarke's loss of faith in God became his undoing. He turned away from God for his greed. I doubt God perceived him as a priest anymore. I sure as hell didn't."

John tilted his head, and Marie smiled. "Please, John, take me home. Please take me to Dunstaffnage. But in our time."

John smiled and glanced at the cross, then at her. "Aye, my love. Nothing would please me more."

Chapter 16

The housekeeper led them to their rooms, and upon arriving at the door, she waved them in.

When John followed Marie, the housekeeper stopped him with her hand on his shoulder. "Ye can't be sharing a room with a woman ye have not wed. 'Tis not proper."

Marie glanced back as John glared at the housekeeper. "Aye, of course. 'Tis not proper."

He turned but gave a last glance at Marie as he left her alone.

She supposed it seemed better this way, a chance for them both to reflect on all that had happened.

The housekeeper eyed her for a moment, then shut the door firmly.

Marie did a full circle of the room, different than hers in the future and not even Brielle's room with the built-in stone bench facing a window. This room didn't exist in the future. Smaller, with no fireplace and a small slit for a window that only held a hide over it. She suspected the wind blew the rain and cold into the room directly onto the bed.

Marie crossed and sat on the bed, more of a straw-stuffed cot if she were honest with herself. The boning in her bodice pinched, and she reached behind her to pull out the lengthened ties, pulled hard on them, and wiggled until the pressure eased around her chest.

She sat in a room alone. Finally free from all the pressure of the last couple of weeks, Marie let loose. A tear escaped and another. A sob came, and more tears rolled down her cheeks. Marie curled up on the bed and allowed the dam to be free. All her pent-up fear of being kidnapped, the worry of Clarke hurting her, the need to escape, and her desire for John to rescue her all poured out in one long, freeing bawl. Sob after sob burst free, and her heart felt raw, her soul stuck, and her mind lost.

After some time and a few sniffles, Marie remained alone. She lay there and found comfort in the solitude, one with herself.

A tapping at the door woke Marie. She must have dozed off. Still in her stained, dirty dress, she slowly rose, crossed to the door, and opened it expecting the housekeeper again. Lady MacDougall stood with a smile and clothing folded over her arm.

Marie stood back, inviting the lady to enter. "M'Lady."

Lady MacDougall entered with a maid who followed, carrying a pitcher and a cloth.

The room not being very large, Lady MacDougall turned close to Marie and signaled the maid, who set down the pitcher and cloth on the bedside table, the only other furniture in the room beside the bed. "John MacArthur assures us ye are his friend."

Once the maid stood upright, the lady waved her out.

Lady MacDougall stood still as she glanced over at Marie. "Kidnapped by a priest." She huffed. "Well, I am certain ye are not up for a social call." She set the clothing on the bed and waved to the pitcher. "Some fresh clothes and something to wash with." The lady passed her and, at the door, turned and held the handle. "Dinner is at sundown in the grand hall. While John MacArthur claims ye're betrothed, my husband refuses the claim as no contract is signed." She eyed her again. "Such a shame the lot us women have in life, is it not? Whether we tell the truth or lie, it's up to the men to decide our fates." She shook herself. "If ye need a friend, my name's Anabelle. Ye may call upon me anytime, Lady Marie."

The door clicking shut announced she left Marie alone. Alone again.

Marie stepped to the pitcher. A sliver of soap sat on the linen, and the water felt warm. After the last weeks on the road, a wash and clean clothing became a welcome gift—given from an unlikely ally.

****

Marie entered the great hall for dinner, fresh, clean, and feeling like a new woman. The crowd shuffled about. Marie, familiar with the seating hierarchy, strode to the front, intent on reaching John at the dais. She spotted him and waved, which he returned. When his attention shifted to her, Laird MacDougall turned and glared.

He waved to someone, and a guard stepped before her. "I do believe yer seat is over there." He nodded his head to the center table amongst the villagers. Her gaze followed his nod, and people crowded the middle table filling it. She glanced back at John, who argued with the laird. Her gaze slid to Lady Anabelle, who shook her head. No support would come from her. Well, it remained only for a short time, till they traveled to the future, and sitting with people from the past should prove interesting.

She tried to sit near the front, but a man slid on the bench.

Marie moved down the long table and stepped over the bench only to have a woman stop her with her hand. " 'Tis my seat beside my husband."

Marie moved farther down the table, and people blocked another two attempts to sit. She found herself nearly at the end of the table, and as she glanced back at the dais, she bet an entire football field remained between her and John.

As she sat down, the call for prayer came, and she stood again. The clergyman gave a short blessing, followed by murmurs, and everyone sat. Servants bustled about carrying platters, but nothing came to her table that she expected. The servants would serve them last being at the end.

She turned to the lady beside her and spoke, but the woman gave Marie her back.

She glanced at the man across from him, who glowered as he sucked his teeth.

Not to be deterred, she spoke aloud. "My, this is so nice. I've traveled so much, and to have a full meal will be a treat."

The man across from her huffed.

The woman on her other side leaned over. "Aren't ye the woman from the priest? The one who killed Dougie?"

Marie gasped. "I didn't kill John's father. The priest did!"

The man before her huffed again.

Platters set before them with trenchers interrupted the exchange, and with the distraction as well as the arrival of needed nourishment, Marie chose to eat in silence.

She reached for the bowl of stew, but the container passed around. When it came to her, she tipped the bowl. Only drops and some lumps slipped out. Half a loaf of bread was before her. Marie turned to the woman who asked if she killed Dougie, and the woman returned her smile. When she turned back, her bowl was half full. Her gaze snapped to the man before her, who glanced away. So, the rumor mill was busy already, and she wasn't even here a whole day. At least some villagers were charitable.

The laird stood and called attention to all in the hall. "Clan MacDougall, we mourn the passing of our great ship captain and his wife. But we also welcome his son, lost for some time, and returned to the bosom of his family. We welcome John MacArthur." John stood and nodded as the women clapped and the men stomped or beat the tables in tribute to him. His gaze roamed the room, and when he squinted, it finally settled on her. A smile passed his face but vanished when Laird MacDougall slapped him on the back, nearly knocking him over.

The laird called out again. "A toast to Dougie, his wife Katherine, and their son, John." Everyone raised a cup, and all shouted, "Slainte'!"

The laird called again. "A story. I need an elder to entertain me. Lift my heavy heart with a good tale!"

All sat, and an older man stood and shuffled to the dais. "M'Laird, in honor of Douglas and Katherine, *The Warrior and Lost Lover*. I'll tell the tale of the lost lovers."

The people in the hall erupted in cheers, stomps,

and the pounding of tables.

The laird yelled, "Silence! I wish to hear this story. I haven't heard it in a long time." He waved to the bent man with the white hair. "Proceed, Hamish."

Hamish and a good tale—memories of her and Brielle at the Dunbeg pub flitted through her mind and warmed her heart. Marie settled into her seat, looking forward to a good tale from the past. She hoped it was one she didn't read, a new story to share with Brielle and add to her collection upon her return home. Home, the future, soon.

Hamish bowed before his laird turned to face the crowd, and his voice started softly. "An unfortunate female wanderer took up residence in a dark vault among the ruins of Dryburgh Abbey. For some time, many in the village wondered about her strange behavior because, during the day, she never left. When night fell, she would emerge from this miserable habitation and wander from house to house in the village, begging for food and clothes. She obtained necessities from their charity and lived in the abbey ruin." A woman in an abbey made Marie nervous, but she stifled it—a coincidence only.

Hamish strolled between the tables, his voice raising as he warmed into telling his tale. "At midnight, each night, she lit her candle and returned to her vault. She assured her friendly neighbors that a spirit arranged her habitation during her absence. She described him as a little man, wearing heavy iron shoes, which he trampled on the clay floor of the vault to dispel the damps. He required her to stay during the day to pray for her lover's return." Marie understood praying for a lover's return. Her gaze shifted to John, whose eyes met hers across the large space.

He quickly turned, his kilt flared and his arm flung out. "Some village people regarded her with compassion from her far-fetched tale, thinking she possessed a deranged mind. But some of the cruder villagers feared her behavior, claimed she became possessed by the devil, and treated her poorly by denying her assistance. The reason she adopted this extraordinary manner of life she never explained."

He shrugged at the last bit, then continued his stroll, coming closer to Marie. "It was later believed she stayed underground all day because she gave a vow to her lover. During his absence, she vowed never to look upon the sun until his return since he promised his return would brighten her soul." Why was he walking toward her? What did this have to do with her? Her gaze shifted from Hamish to John as he leaned over to see her better.

Hamish stopped next to Marie. She had turned as he told the story and nearly faced the back of the bench. Now this wasn't a coincidence. He did this on purpose. Her breaths came faster as heat flashed over her body.

Hamish stood beside her as he spoke. "Sadly, her lover never returned, leaving her alone. She never would behold the light of day again. Many claim the spirit who kept her in her prison was no one other than the spirit of her lover's father, haunting her as he blamed her for his son's death." Everyone in the hall turned their gazes upon her. The weight of so many became hard to bear, but Marie straightened her back and returned the glares. She scanned the room, and her eyes landed on John, who looked ready to kill. Was it her or Hamish John was upset with?

Hamish's voice continued softer. "The Dryburgh Abbey vault, or rather dungeon, in which this unfortunate woman lived and died, goes by *Leannan Caillte, lover lost*. With which her gloom many claimed caused her disturbed imagination, and few villagers dared enter the area by night."

Hamish strolled back to the dais. "They say her ghost walks the ground at night, calling for her lover. *Leannan caillte, Leannan caillte, Leannan Caillte*." The last, he cupped his hands to his mouth and yelled out as if calling across the loch.

Hamish momentarily paused as he lowered his hands and gazed across the room. "She cries into the night. She searches for her lost love, and many a man who wanders too near at midnight never returns."

Hamish strolled the rest of the way to the dais and turned to face the crowd as he spoke. "A priest visited the village and told all who would listen...

" *'And on all hills that shall be dug for the place of God.*

No fear shall be cast upon anyone on his hallowed ground.

For there you shall bury all fear, hiding it from the doom of man.

This is our cross to bear.' "

Marie gasped, but her reaction became drowned out by the crowd's roar at the finishing of Hamish's tale. The quote was the same as the priest chanted over the crosses. Was this a sign?

Chatter from around her broke through the noise.

The woman beside her spoke loudly. "They say she died a lover's death, one lonely with a broken heart."

The man across from her slammed his hand on the

table. "Bah, the hag got what she deserved. The real story says she betrayed her lover, and the father's ghost caved in the vault, burying her alive."

Buried alive. Marie's breaths came short, and her vision dimmed. The clergyman approached her and patted her on the shoulder. "I understand ye've had a trial, my dear. Maybe ye should stop by for some counsel tomorrow?" But the words never reached Marie, or they didn't register. All she saw was the dirt piling in and the priest screaming from above.

Her fingers grazed the dirt as more dropped upon her face. She clawed the walls repeatedly as the soil packed under her nails, but she didn't care. Grime landed on her head, stuck in her hair. She leaned back and tried to find fresh air, but more dirt fell.

Marie shifted away but bumped into the woman beside her, who shoved her back. She jumped from the bench and moved away as someone grabbed her. When she turned, she stared into the clergyman's face.

She stretched toward the opening again, like a lost soul who reached for heaven, but a shout answered, "Women are the temptation placed on the earth to foul men. You shall pay the price of the priest's sin. Die, whore!"

She jerked away from him and stumbled into people on the bench behind her as she cried out.

The soil covered her chest, pressed in, and she struggled for air. She couldn't stop the dirt's fall, and the mound trapped her arms. She couldn't reach her face. Earth piled around and covered her. She drew in a breath but couldn't. Left suspended, her lungs desperately burned as she tried to breathe.

She lay on the floor, among the rushes, and curled

into a ball.

Strong arms grabbed her. She screamed and struggled until a familiar voice whispered in her ear.

The sea fairy swam fast away,
Safely over the wave and sea.
Gave her heart to her human love,
Will she ne'er come back to me.

The male timbre was familiar, and his scent, male musk mixed with the salt of the ocean familiar as well.

Will ye come back to me?
Will ye come back to me?
Better loved ye canna be,
Will ye come back to me?

John held her in his arms as she shook. He slightly rocked as they sat on the floor. John spoke softly the poem he recited when she experienced the nightmare. When he came to comfort her as he had now.

Marie tilted her head till she saw his eyes, and tears threatened to fall.

He brushed her hair away from her face. "Donna, worry Marie. I have ye."

Awareness came back, and the people in the great hall stood and stared.

Lady Anabelle approached, bent beside them, and her hand touched John's arm. "Let me take her to her room, John."

His arms tightened around her, his refusal she felt build.

Laird MacDougall stepped behind Anabelle. "John, allow the women to do their work. Let them care for the infirm woman."

John's arms loosened, and he picked her up as he stood. His arm around her waist held her steady.

Anabelle smiled as she transferred Marie to her side.

They made for the stairs as murmurs from the crowd filtered in. "Poor lass, gone with her mind she is."

Another few steps and another comment flitted to her. "The priest who took her abused her. She said *he* killed Dougie, not her."

She allowed Lady MacDougall to take her upstairs and into her room, numb to all around. All she wanted was to sleep and wake back home. *Home and John.*

Chapter 17

Marie sat in front of the fireplace in the great hall at Dunstaffnage, but it wasn't in the present as she had hoped. Their travel back through the portal had been delayed longer than she believed.

Now over two weeks had passed since the dinner incident. The funeral preparations and castle business kept John busy. Laird MacDougall acted like John became the secondary captain, often including him in all castle and clan business, which left little to no time for them to see each other.

But today, it was different. John's parents' funeral had finally arrived. John had sent a message to her. She held the note in her hand now. She read it often.

Marie,

It is my sincerest wish you join me in the funeral procession for my parents. Please stand by my side. For this day, I will need your strength and wisdom. It is my dearest hope with the conclusion of my parents' funeral we can finally return home. Home to the future.

Forever yours

John

No declaration of love, no mention of becoming his future bride, he only spoke of his need for her.

She sat and held the letter as she waited for John to arrive. So, they attended his parents' funeral, his second funeral for each. She folded the note and put it in her pouch. Was the thread left of their relationship enough? Was his need for her and love sufficient along with her desperate need and love for him?

"Marie, are ye ready?" John's voice startled her.

****

John stood as he stared at her in the main hall by the fireplace, much as he had that night in the future. The one where he sent Colin to the past when he understood so many things. His duty to the stones and how it affected all those he served—how the rocks might put Marie in danger. If he kept her from them would be the only way he kept her safe.

He understood differently now. The evil Fae would use anyone close to those who protected the stones as a weapon if they believed it would get them a Stone of Iona. He knew then he loved her, but life was much simpler.

Now everything seemed so complicated. The stones, the magic, his parents' death, Marie—if he kept her close, loved her, would she constantly be a target, in jeopardy from the Fae, the stones? Would he be able to keep her safe and get to her in time?

He loved her too much to place her in the path of danger, and he wasn't sure if he asked her to be with him was the best choice for her. But he loved her with all his heart and soul. He wanted her near, wanted to touch her, hold her, love her. But if the price became her death at the hand of his duty, he didn't know if he could live with the guilt. He gazed at her again, finding solace when she stayed with him today. He would sort out the rest later. Today, he buried his parents for the last time, his final goodbye, and he wanted his love beside him.

He stepped forward, close to her. She was more beautiful in period clothing than any woman he had seen before and would ever see again.

"Marie, are ye ready?"

She jolted and whipped around in the chair.

John strode to her and offered his hand. " 'Tis time. I am happy ye are joining me today."

She glanced at his hand, then back at his face. Streaks of tears stained her cheeks. Were they tears for his parents or him? He couldn't tell.

Laird MacDougall entered the hall with the rest of the funeral procession. "Aye, here we are. A solemn day for ye, John, it is."

John took Marie's hand and guided her to stand next to him.

As Laird MacDougall approached, his eyes went to their joined hands. "She will be joining us today, lad? She's not yer wife. 'Tis highly inappropriate."

John held Marie firm, even when she tried to remove her hand. "Aye, she's joining me, my laird."

Laird MacDougall glanced between them both. Lady MacDougall took his arm as she whispered in his ear. Laird MacDougall nodded and turned to the castle's main door.

The group gathered at the castle entrance and formed the funeral procession with the caskets lined up, ready to go. The village gathered outside to bid farewell to their favored boat captain and his loving wife.

Marie sniffled next to him as they started forward and followed the group. He squeezed her hand and turned to tell her it would be okay, but they emerged outside the castle to the crowd of mourners.

The first person to stop John and shake his hand

was his da's first mate from the ship. "Yer da was a right man. It was, John. Ye should be proud ye found him before he died."

John turned and used his free hand to shake, but Marie tried to tug hers free. He gripped her harder and refused to give in. The next man shook his hand, wished him well, and so on down the line of villagers as they followed behind the laird and lady of the castle. Each time John tried to turn to Marie, another villager hailed him and expressed sorrow for his parents' passing.

While no one found their passing strange, his da at the hands of an evil priest and his wife, in her sleep, both died at the exact moment. John found it odd. He recognized their deaths occurred as a Fae spell, but he liked to think of them happy together in heaven.

A woman approached and took John's hand in hers. "Yer ma, she was my best friend. Hers was a death of heartbreak for her. It was as if she understood her lover's spirit had left the earth, and her time had arrived to join him in heaven. It was true love. Ye must know that. I'll miss them. God go with ye."

As she turned away, she stared Marie down and flashed the sign of the crow to ward off evil. Marie stiffened beside him, but he placed his free hand on her arm. This became his first glance at her face since they left the castle. Her eyes filled with tears, and she looked tired and worn. He wanted nothing more than to take her in his arms and kiss her concerns away.

He leaned down and whispered, "Marie, I am glad ye are with me today. Ye bring me strength."

She glanced away from him but nodded.

The crowd filed into the chapel yard behind the

laird and lady for a brief graveside service. The laird insisted on something grander for his favorite boat captain, but John's parents would want something private yet reserved for close friends and family.

As the priest began a short sermon, John stood over his parents' coffins for the second time in his life. The surreal feeling wouldn't leave him. He glanced at Marie. Her head bowed as if in prayer. He squeezed her hand in his once, and she clasped back once—reassurance.

He gazed out over the loch, quiet and smooth as if the waters bowed in reverence to the sea captain who once sailed its waters. He remembered all his parents sacrificed to be together, for love. Was love enough? For him and Marie, would love be enough? A breeze lifted his hair, then flowed down his neck. A brush against his cheek and his mother's voice spoke as if she stood before him.

"John, my sweet son. Yes, dear, it is enough. It remained enough for me to see ye for those last moments and know I will carry them forever in my heart. Ye always questioned so much, son, instead of embracing life, living life. Yer true love, I can see her, ye know. She's a beauty. Don't lose her. I'll always be here for ye, in yer prayers."

John gasped and peeked at Marie, whose head remained bowed. He tried tilting his head to see her face, but the priest's call grabbed his attention.

"My son, please step forward and give yer last prayer for yer parents." Marie tried to drop his hand, but he drew her with him. He stood there bowed over his parents' coffins.

He couldn't say out loud what he wanted. The

people present didn't know of the Fae spell, the bargain his da made in exchange for his and his love's lives. *Ma, Da. I love ye. Thank ye for all my blessings in life. Da, thank ye for yer sacrifice. I'll make it matter.*

His da reply whispered in the wind. *John, I love ye so. This remained worth it, one last adventure, eh? Keep yer Marie safe. The duty is yers now. The stones and Marie, ye must keep them safe.*

Marie sniffled beside him. He pulled a handkerchief from his pocket and offered it to her. She glanced at him as tears ran down her cheeks.

He dried them for her and whispered, "Marie. I promise everything will be all right."

Chapter 18

Dunstaffnage, Present day

John looked over at the *Fae Fable Book*. Mere days ago, he saw it in the past, almost new. The book, older in the future, made the time between John leaving and arriving back seem even longer. The glass case was gone, and he touched and read from the book at leisure. He supposed Morrigan wanted it that way, so he stayed a willing participant. He skimmed the pages until he got to the Stone of Fear fable.

"Here it is. God, Da."

John read aloud so everyone in the room heard.

The father faced the devil, and his son's love strengthened him. The devil perceived the man's love for his son and turned his destruction upon his son's true love. The father's fears grew, and he called upon God's help. God asked, "Do ye believe in me?"

The father yelled, "Yes!" and the cross from his vision appeared in his hands. For his fear of losing his son became great, the father prayed harder than before. The Stone of Fear glowed purple, and the father cast his fear out through the stone. But the devil hadn't finished. He thrust the fear back toward the son's true love to kill her. The man covered his son and his love with faith and love. The man destroyed the devil, thus sending him back to hell, but he suffered a death wound.

As the man lay dying, he realized he had gained the love and respect of his son. The father became content to die in exchange for his son and the son's true love's life. He told his son as much and died peacefully, knowing he spent eternity with his true love, his wife. He felt blessed to have his true love and such a dutiful son.

The father thanked God, for our best blessings are often the least appreciated.

The room remained silent as John whispered, "God, Da, I hope this is worth it."

John stood over the book. He blinked, and the glass casing reappeared. John took a deep breath, then another. He turned and faced the room's occupants.

Colin leaned against his desk, arms and feet crossed in his all too familiar stance as he regarded his wife. His wife, Bree, sat in a chair before the desk and looked at John with tears. Marie, his true love, sat next to Bree. His gaze fell on Marie, and a tear rolled down her cheek, but she smiled.

John took a deep breath. "The last thing he said to me was he loved me. God, I miss him. 'Tis been hard to find them both and then lose them again."

John turned and stared out the window. Memories of his parents echoed. His mother looked happy and smiled with his da in the past. The extra time his da bargained for—was it worth it?

His gaze focused on the window's reflection and the room's occupants reflected in the glass. His eyes roamed over each one, and he observed their expressions clear as the day before him. Colin was composed as he watched his wife. Bree held Marie's hand and patted it as she whispered to her good friend. Marie. His gaze finally settled on her. Her eyes connected with his, and another tear trailed down her cheek.

Colin approached John and patted him on the back. "It was how he wanted it, John. I can understand the love a father has for his children. Aye, ye would do anything for them."

John nodded in silence. Bree handed Marie a tissue and hugged her. As she stood, she nodded at Colin toward the door.

Bree whispered to Marie, "If you need anything, just ask."

Colin cleared his throat. "Aye, well, Bree and I must check on the hellions."

Bree rolled her eyes. "Your children, and you love them."

She took Colin's arm, but he stopped at the door. "Ye both know we love ye and will be here if ye need anything."

When neither responded, she and Colin left the room and closed the door softly. The click announced he and Marie were alone.

****

Marie rolled the tissue in her hand as she stared at the reflection of John in the window. His expression did not indicate his inner emotions, only a stoic glare. They returned to the present a couple of days ago—the time from her rescue at the priory to Dunstaffnage and the trip through the portal, a blur. She knew the experience continued as turmoil for John.

He gathered his parents' bodies and worked with Laird MacDougall in the fifteenth century on arranging funerals and burials. John insisted they stay until the end of the memorial service. Marie never questioned his choice. John needed a last moment with his parents.

Laird MacDougall wouldn't permit them to remain in the same room because she and John hadn't wed. They spent little time together as John prepared for his parents' funeral. What time they spent together, he hadn't brought up the subject of his proposal or his desire to wed since the night he proposed, the night before the priest kidnapped her. That night seemed so long ago to her, and Marie wasn't sure if he had changed his mind. John's father saved her life by sacrificing himself. Did John hold resentment against her? If he did, she wasn't sure she could handle it.

Marie stood and took a deep breath. She stared at John's back, broad and firm, as he gazed out the window. Her gaze traveled over him as she took in each detail. The light shone on his warm brown hair. It was lighter than usual. His powerful legs stood braced apart. His stance looked firm as if he carried the world of Dunstaffnage on his shoulders. Her gaze traveled to his hands at his sides as they clenched and unclenched, the only movement about him. She wanted to say so much, thank him for his father's sacrifice. Express gratitude since he risked his life when he traveled in time to find her, save her, and bring her home safely. To tell him she loved him with all her heart. She remained ready to wed him and start a new life together—the two of them together to conquer the world. Yet as she stood there, everything paled in comparison. He had lost his parents, and he needed more time. Maybe time alone wouldn't be enough. Perhaps she had lost him and, with that, a bit of herself.

She sighed and turned toward the door, quietly opened it, then paused as she glanced at John. A tear rolled down her cheek, and she turned and left the man she loved with all her heart.

****

Much later in the night, Colin held Bree in his arms. The tang of a fresh, loved woman floated through the air, making Colin feel satiated.

Bree stirred in his arms and mumbled a little.

Colin whispered in her ear, "*Mo chridhe*, what is it?"

Bree shifted and sighed. "Nothing, dear. Go to sleep."

Colin smiled into the darkness. He knew his wee Bree better than that.

He flipped her over, so he stared into her eyes, glossy orbs in the darkness. "If ye don't tell me, I will torture it out of ye." He kissed her, but she didn't return the kiss.

Colin pulled back and brushed a curl away from her face. "Bree, what is troubling ye?" She sighed, and a tear rolled down her cheek. Colin brushed it away with his thumb and kissed the wet spot.

Bree took a breath, and it hitched. "I don't know what is wrong. Only something has bothered me since John and Marie's return."

Colin rolled to his back and pulled Bree to his side so her head lay on his chest. "Try to tell me. Ye'd be surprised what I can understand these days."

She blew out a laugh, but it came as more of a huff. "A feeling of doom. I sense evil has returned, or doom is upon us."

Colin hugged her tightly. "Now, Bree, nothing has

happened, and their return signals the return of a stone. The Fae should be happy."

Bree sighed, "I know, and yes, finding the Stone of Fear is good. But I can't shake the feeling we head toward disaster."

Colin kissed her forehead. " 'Tis likely the fact they haven't returned that damn stone yet. Anytime I get near it, my greatest fears surface. John says the same. Once we return it to the chapel, all will be well."

Bree nodded. "I know. Marie wanted to study and record the cross, since we aren't sure if the cross will disappear with the Stone of Fear." She shivered, and he hugged her closer as she whispered, "It still bothers me."

Colin yawned and mumbled as his wife carried on with her commentary.

She often rambled about her work, and Colin loved her for it, but tonight he felt tired.

"The cross and the remaining stone are a mystery. One Marie believes she needs to solve. I told her I feared there was more to it than that." She lay silent momentarily, and Colin hoped she drifted off to sleep.

Bree jolted in the bed.

Colin sat up and pulled her into his embrace.

She patted his arm. "It's okay, Colin. Go back to sleep."

He grumbled and kissed her as he lay down.

Bree whispered in his ear, "Colin?"

He mumbled a half-asleep reply. "Um, mm."

"Colin, I want you to keep the broach, the Brooch of Lorne. I want you to keep it with you wherever you go."

Colin's eyes snapped open; he remained wide

awake now. The Brooch of Lorne remained a MacDougall trinket lost after the Battle of Dalrigh in thirteen hundred and six. John of Argyll, chief of the Clan MacDougall, ambushed Robert the Bruce of Scotland, where he ripped Bruce's cloak off and kept the brooch for the family. Colin recalled the story well, and the family believed they had lost the pin until Marie dug it up a few weeks ago. Designed to carry two magic stones, one atop another, they claimed the pin held powers. The base stone setting was shaped like a heart, and the top showed an oval.

Colin's heart dropped. "Why would I be needing the brooch, Bree?"

She sighed, "A feeling I have. You must keep it nearby. Promise me."

Colin's brow frowned. "Aye, if keeping one of yer old things will make ye happy. Aye, I promise." He tried to make light of her worry, but her request sent chills though him.

Bree sighed and curled up in his arms. But the sense of doom didn't leave Colin.

Chapter 19

John arrived at Granny's door, unable to recall the trip from the castle to her cottage in Dunbeg, the village near Dunstaffnage castle. He shook his head and raised his hand to knock. Granny opened the door. She gave him chills when she did that.

She waved him in. "About time ye made it over here. Leaving yer wee granny to guess at all the fun ye and Marie have had."

John strode into the cottage as Granny led him to the kitchen. They always sat at the kitchen table and visited over tea. When he arrived in the kitchen, she already had set everything up. He used to be shocked when she did this, but he came to expect this from Granny these days.

He stood in the doorway and studied her for a moment. He wondered at her age. She had to be in her nineties, at least. Granny always realized when he needed to speak of the Fae. Had Morrigan, his family Fae, been in contact with Granny?

She rapped her knuckles on the table loud enough to grab his attention. "Stop yer wool-gathering and come tell me what yer adventure was."

He shrugged and crossed the kitchen.

As he sat, she poured some fresh tea. "No, I haven't seen Morrigan, and yes, I might be a little crazy." She smiled and patted his knee. "Aren't we all a little crazy, dearie?"

John smiled at her and sipped his tea.

She picked up her drink and eyed him over the rim. "Now start from the beginning and don't leave any details out. I love a good story."

John told her everything from when Marie went missing to today when he woke. How he found his parents in the past, how his father captained a ship, something he didn't know his da did.

His granny laughed and patted his knee. "Ah, John, yer father was always an expert sailor. It runs in yer blood, ye know."

John ran everything back through his mind—Marie's kidnapping, the priest who chased after a Fae stone of Iona, the trip back in time, and his parents found in the past. *Marie*—he never imagined his duty to the Fae stones would take such a turn, such a toll on his life, but it had. The events took a more significant toll on Marie, and he worried if their love would survive his duty to the stones. It all came down to him. He must ensure he cared for everyone at Dunstaffnage and kept them safe.

He shook his head. "Granny, I am just not sure what all this means."

She made a guttural noise in the back of her throat. "Ah, my boy, this isn't supposed to make sense. The Fae never make sense. If they do, ye run like mad away, for they are about to trick ye." She sighed. "What was he like when ye visited him?"

John smiled. He pictured his da as he had seen him in the past. The wind blew his hair as he walked down the ship's plank. He looked years younger than John ever remembered. His da had to be at least twelve years older from when he disappeared to when John found him in the past.

Granny cleared her throat loudly and raised her eyebrow at him.

John shook himself. "Granny, he was so joyful. At times, he looked like I remembered him before Ma died. So happy and full of life, if that makes sense. His body looked older but appeared years younger."

Granny smiled. "Aye, dearie. That makes perfect sense. I'm glad ye got to see him, spend time with him, with yer ma too. This was meant to be."

John sighed. Meant to be. There the phrase came again, that quote. His da used it when he confronted the priest like he knew all along what the future held.

He glanced at Granny, who sat and smiled when his gaze met hers. "That's what I am having trouble with. His resignation to his fate, his death. And how he did it for me."

Granny studied him for a moment.

He took a sip of tea. It got stuck in his mouth. He swallowed it hard, and a rock went down his throat instead.

Granny gazed out the window and spoke softly. "Ye should not feel guilt. This was his choice, his life to give. He made the bargain with the Fae." She turned and eyed him. "He tricked them good, for he gave ye life twice now."

She rapped the table, her voice harder. "Yer da gave yer true love life."

She rapped it again. "He made sure ye both would have a long life together."

She laughed loudly. "And all that damn Fae Morrigan got was a rock."

John sighed. "A Stone of Iona Granny, a powerful magic Fae stone."

Granny stared into his eyes for a moment. He sensed she searched through his mind, viewed all his thoughts, peered into his soul, and knew all the secrets he kept.

She nodded once and pointed her finger at him. "Aye, a powerful stone. One ye need to put back. Today. No more bargains with the Fae. Lucky once is enough. The next time won't be so fortunate."

John nodded but didn't seem convinced.

Granny turned toward him and took his hand in hers. "John, ye have the fortune of love. Love from yer family. Love from yer friends. But more important, yer true love loves ye deeply. Don't turn yer back on her, on yer love. True love is a gift, one that ye should cherish."

John stared at the weathered old hands that cradled his young ones. A picture flashed in his mind. His old and battered hand as he held his granddaughter's soft young hand. They sipped tea in a cottage kitchen. He blinked, and the vision vanished.

His granny patted him. "Go to Marie, tell her of the love in yer heart. I promise it will all make sense when ye do."

John nodded and rose to clear away the dishes, but Granny waved him off. "Ah, just put yer cup in the sink."

She swayed her hips as she stood and giggled. "I've got a gentleman caller coming. Got to make some more tea."

As he turned to leave, Granny hugged him. They stood there a moment, and John sensed peace. As he backed away, she winked and batted his sleeve.

****

When John returned to the castle, he sought out Colin and found him in the study. Fortunately, Colin sat alone. The kids and Bree must be out; the castle remained as quiet as a tomb. John strode in and slumped in the chair before Colin's desk. Colin glanced up from some documents he studied and set them aside.

Colin sat and looked at John for a moment. The silence seemed welcome as John had much on his mind. Colin rose, stepped to the table behind the desk, and poured two whisky glasses.

He crossed to John and handed him one. "I can tell from the look on yer face ye need this." Colin sat in the chair next to John, took a sip of whisky, and sat silently.

John sipped his whisky, held the liquor in his mouth for a minute, and savored the flavor as he swallowed. He opened his mouth to allow air in and smacked his mouth shut. As he rolled his tongue around, he relished the aftertaste.

"Ye know, the whisky in the fifteenth century doesn't taste the same."

Colin laughed. "I know it doesn't. Same for the eighteenth."

John gazed at his glass. "Same distillery, same process. Peat smoked over barley, fresh water from an icy stream, a century-old process repeated today. And it tastes different."

Colin glanced at his whisky, then at John. "Aye, John, I imagine many things look different to ye now. They did for me, too."

John sat and reflected for a moment. Different. The castle looked the same, but every job he performed since returning seemed monumental. The weight of responsibility to those around him more crucial, their faith in him more profound. Marie, their relationship, secure the day the priest took her, now left in disarray. Did she still want him as her husband? Did she still want a life with him if it meant she might be in danger from the evil Fae, her life possibly at risk again for his duty? Different—everything felt different.

John sighed. "I'm uncertain anymore."

Colin set his glass down and sat back in his chair. "How so?"

John shrugged. "I don't know. Maybe that's just it. I don't know about a lot of things."

Colin nodded. "I can understand. After I returned from the eighteenth century, it took me time to sort out all my thoughts. But I can tell ye, the one thing which kept me going was Bree." He sighed. "Just her. Knowing she stayed there. It became enough until I got the rest figured out."

John sat there and held his glass as he contemplated what Colin shared. Marie, he had Marie. Everyone kept telling him, ye have Marie, and she would be enough. Was Marie enough?

An image popped into his head. He and Marie at Ardchattan Priory as they walked the grounds. But it wasn't a memory. They were older, and their smiles were broad. Children laughed. He glanced up, and they ran ahead of him—a young boy, his spitting image, and an even younger girl with Marie's blonde hair.

Marie called out, "Kids, don't go near the loch."

The girl called back, "Okay, Ma."

He turned to Marie, and she smiled at him. The corners of her eyes creased with her smile, and her cheeks filled in more. She appeared older but held the same warm smile he grew to love. It hit him and made his breath come out in a whoosh. He loved her, and he always would.

A boy shouted, "Come on, Da. Ye promised us a picnic. One in the garden ye and Ma love." The warmest feeling washed over him, of immense pride and joy. The sensation made him think of his da and sense him near him.

He blinked, and the vision faded.

Colin stared at him intently and nodded. "Ye need to talk to Marie, John."

John blinked again, and the vision still echoed in his mind.

Colin patted his knee. "Ye need to talk to yer true love. Things will be clear. I promise, my friend."

John nodded. Colin remained right. He needed to talk to Marie, express his love, and discover her thoughts with all the changes.

Colin peered at his desk and back at John. "Ye know, my offer to live at Ardchattan Priory for ye and Marie still stands. It would mean a lot to her, especially after I read her renovation proposal. She made a damn good case."

John stared into his glass. He and Colin spoke about the priory arrangement shortly after his return to the future. The project remained Colin's idea at Bree's suggestion, her very strong suggestion. They worked on the planning, but John still needed time. He hadn't spoken to Marie about the priory project, about them. Would she still have him after all that had happened? Would she still want to be his wife?

He shook himself and needed to focus. "Aye, we

will meet in the chapel today to return the Stone of Fear. She wanted to do that together, and I admit it seems fitting."

Colin nodded, his voice firm. "Aye, that damn stone needs to return to the Fae." Colin picked up his glass and drained the rest of his whisky.

John drained his and set his glass on the desk as he rose to leave.

When he reached the door, Colin said, "If ye see that damned sprite of yers, tell her we've had enough adventure for a lifetime."

John huffed a laugh. Colin didn't like his Fae, Brigid, who teased him at every given opportunity. John's Fae Morrigan wasn't so spiteful.

He smirked. "If I see either, I'll tell them ye *miss them* something *terrible*."

He quickly stepped out the door and closed it. After the door clicked closed, glass crashed against it.

Colin yelled from the other side, "Ye tell that wee gnome to go to hell."

John laughed out loud. Things were better already.

Chapter 20

John entered the chapel and stood at the back. Marie sat in the front pew and stared at the altar. She hadn't noticed he entered, and he took a moment as he studied her. She was beautiful in the setting sun's light. The separate rays touched her like angels blessed her with golden glimmers.

They agreed to replace the stone at dusk as Emily MacDougall, Colin's mom, suspected some magic occurred when the shadow of the top window aligned with the mosaic cross on the floor. Colin and Bree swore the cross windows became part of the power which returned Colin from purgatory. But really the power came from Bree's love for Colin. True love remained the greatest power of all. Wasn't it enough for him? Was it sufficient for them?

How would he bridge the gap between them since they returned? How did one show love, admiration, and respect for the woman he wanted to spend forever with, his one true love? He searched his mind and heart, and he had the answer all along.

****

Marie sat in the Chapel in the Woods, this being the first time she came to the chapel since her and John's return to the twenty-first century. She recalled Bree used to fear the doorway, and with good reason. It was a portal in time. Marie never feared the entrance or the chapel. But today, she feared many things.

Would John still want her as his wife? Did he still love her as he declared before her kidnapping and their trip back in time?

The fifteenth-century events ran through her mind. Could John put aside her kidnapping and the priest's quest to find a powerful Fae stone that cost his parents' lives? If she begged him to forgive her, would he?

Marie held the cross in her hands. She didn't carry the relic much since she returned to the future. A mere touch and her fears rushed to the front of her mind and screamed all at once. She needed to focus on something else to quiet them. Today the feeling happened easily— her love for John. Her love for John always worked.

Marie turned the cross over in her hands. She took photographs of it for historical purposes since she feared the cross would disappear when they returned the stone to the Fae. She rotated it again and she stared at the Stone of Fear.

The last time she examined the stone this close, a vision was of a priest who yelled at her like in her dreams. Today, only the flicker of light through the deep purple stone glittered back at her.

An awareness overcame her, a sensation at the nape of her neck that spread through her shoulders and warmed her heart. A flutter of air caressed her hand, like a hand on hers in the last sunlight. A shuffle and a step up the aisle—those were his boot treads. The bench rocked as his weight settled beside her.

She recognized who it was without looking, realized when John entered the chapel. She always felt an awareness when he came close. He stood in the back for some time. She sensed him, detected his troubled thoughts, and feared what his judgements were—feared what his heart led him to decide.

She couldn't look at him, so she handed him the cross and rose to leave. As she strode away, she sensed the power from the Stone of Fear leave her and her fears faded.

Marie took a few steps down the aisle, and the bench creaked. "Marie."

She stopped but didn't turn around. Her eyes watered, and her throat closed. She couldn't face John, not now. If she did, she might fall apart.

"Marie, I've had time to think over things. Events in the past, our situation in the present—and about the future."

He took a deep breath. "Our future."

Marie's breath caught. A tear slipped out and fell down her cheek. She still didn't turn, understood what would come, his rejection. She couldn't face him if he told her he no longer loved her.

The clunk of the cross on the pew and the shuffle of a step let her know John moved. Heat on her back told her he stood close behind her. She wanted John to wrap her in his arms and hold, kiss, and love her.

He inhaled and released his breath. "Marie, I've thought about what happened in the past. What my father did."

Marie's head dropped, and she stifled a sob. *God, here it comes.*

"Marie, I don't want his sacrifice to stand between us." Was this a trick? Had she heard him right? She glanced up at the window as the sunbeam shone on her face.

John sucked in his breath.

The sun cast her in a circle of warm sunlight that lit her, warmed her. Marie's fears faded, and her heart melted.

"Marie, please don't feel guilty. My da made his choice, but I think he chose based on what he realized about me." She took a deep breath and stared at her hands as she sniffled.

He took a sudden breath.

Was that a gasp? This whole conversation tore at her heart.

"Marie, he realized how I felt about ye. How ye being missing tore me apart. He witnessed how much I loved ye. And he understood losing ye would be the death of me."

She stiffened her shoulders.

John's hands rested on them as he smoothed both his hands over her.

She took a cleansing breath. Could John mean what he said? Did he love her still?

He whispered in her ear, "He recognized ye were my true love. He sacrificed himself not just for me but for us, our future."

She whirled around. "Ye aren't leaving me?"

John smiled as he wiped the tears from her face. He shook his head and took her face in his hands. The sun shone on them a cast them in the glow of a halo.

John whispered as he held her.

The sea fairy swam fast away,
Safely over the wave and sea.
Gave her heart to her human love,
Will she ne'er come back to me.
Will ye come back to me?
Will ye come back to me?

Better loved ye canna be,
Will ye come back to me?

Marie smiled. "John, yer poem."

John caressed her cheek. "Aye, I finished it." He took a breath and gazed into her eyes as he recited the rest of his poem.

Ye trusted yer heart to yer lover,
I trusted ye, dear sweet Fae.
I kent yer hidin' in the glen,
Your crying echoed my way.
Asked her to be my bride,
An even tho purer we may be.
Silver canna buy my heart,
That beats hard for her beauty.
Sweet the love stone's note held long,
Lilting wildly up the glen.
But aye to me I regret she has gone,
Will she not come back again?

She gazed into his eyes and saw her love reflected.

He bent and kissed her deeply.

She wrapped her arms around the man she loved and returned his kiss with all her heart.

John lifted his head and gazed into her eyes. His hand cupped her cheek, and he whispered, "Marie, I love ye. Please be my wife?"

Marie smiled as a new tear trailed down her cheek. She laughed in a sob, and John wiped her tears.

Marie sighed and she whispered back, "Aye, I'd love that." They kissed again as the sound of tinkling laughter filled the chapel.

John jerked Marie behind him as he glanced around the chapel. His gaze landed on the altar.

Marie peeked from behind him, and a short, slight

woman sat on the altar dressed in all white with shining jet-black hair. When she turned her head the point of an ear peeked out, and translucent wings fluttered from her back in the light. To Marie, she resembled one of the Fae in Scottish fables. *Wait, she is a Fae in the flesh!*

Marie gasped. "Holy shit."

John glanced at her. "Ye can see her?"

Marie nodded. "The sprite sitting on the altar twirling the cross from its chain. Aye, I do."

The Fae smirked with a knowing glare as she held the cross, the one with the Stone of Fear.

She laughed. "Hello, John, introduce me to yer true love."

John shook his head. "I'd rather not if ye don't mind. I like her here in my arms. There's no telling what ye and yer sister may do."

The Fae shrugged. "That's okay. My sis isn't with me today."

The wee woman glanced past John and stared directly at her. "Hello, Marie. I'm glad we finally met. I'm Morrigan, the MacArthur Fae. We'll become fast friends; we will."

When their eyes locked, Marie's heart skipped. Was this an evil Fae? An awareness came upon her. She was no evil Fae, far from it. Marie sensed her goodness and kindness, all light. For the first time since she returned from the past, Marie became…hopeful.

Morrigan's gaze returned to John and took on a devilish grin as she held up the cross. "Ye really shouldn't leave this thing lying around. An evil Fae might pick it up."

John waved his hand. "Ye have the stone. Now be off with ye. Ye've finished yer business."

Morrigan flew up near the ceiling and floated there for a moment. "Actually, my business isn't done." Her gaze shifted back to Marie. John moved between them and blocked Marie's view. Morrigan flew above the altar, and her eyes connected with Marie's. What did this Fae mean? Her business isn't done. She had the stone.

John turned, took her in his arms, and held her tight. "Don't fall for her tricks Marie. I don't want anything happening to ye."

Morrigan giggled in her tinkling laugh. "John, she has nothing to fear now. I'm also here to thank her. It's Marie the Fae owe a thank ye to."

John held Marie tighter. "How so?"

Morrigan's gaze went to John, then back to Marie.

Marie stood stunned. The Fae desired to thank her. But wait, because of her John's parents died. The priest kidnapped her. She was the one who caused all the issues.

Morrigan stared at Marie, and calmness covered her.

Morrigan shook her head. "Marie, ye are wrong, dear."

Wait, did she read my mind? Holy hell!

The Fae's focus shifted to John. "If it weren't for Marie, we would never know where the evil Fae placed the Stone of Fear. There wasn't another stone tracking it like the Stone of Love, and since Colin lost it while in purgatory, we had no idea where the Stone of Fear went."

John's grip loosened, but he still held her.

Marie blinked at Morrigan. She found the stone for the Fae.

Morrigan twirled the cross. "Ye see, the evil Fae placed their version of the Kells book, bad as it was, in the priest's path along with the Stone of Fear, hoping they would find another Iona stone." She sighed. "And it almost worked."

Marie tilted her head, "But I don't understand. Why thank me? It was John's da who recognized the stone. He found it."

Morrigan nodded. "Aye, and he understood he would find the Stone of Fear one day, just not exactly when."

As Morrigan smiled at Marie, she became warm.

Morrigan grabbed the cross and pointed the end at Marie. "But it was ye who made the magic in the stone work. It was yer emotions for John, fear for his life, desire for yer life together, and love that powered the stone. While Douglas sacrificed himself, it was ye who used the stone's power to injure the priest, all while ye kept possession of the stone."

Marie gaped at Morrigan. "Ye mean I did it? I recovered the stone for the Fae?"

John shifted beside her and squeezed her once.

She turned, and he beamed at her. "It was ye, Marie, all along. Ye're the one, my one true love."

She hiccupped and hugged him. "Oh, John, I love ye."

Morrigan fluttered as the tinkling laughter filled the chapel.

Marie glanced at the altar where the Fae settled again. "Now, one last task, and *then* my business is finished."

She twirled the cross from its chain, and it spun fast. As the cross rotated quicker, a purple light shone from the circle. The violet light grew and spread through the interior of the chapel. A bright burst of light shot through the chapel in a crash of musical tinkling glass. The light blinded Marie. As her hand reached for her face, John's hands shifted and covered both their faces.

When the light faded, and all was quiet, they both glanced around the chapel. Marie turned to the stained-glass window looking for the Stone of Fear, and the purple stone sat in the box at the bottom. When she stepped toward it, the box disappeared along with the deep purple stone.

John and Marie stood alone in the chapel in the setting sun's light.

John heaved a deep sigh. "Well, thank God the stone's returned."

Marie shook her head. "I don't think so, John." Marie held up both her hands. In one, she held the gold cross, empty of all stones.

John took the cross and rotated it as he checked each side.

Marie held out her other hand and fisted tight.

John glared at Marie as his brow drew down.

Marie smiled back. "Just before the stone burst, Morrigan whispered in my ear."

John's eyebrows shot to his hairline. "Dear God, please tell me it is good news. I don't think we can survive another bargain with the Fae."

Marie giggled. "She said yer father's spirit made one last bargain."

John gasped. "Lord, what bargain has he made now?"

Marie patted his face. "Morrigan said this is his

wedding gift to us." She opened her palm, and the last bright red ruby stone from the cross twinkled in the dusk light.

"Morrigan said her father, Dagda, king of the Good Fae, blessed the stone. They named it the Stone of Eternal Love to represent our love for each other. Morrigan said this is for my wedding ring."

John peered at the stone and then at Marie. "Are ye sure ye'll want a stone from the Fae as yer wedding ring?"

She smiled. "Ye said I got to pick out my stone. This one is from yer da, so this is the one I want."

John closed her hand around the stone and squeezed it once.

His gaze met hers as he smirked. "What did the new rock say when it met its new owner?"

Marie shrugged.

John smiled. "Let's start with a clean slate."

Chapter 21

A few months later

"I'm so excited someone gets to use Rose's wedding dress from the past. It still looks brand new." Bree grinned as she stared at Marie.

Marie fingered the embroidery on the bodice as she admired the floral detail. She would have the wedding of her dreams. This year, a historical wedding in the fully renovated Chapel in the Woods kicked off the reenactment event. They planned the event for months. Bree enlisted the Historical Society of Scotland as they replicated the thirteenth century.

Marie and Bree stood in Marie's room. The handlers from the Historical Society flitted around the dress for the last fitting and used white gloves, keeping it in pristine condition. Her friend Bree hugged her from the side. Her excitement made Marie's heart light.

Marie hugged her friend back. "Aye, thank ye for letting me use it. This is the wedding I have dreamed of my entire life, a fifteenth-century wedding." Marie gazed at her dearest friend and smiled.

Bree patted her arm. "You deserve to have the wedding of your dreams. It almost feels like we are celebrating your wedding and John's parents. It was such a great idea that you and John chose not only the reenactment event but the same date when John's parents wed." Bree giggled. "It's so romantic. I hope it will be the highlight of the historical event."

Marie laughed. "Aye, ye also hope it will be the highlight of yer museum exhibit."

Bree smiled. "Well, yes, and a perfect replication of a historical highland wedding. And let's remember the Historical Society of Scotland is footing part of the bill. The photographers will capture every moment. Not just for you, but for the exhibit as well."

Marie smiled. "Aye, well, I suspect Colin would've gladly paid for everything if they hadn't."

Bree smiled. "Aye, he would've for our best friends."

The twins burst into the room and toddled around the bed with a harried Ainslie, who followed closely behind. "Sorry, Bree, they got away from me again."

Bree bent and swept Evie into her arms before fingers sticky with lord knows what touched the delicate fabric of the wedding dress.

Ainslie grabbed Ewan and tickled him till he squealed.

The handlers quickly picked up the dress and shifted away with it.

Marie sat in her chair before the fire, gazing at her best friends, now her family. Things couldn't be better. Since she and John returned the Stone of Fear to the Fae's hiding place, a sense of peace descended over Dunstaffnage Castle. Life moved on, and no Fae activities disrupted the natural flow of life. The last historical dig on the castle grounds had wrapped up, and Bree's museum tour started soon with the artifacts cataloged and ready for the Scottish Historical Society.

Marie and John's love blossomed, and their

wedding remained a mere two days away. John asked her to meet him in the chapel today at dusk. He worked on a project these last months that he and Colin remained very secretive about.

She looked at her friends and smiled. "I must change and head to the chapel now. It's time to meet John."

Ainslie and Bree exchanged a look as they giggled. They had done that a lot recently, and Marie figured they were in on the secret John kept from Marie.

****

John sat in the Chapel in the Woods, waiting for Marie to arrive. He and Colin had worked on this plan since he returned the Stone of Fear to the Fae, and he hoped he had guessed Marie's desires correctly. Of course, he had. Bree harassed him to no end to get his gift ready in time for the wedding. He wanted to surprise Marie and hoped she would become ecstatic about his plan.

A light footfall sounded behind him, and he took a deep breath. He patted his jacket pocket and made sure his present remained there. He rose and turned to greet the love of his life, excited to share his plan for their future.

Marie stood near the door as she smiled. "It's dusk, just as ye asked." She waved her arms to her sides. "Here I am."

John smiled. She seemed radiant, and happy. He would never tire of her smile. He recalled the first time they were in the chapel when she arrived for the restoration project. It was the first time they had seen each other in person. He wanted so badly to meet her, and when he did, he couldn't resist the urge to kiss her, so he had.

"Do ye remember the day we first came here?"

Marie glanced down in a blush. "Aye, that was the first day ye kissed me."

John returned her smile.

Marie took a step toward him.

He took a step toward her. "Aye, did I sweep ye off yer feet as I intended?"

They continued to step slowly toward each other and met in the center of the chapel.

Marie blushed, "Aye, ye did at that."

John took her hands in his, bent and kissed her lightly on the lips. God, she was so pretty, and she was his, his wife, forever.

"I have a wedding gift to give ye."

Marie looked at their hands, then back at John. "John, it's too early for gifts. The wedding is still two days away."

John cupped her face with his hand. "It's never too early for gifts, and I wanted to give ye my wedding gift in private."

Marie blushed. "John, it's not right to do *that* in a church."

John barked a laugh. "That's not what I mean, ye sexy woman. But I will take ye up on the offer later tonight."

John pulled the box from his coat pocket. He took a moment and stared at the long slender box.

Marie's gaze traveled from the box to her left hand, where the red ruby sat in an intricate setting which matched the scrolls on the cross.

John smiled. He confused her and planned it that way on purpose. What sat in the box wasn't a bracelet.

It was so much more. He understood his gift would mean the world to her.

He held the box before him as he gazed into her face. "Marie, do ye remember what ye said to me that day we first had lunch at the priory?"

Marie tilted her head and shook it.

He smiled as he recalled that day. He almost wanted to tease her to drag out his surprise but figured that would torture him as much as it would her. Now was the time.

John took each of her hands, placed the box in both, and released it. "My gift to ye for our wedding." He kissed her cheek. "My gift to ye for our future." He kissed her other cheek. "And my gift to ye for our family." He kissed her lips, and Marie's eyebrows lifted. She blinked, then blushed.

John smiled. "Open it, Marie." Marie pulled the ribbon, and it fell in her hand. She opened the box and peered inside. Set upon purple velvet sat an old skeleton key.

She took the key out, held it between them, and raised an eyebrow. "An old key, John? The castle's locks were changed years ago with the modernization." She glanced at the key and then back at John. "What's this one to?"

He gazed at her lovingly. "Do ye remember telling me how it was yer greatest dream to remodel an entire church or abbey?"

Marie gasped, peered at the key and back at John. "Well, yer wish is mine to grant."

Marie's mouth opened, then she shut it with a click of her teeth.

John beamed at her. "Colin has permitted ye to

remodel Ardchattan Priory."

Marie gasped. "John, really? The proposal? He will do it?"

John nodded. "Aye, here's the best part." He paused for a moment, unable to resist teasing her. He enlisted Bree's help for this one as it became near impossible that they kept it from Marie. The entire Historical Society remained abuzz with the project and excited for Marie.

"Bree contacted the Historical Society of Scotland. Ye will lead the restoration, yers to manage, oversee, and remain as caretaker for the future. We will live there permanently while I remain Captain of the Castle for Dunstaffnage."

Marie squealed, jumped into John's arms, and hugged him. He picked her up and spun her in a circle. His heart became whole, his surprise and gift for Marie an evident success.

When he set her down, her head bowed, and she sniffled. "*Mo ghràdh*, what is it? What is wrong?"

Marie handed the key and the box back to John and stepped back. "John, I can't live there. I can't, knowing who's buried there and how it happened."

John set the box on the pew and took the key, placed it in Marie's hand, then closed his hands around them and held them momentarily. "Marie, I know about how Father Clarke died. I also know that was yer nightmare. Being the nun buried alive in the priory."

He gazed into her eyes. "That is what Colin and I've been busy fixing."

Marie gasped.

"We arranged to have his grave relocated. I would never ask ye to live someplace that bastard rested. He's gone. The clergy arrived and blessed the ground. The priory is all ready for ye, for us."

A tear escaped Marie's eye. John wiped it away and gathered her in his arms. He kissed her deeply as he let all his love flow through the kiss.

When he raised his head, Marie smiled. "My geologist friend had some great news for us, which he just couldn't wait to *talus!*"

"Talus." John barked a laugh at her pun. Talus was a jumble of loose rocks. She impressed him since she likely looked up talus to make a joke. "*Tell us*. Okay, ye have some news for me?"

Marie glanced down and blushed. "I have my wedding present for ye today as well."

John's eyebrows rose. "Well, what's my present?"

Swinging from side to side, she peeked at him with a smile. "What do baby rocks wear?"

At a loss as John racked his brain for what she hinted. *Baby rocks? Did she mean pebbles, crags, or marbles? Wait, I've got it!*

He tilted his head and replied. "Diapirs." *Diapirs were piercement structures resulting from the penetration of overlaying material. Diapirs can form anticlines, salt domes, and other structures by pushing upward and piercing overlying rock layers. Wait. What does this have to do with them and how is a rock a present?*

He stared back at Marie; she stood with a smile. They were to marry, start a family, diapirs…*diapers*. His breath whooshed out, and he became a little dizzy. She meant diapers, as in for a baby.

John grabbed her shoulders. "Marie, are ye saying…I mean, does this mean…"

Marie took his hand and placed it over her stomach and nodded.

John picked her up spun her again and laughed as he set her down. He gazed into her eyes; their happiness spread through the chapel.

When the setting sun shone through the chapel window, and a beam of light glowed around the couple, he kissed her with all his heart. As they kissed, John remembered the Stone of Fear Fae Fable ending.

The father thanked God, for our best blessings are often the least appreciated.

He sent a prayer to his parents. *Thank ye for my best blessing, the greatest gift ye gave me, my true love, and my family.*

Chapter 22

Dunstaffnage Reenactment Event - present

Today, the day before their wedding, and Marie stood on top of the wall walk, as the reenactment events unfolded on the grounds below. She giggled as John carried a large "creel" or basket filled with stones from one end of a castle yard to the other. Groups of villagers and guests for the reenactment event cheered him on. Colin and a group of men teased him as they piled more rocks into his basket.

He stumbled, and Marie gasped. If he dropped the basket, he would have to start over again. He duplicated an old Highland custom where the groom carried rocks. The rules required him to continue with this arduous task until his bride walked out of her house and kissed him. When she did, his friends allowed him to escape from the "creeling". If not, he would continue until he completed the circuit of the town, in today's case, the castle yard. This remained his third time already.

Bree stood beside her and sighed. "You really should put him out of his misery."

Ainslie, Colin's sister, stood on her other side and huffed a laugh. "And miss all this fun? If she ends it too soon, the reenactment will be over."

Marie gasped as John stumbled again and almost fell to his knees.

The men in the crowd cheered loud enough to echo across Loch Etive.

Marie turned and started down the wall walk. "Okay, fun's over. I need to stop this, or there will be no husband for the wedding."

Bree and Ainslie's laughter followed her as Marie smiled.

****

The following day, Marie stood at the castle doors, ready for her parade through the yard to the chapel. Finally, the day of her wedding had arrived. Her highland historical wedding occurred for the reenactment event, and the Scottish Historical Society remained on hand with a team of photographers who captured the events for Bree's upcoming museum tour.

She wiped her hands on the towel again to keep the historical dress clean. After the wedding, it would become part of the museum's display. She fingered the embroidery. The dress seemed perfect.

They took the past year to plan this event and waited for the right date, the same as his parents' wedding. Her love for John grew daily, and only yesterday, she shared news of her pregnancy with John. Ecstatic about becoming a father and husband, he raided Colin's cigar case and the men sat up as they smoked and drank whisky.

When she first arrived at Dunstaffnage, she wasn't sure if this remained where her life would take her. During her abduction, she wasn't sure she would make it back, back to John. His steadfast pursuit and devotion, her rescue, and the recovery of an Iona Stone, the Stone of Fear all led to this moment; everything seemed perfect.

The lead piper glanced over his shoulder and nodded at her the signal that they begin. Her bride's parade followed. In the past, people would line the streets to the church to cheer on the happy couple before they took their vows. Today she paraded through the castle yard led by bagpipers in the highland tradition to meet John on the steps of the Chapel in the Woods.

The pipers lifted their instruments and began to fill their bags with air. Marie took a deep breath—this was it. The two pipers started the bass tone, deep and low. The melody began with a traditional wedding march that had Marie near skipping as they led her out the castle doors and into the yard as she made her way to the chapel. Her heart swelled; this embodied the wedding of her dreams. As she walked through the crowd, she recognized many people from the village. The lads from the wharf waved enthusiastically, and Hamish McLean, the pub owner, stood by their side. The Historical Society photographers progressed behind the crowd as they snapped shots, and halfway there, video cameras stood on platforms as they captured every moment. As she drew closer to the chapel, she spotted friends from college who all wore highland dresses which fit into the reenactment wedding perfectly. She waved as she passed them by.

Bree and Colin stood upon the church steps, dressed for the historic occasion with the twins held between Bree and Ainslie. Evie and Ewan were dressed in historical clothing as well. They were calm, likely under threat from their father. Her gaze traveled to the chapel doorway, and in full highland regalia waited her love, John MacArthur.

He stood alone with no family member beside him. Granny died the day after they returned the Stone of Fear to the Fae. John said it seemed fitting, as she performed her duty by staying alive long enough to guide John on his quest for an Iona Stone.

Marie stood also alone on the chapel steps with no family left to give her away as well. They both planned to start their new life with each other, together.

As she stepped onto the chapel entry, John took her hand and kissed the back. "Ye look as bonnie today as the first time I met ye."

Marie returned his smile. "Ye look wonderful in a kilt."

John laughed. "Like me skirt, do ye?"

"Aye, yer knees are sexy."

The minister cleared his throat, and John and Marie turned to face him, arms linked.

Their service occurred on the chapel steps, as remained the custom in the old Highland way. Plus, not all of the guests would fit in the small chapel. The location gave the historical photographers a perfect setting for her dream wedding and plenty of space as they captured every moment.

When it came time to exchange the rings, Marie's stomach fluttered. The exchange of rings remained a key feature of any wedding. A circle with no beginning and no end symbolized the love within a marriage. She gazed at John as he spoke his vows in Gaelic and slid the extra band with matching scrolls to the ruby ring on her finger.

I vow ye the first cut of my meat, the first sip of my wine.

From this day on, it shall only be yer name I cry

out into the night.

Into yer eyes, I shall smile each morning.
I will be a shield for yer back as ye are for mine,
Never shall a grievous word be spoken between us,
For our marriage is sacred between us.

Above and beyond this, I will cherish and honor ye
through this life

And into the next.

The minister repeated the vows in English, but John insisted they each spoke them in Gaelic so her dream historical wedding was authentic. John ensured every detail was what Marie wanted, and his care touched her. Marie's eyes watered with emotion as she spoke her vows, the same as John's.

Holding a larger version of her band with the same decorative scrolls, she repeated Gaelic vows as she slid his ring on his finger. As the minister recited the vows in English, John smiled, bent, and kissed her. A loud cheer rose from the people gathered in the yard.

The minister huffed. "Well, I guess you can kiss yer bride now, John."

Everyone within their hearing laughed.

Marie and John turned together and held their hands high as Colin announced, "As Laird, I am pleased to present to ye, Mr. and Mrs. John MacArthur, Captain of Dunstaffnage."

The crowd erupted in cheers as the bagpipers picked up a lively tune of an old Scottish folk song, for the parade back to the castle. Prepared for the guests sat a traditional wedding feast of duplicate buffets set out in the castle yard. Roast beef, chicken, and pork accompanied by roasted potatoes, mixed vegetables, fruit, and nuts weighed down the tables. Wine and spirits sat prepared at the bar, the MacDougall whisky a feature.

In tradition, the feasting carried on into the night or until the men passed out where they sat. Today, the reenactment organizers planned to close the festivities around midnight.

John bent and kissed her at the castle steps. "Ye head up and change, so ye don't have to worry about messing up the historical dress."

Marie smiled and turned to the castle entry.

John held her hand tightly and pulled her back into his embrace as he whispered in her ear, "I love ye, Mrs. MacArthur, but don't take too long. Our exit will be early. I have a surprise for ye."

Marie couldn't change fast enough. Wearing another historical dress she planned to dine in, she strode to the castle steps where her husband awaited her. *My husband.*

He smiled as his hand reached for hers. Marie gasped when he shifted aside, and she cleared the doorway.

An antique horse-drawn carriage awaited them at the steps of the castle. Men dressed in traditional highland garb stood ready for another highland tradition—an escort who would attend the wedding couple to their new home. Marie and John stood at the entry landing, which overlooked the castle grounds. Colin and Bree stepped up beside them.

Colin leaned over and spoke to the couple as the crowd gathered below. "Congratulations, ye two. I am truly happy for ye."

John smiled and hugged Colin. "Thanks for all ye have done, for everything."

A teary Bree hugged Marie. "Are ye ready for the bouquet toss?" Marie gazed back at her very best friend.

Beyond her, Ainslie stood, and Marie leaned over to her. "Ainslie, aren't ye going to go down to be with all the single ladies to have a chance at catching the bouquet? Who knows, ye might be the next to marry?"

Ainslie scoffed a laugh. "Not in this lifetime, nor the next!"

Colin winked at Marie, who only smiled. Well, Marie would ensure their plan for Ainslie to catch the bouquet would happen whether she stood with the women or not.

Colin turned to the crowd of women who gathered beneath the castle steps and announced loud enough for all present, "Are all the single maidens ready for the bouquet toss?"

High-pitched squeals radiated from the woman below.

Bree turned to Marie and switched bouquets for a smaller one of flowers tied with a ribbon since the tossed bouquet usually ended up being involved in a tug-of-war match between women, each vying for the honor since a caught bridal bouquet meant the promise of the next to wed.

Marie gathered herself, spotted Ainslie from the corner of her eye, and tossed the bouquet. The flowers tumbled in her hands only to be caught by Bree, who also fumbled with the bunch once, then again. The flowers tipped into Ainslie's hands and landed there.

The crowd roared, and Ainslie yelled, "Well, damn if I didn't catch the stupid bouquet!"

Everyone on the entry landing launched into

laughter.

Ainslie folded her arms. "Oh, the hell with it! I don't need a man!" She tossed the bouquet to the crowd of women below, who tumbled into a flurry of activity to capture the flowers.

John led Marie to the waiting carriage, helped her in, and climbed in after. As John and Marie waved to the crowd, the carriage started down the cliff's road.

Marie snuggled into John's arms. "Well, husband, this is a nice surprise."

John kissed her cheek. "It's not over yet, wife."

Marie smiled. "Well, I hope not. I'm looking forward to my wedding night, but where are we staying? I thought the plan was the castle?"

John bent and brushed his lips against her, then kissed her deeper. It was over two years since their first kiss, and she still got tingly when he kissed her.

The horse-drawn carriage progress stayed slow, and the view from the window changed as they traveled through Dunbeg. Soon Marie recognized where the procession headed.

She turned from the window. "John, are we headed to the priory? The renovation project doesn't begin for another few weeks. Only one building is livable, with a small living area, kitchen, and bedroom, and the roof leaks. What if it rains?"

John glanced out the window then at Marie. "Then I will have to hold ye to keep ye warm, wife."

She huffed, not convinced. John's finger on her chin turned her gaze to meet his. "Trust me, wife. We still have some traditions to tend to. I want to ensure we begin our lives right, and Colin and I got the place ready."

When they pulled up to the priory steps, John jumped from the carriage and held his hand for Marie. He helped her down, escorted her to the door, and opened it but stopped Marie from entering.

"Wait, wife. We must honor the ancient tradition of carrying the bride over the doorstep. This tradition will ensure that we step over the evil spirits that might inhabit the thresholds of doors. Considering the priory's history, I didn't want to take any chances."

Marie teared up. He wanted to ensure she felt safe as their life started at the priory, a place which in the past held terrible memories—her kidnapping, the priest's capture, and John's parents' deaths. But in the present, the priory represented hope—a promise for their future together.

John swooped Marie into his arms and paused at the doorway. "What did the miner say when he had to carry his new wife over the threshold?"

Marie smiled as she waited for the punchline.

John kissed her lips and replied, "Don't quarry. I've got this!"

He carried her across the threshold and lowered her in his arms.

He caressed her cheek as he gazed into her eyes. "Marie, ye are my greatest gift, my best blessing. Ye and the bairn, ye are my future."

Marie stared back at the love of her life and recognized she had no fear if John stayed with her. Together, they would conquer anything.

"John, I love ye. *Ye* are my best blessing, the greatest gift, true love, and my family."

Epilogue

Marie lifted another rock from the rubble by the priory and shifted it so she got into the old refectory. She huffed a groan and rubbed her lower back. As she stood, her very pregnant belly stuck out.

John came by her side in an instant. "I told ye not to lift anything heavy." He cradled her belly and rubbed her lower back.

She sighed in relief. "I know, but I can't seem to wait. I want to get everything done before the babe arrives."

John smiled as he held her. "Ye can't possibly get all this done, and the babe will be here soon, long before we finish the total renovation. We have the main building already done and a place to live until it's all finished."

Marie sighed as John guided her out the doorway into the garden. "Plus, I have a surprise for ye."

Marie smiled as she allowed her husband to distract her from her work. The lads from the wharf worked on the rubble and planned to finish the clearing today. John led her around the bend of the main priory, and set out in the garden area by Loch Etive sat a MacArthur plaid, an array of food bins, and a bottle of Marie's favorite water setting in ice. She constantly craved iced water during her pregnancy, and John always kept a supply close at hand.

She smiled and looked at her husband. "A picnic. Ye know I love picnics."

John took her hand in his and kissed it. "Aye, the first of many we'll have at our new home at Ardchattan Priory."

****

The Fae Realm, Purgatory Prison

Balor, King of Fomoire, the evil Fae, viewed her, clear as day, from his prison in purgatory. If he concentrated hard enough, he got through the prison's energy wall and connected with the evil Fae he sent to the eighteenth century. He ordered the dumb chit to search for the Stone of Love, but she screwed that up. Now the human his Fae occupied sat in the Chapel in the Woods at Dunstaffnage Castle in Scotland. The bitch attended a damned wedding—the wedding of Roderick MacDougall and Brielle DeVolt.

Bless the Gods. She was beautiful. Her aura shone from her body—a light pink showing her true love for the man before her. But when she turned, the light flashed a rainbow that occurred, uncommon in any human. She existed as a rarity in any realm. Balor wanted her, and he would have her. She resembled his previous human wife. He craved the power and strength gained from mating with a human. He shivered when that familiar feeling rose through his Fae body.

Once he escaped, he would find a way—a way to her. Nothing would stop him. She would be his and his alone. He gripped the Stone of Lust, and the magic Fae stone's power surged through him—lust for power, lust for control, lust that remained his for the taking. He gazed at Bree, and a craving for her rose, a call he must answer. He would take her, possess her, and never let go. The Stone of Lust glowed black. His escape plan now manifested in his mind.

He grinned into the darkness. "I'm coming for ye, Brielle, and ye will be mine."

A word about the author…

Margaret Izard is an award-winning author of historical fantasy and paranormal romance novels. She spent her early years through college to adulthood dedicated to dance, theater, and performing. Over the years, she developed a love for great storytelling in different mediums. She does not waste a good story, be it movement, the spoken, or the written word. She discovered historical romance novels in middle school, which combined her passion for romance, drama, and fantasy. She writes exciting plot lines, steamy love scenes and always falls for a strong male with a soft heart. She lives in Houston, Texas, with her husband and adult triplets and loves to hear from readers.

You can email me at:
info@margaretizardauthor.com